Fool's Run

PATRICIA A. MCKILLIP

POPULAR LIBRARY

An Imprint of Warner Books, Inc.

A Warner Communications Company

POPULAR LIBRARY EDITION

Popular Library®, the fanciful P design, and Questar® are registered
trademarks of Warner Books, Inc.

Cover illustration by Michael Whelan

Popular Library books are published by
Warner Books, Inc.
666 Fifth Avenue
New York, N.Y. 10103

 A Warner Communications Company

Printed in the United States of America

This book was originally published in hardcover by Warner Books.
First Printed in Paperback: February, 1988

10 9 8 7 6 5 4 3 2 1

The Magician stumbled down the transport passage in a dreamlike haze of amethyst and blood. The fused and shattered bodies of robots lay like broken dolls along the track. The security cameras had been blinded by Terra Viridian. She had found him; she had given him no choices. She had shown him the way through the maze of the Underworld, her mind a thread he had followed. Now she had vanished again, moving secretly before him or behind him, somewhere along his impossible path. He had played music for his freedom; what he needed now was an idiot's luck.

"Fool's Run," he whispered. His head throbbed; blood kept falling into his eye. His throat burned with thirst. He ran expecting to be killed at every step, expecting a fallen robot to move, turn toward him, eject light like a dying breath.

The transport door opened with a rend of metal. The Magician continued doggedly toward it. A small army of guards leaped past him. He felt a rifle behind his ear . . .

* * * * *

"*Fool's Run* soars using glorious imagery to tell an intriguing story. The completion of the Vision is the chilling climax of the book; both it, and the narrative journey to attain it, make highly enjoyable reading."

—*Rave Reviews*

Please turn this page for acclaim for *Fool's Run*.

"There are no better writers than Patricia A. McKillip. If you don't believe me, read *Fool's Run*. Like a shimmer of oil on water, her work is at once beautiful and evanescent, translucent and distinct; a sheen of calm over a vast depth. Some writers can paint the surface: some go deep. McKillip does both."

—Stephen R. Donaldson,
author of *The Mirror of her Dreams*
and *The Chronicles of Thomas Covenant*

* * * * *

"One of the more powerful and evocative science fiction visions to have come my way. McKillip weaves a poetic tale, threading what might otherwise be too much predictability and coincidence into a pattern of order and beauty. *Fool's Run* deserves to be read, not to be described. . . . the novel will long be remembered."

—Debbie Notkin, *Locus*

For all the musicians and patrollers of the 23 Club.
With my very special thanks to Don Harriss.

PROLOGUE

Silence. A cliff face black as deep space. A dim, reddish sky beyond it. An oval bent back on itself, all colors or no color, lying on amethyst sand. A concave vision of a red star. The cliff. The oval. The red sun. The vision.

Silence. Darkness.

A sound. The prisoner moved her eyes, saw grey. A cushioned chair back angling into a grey uniform sleeve. Wrist. Fingers. A control panel with a Milky Way of glittering lights. Transparent ovals set into grey walls. Oval weapon lockers. She shifted slightly, heard her own breath, then radio static.

"Identify."

"Voice code six: 'I must go down to the sea again, to the lonely sea and the sky.' *Jailbird*, coming home to roost. One prisoner."

"Status."

"Extremely dangerous. Request double guard at the dock. Request entry code."

"Challenge."

" 'To drift in a world of dreamers, to see no sun.' "

"Challenge."

"4.057×10^{13}."

"Challenge."

"Betty Grable. *Jailbird*, WGC909Z, request permission to enter."

"Entry code C. Channel three. *Jailbird*. Permission to enter the Underworld."

A gigantic circle slowly turning against the stars, two

rings twisting around each other, one light, one dark. Minute lights flashed from a section of the light ring; the cruiser *Jailbird* turned toward them. The prisoner stared at the floor. A crystal filament was looped loosely around her wrists. If she moved too abruptly, she would cut off her hands. From the polished grey wasteland grew four boots. If she lifted her eyes from them, she would see laser-rifles. A star exploded in some galaxy in the dark at the back of her mind. Light dazzled across her brain. She made some sound; a rifle shifted. She raised her head slowly, slowly in the wild light.

The static again. A different voice. "*Jailbird*. This is Records. Name of prisoner?"

"Terra Viridian."

The com whistled. "You've got her."

"Affirmative."

"Legal status."

"Her status-sheet is a mile long, can I give—"

"Give us a printout when you dock. *Jailbird*. Is she sane?"

"Legally."

"Off-record."

A breath of silence. "You ask her. Look into her eyes and ask her. Records. Shifting to entry channel."

The ring-wall loomed before them. The shielding opened to a blazing oval of lights. The prisoner rose. Six feet tall, bald, emaciated, she looked inconsequential enough to be borne away on a solar wind. But the unnatural stillness of her face, the enormous, smoky grey eyes touching the face of one guard, then the other, made them raise their weapons. She said tiredly, with a curious logic, "You cut off my hair. How could I harm you?"

They didn't answer. Two faces: one male, one female, one light, one dark, identical in their expressions. The cruiser-commander swiveled to look at her; beside him, the navigator eased the vessel toward the lights.

"Sit down," the commander said.

"True or false," she said to him, like an ancient conundrum. "I am sane."

He met her eyes a moment longer, trying to find an answer in them, then shook his head. "In there, in the Dark Ring, it won't matter." He added almost gently, "How old are you?"

"Twenty-one."

"Christ. Godchrist. A hundred years here. You can't be sane. They should have sent you to New Horizon, repatterned your brain."

"I am sane."

"You murdered one thousand five hundred and nine people. Is that sane?"

She gazed at him, hearing him as from the small end of a funnel. "You belong to one pattern," she said, as she had repeated a hundred times during her trials. "I am caught in another."

He turned away impatiently. The great oval doors yawned wider; dock lights flared below them. "Drugs," he said. But she hadn't finished.

"The vision is different." Her thin voice was careful, insistent. "The Dark Ring is not in the vision."

He looked back at her, quiet again, still trying to comprehend her. "What color was your hair? Before they shaved you? When you were a child?"

"I don't remember."

"Do you remember being a child?"

"I was never a child."

"Are you a killer?"

"Yes."

The navigator touched his arm when he didn't move. "We're here. You want to program the entry code before we blow up?"

The commander turned, fingered lights savagely. "Some days I hate this job." The red warning lights around them turned to gold. The cruiser settled in the vast, metallic silence. The prisoner hid behind her eyes, listening.

ONE

THE QUEEN OF HEARTS

O N E

The Magician sat alone on a stage in the Constellation Club, playing Bach to the robots whirling a grave minuet around him as they sucked cigarette butts off the floor. Though the walls of the vast club were a polished, starless black, in the world outside, the sun was just rising. He changed key in a sarabande, and the blackness washed away in a sudden tide of color. The walls, now glowing chartreuse, proclaimed it six o'clock in the morning. The Magician and the robots remained oblivious. Only Sidney Halleck, polishing the oak slab of one of the dozen bars in the place, gave the change any attention. Something closer to the color of mud, his wincing eyes told him, would have been easier on the eyes after a night like that.

The Magician's fingers wrapped chords neatly together into a resolution, then leaped forward three centuries. The piano, made over 150 years before, a pre-FWG antique, sounded gentle but precise in the empty cavern of the club. Sidney stopped caressing the oak and leaned on it, listening: a big man with a plump, benign face, a massive nose and shrewd, serene eyes. With its twenty oval stages scattered across the floor, most of them littered with equipment, the Constellation Club by day resembled a hanger for UFOs. The Magician and the antique grand, producing weird music in solitary abstraction, like a kind of exhaust, seemed suddenly to Sidney as unidentifiable as any object that might have descended out of the stars to land in his club.

The patternless spatter of notes came to an end. The Magician sat still, gazing at nothing, softly pressing one key over and over. Sidney waited; the B-flat led nowhere. He broke gently into the Magician's reverie.

"Was that Hanro you just played? 'Aurora Borealis Cocktail'?"

The Magician nodded absently. "Doesn't translate well to the piano . . ." He was still sounding the key. Half his spare, high-boned face was magenta from the night before. He trailed a couple of disconnected body-wires from his belt and from his neck-ring. A stardust of green and magenta glittered in his hair, on the piano keys.

His ear focused finally on the sound he was making; he listened as the air trembled and stilled. His face, of a chameleon type that changed with every thought, lost its clinical detachment from the noise he'd been making and somehow became more magenta.

"I swear every time I breathe on this thing it goes out of tune . . ."

"It's had a long and weary life," Sidney said. "It was up in an attic in Prairie Sector for seventy-five years until I tracked it down. Mice were nesting among the strings." He added, when the Magician seemed no longer in danger of vanishing back into his music, "Coffee? Beer?"

The Magician shook his head, then blew the glitter off

the keys. "Thanks, it's bedtime. What are you doing here so late, Sidney? It's—whatever hour that god-awful green in the walls is."

"It's dawn," Sidney said, and the Magician stopped breathing. He gazed at Sidney expressionlessly over the piano. "I stayed to listen to you. How often do I get a free Bach concert? I had to stay after hours anyway. One of the bands nearly went Full Primal at closing time." The Magician made a garbled noise that Sidney took to be a question. "You were playing, then. You didn't notice the patrollers and the ambulances."

"What—who—"

Sidney waved a hand vaguely toward a distant stage. "A new band called Desperate Sun. They seemed innocuous when they auditioned . . . They were planning to electrocute themselves with their instruments as a gesture of support for the National Regression Coalition of Sundown Sector. One of my bouncers cut off their electricity before they hurt themselves too badly. They kept making speeches to the patrollers about Sundown Sector's right to bear arms, tax itself and call itself Australia again. Though why they wanted to die for Australia in my club eluded me."

The Magician's harlequin face was a patchwork of expressions. "What was I doing through all this?"

"You played a lot of fugues and toccatas. Then you played the Inventions. All of them. That was a little dry," he admitted. "Then you played the Fourth English Suite. Then most of the Fifth, and then parts of the French Suites—"

"I didn't—"

"And you finished up with Hanro's 'Cocktail.' Four hours, nonstop, with patrollers taking statements and injured bodies being borne away under your nose. What on earth were you thinking about?"

The Magician's eyes lingered, wide, on Sidney's face. His right hand slid to the keyboard; the soft, single note sounded again. His eyes, still on Sidney's face, grew opaque.

The walls blackened around him once again. They had

lost their angles; in the cold, pristine night of space, something minute, flashing dark and light, followed its changeless orbit around him . . .

"Magic-Man," Sidney said gently and he blinked. He stopped playing the note after a moment, stared down at it.

"B-flat." He ran his hands over his face, smearing the paint, and stood up stiffly. "I think I need that beer."

"I'll join you. I don't have to be anywhere until ten."

The Magician crossed the floor to the bar: Sidney's favorite, an old-fashioned corner of oak and brass, polished mirrors and mellow light. He started to sit and changed his mind. "You waited for me all night," he said amazedly. "Why didn't you stop me?"

Sidney hesitated, building a head on their beers with artistry. "I was too fascinated," he said finally. "I've never seen anyone play classical music in such a trance. Besides, you were playing very well. Once I got the debris off the floor and the place emptied, it was soothing."

"I'm glad." He sipped the cold beer bemusedly and asked, because it was an uncomplicated question, "Where are you going this morning? Are you lecturing somewhere, or searching Amazon Sector for the first penny-whistle?"

"I'm going home," Sidney said simply. "I had a message yesterday that I'd receive a call at ten this morning from the Underworld."

"The Un—" He swallowed beer too fast; Sidney handed him a towel. "Why?" he asked, breathing again. Sidney shrugged cheerfully.

"I can't imagine. I've worked with several FWG institutions, but never with a prison."

"You own the busiest and most famous club in Suncoast Sector; maybe you're beginning to attract attention in the wrong places. Have you bounced any crime-lords lately?"

"Aaron would tell me. He keeps an eye on everyone."

"Aaron . . ." the Magician said oddly, and Sidney, swallowing beer, glanced at him.

"He was here last night. Or rather, this morning."

"He was on duty?"

"You didn't see him."

"I could have sworn I was alone . . ."

"Have you ever done that before? Played in a trance?"

The Magician looked at him incredulously. "While a band tries to fry itself in front of me? I wouldn't have thought I could play all the Inventions if you paid me. I don't even remember learning them all."

Sidney propped his chin on his fist. "It was a remarkable performance."

"It's a wonder the patrollers didn't shoot me for some peace and quiet."

"Aaron told them you were demented but harmless."

The Magician's mouth quirked. He caught sight of his face in the ornate mirror behind Sidney, a garish blur of paint and sweat, and ran the bar towel over it. The face that emerged, tense, alert, questing, seemed only remotely his own; the eyes, of the indeterminate color of water at twilight, waited for something just beyond the Magician's vision.

He dropped the towel and drank beer, his fingers colder than the glass. He felt it then: the sudden drag of sleeplessness, the chilly dampness of his body, which had pursued music with energy and passion for four hours without him. Sidney was still regarding him curiously.

"You don't remember what you were thinking about."

He shook his head, yawning. "I wasn't thinking."

"Something must have triggered it," Sidney said with gentle insistence, and the Magician felt the tug of Sidney's mind, brilliant, generous and painstaking, toward the scent of a musical mystery. Such things were his career, his passion, and the Magician stirred his own weary brain to give him something valuable.

But there was nothing: the smoothly revolving chip of light and shadow against deeper shadow, the slow rhythm against which he had ordered his playing . . .

"Just . . ." He gave up, shaking his head again. "I'm sorry."

"There was something."

"Yes. But there's no context."

"The B-flat."

"It was slightly out of tune. That's all." He said again, "I'm sorry."

"You'll remember," Sidney said tranquilly. "I don't believe anything is ever really lost. Not a note of it. I think we dwell among the echoes of all the music ever played just as surely as we dwell among our ghosts. No instrument is ever obsolete; someone is always born to play it. You play music hundreds of years older than you are; it lingered for that long in the air, beyond all the noises of the world, until you heard a fragment of it, between noise and noise, an intimation of its existence. Then came the quest for it. The hunger."

The Magician, lulled into a pleasant half-trance by Sidney's voice, was jarred by the word. He lifted his eyes from his shadow on the oak.

"Hunger . . ." His face seemed vulnerable suddenly, undefended by experience, open to suggestion.

"I'm just rambling . . . thinking about the point where things begin."

"Where what begins?"

"The search for anything loved, desired, sacrificed for. What possessed you, for example, to learn those millions of notes when you were young?"

"No—"

Sidney was silent, puzzled by the Magician's intensity. "What is it?" he asked finally. The Magician heard him from a distance.

"Something," he whispered.

"What? Are you remembering?"

"No. You said it. Your words. Something begins." He was still again, his body tense, listening to the words in his head. Slowly the lines of his face changed, became defined, familiar. The beer focused under his eyes; he drained it. Sidney poured him another.

"A ghost was nesting along with the mice in that piano and crawled out into me tonight, gave itself a good time for four hours, then crawled back to bed. There's your answer, Sidney.''

''What,'' Sidney objected, ''was a seventy-five-year-old ghost doing playing Hanro's 'Cocktail'?''

''Then Aaron is right. I am demented. I've been here too long.''

''Nonsense. You've only been here five years.''

The Magician eyed him quizzically. ''Five years. Which is three years longer than you've kept any other band here.''

''I can't help it if Nova is the only band besides Historical Curiosity I can stand listening to after six weeks.''

The Magician smiled. ''In vino veritas, as the Scholar would say. Famous club owner admits he would rather drink flat beer than listen to the music he pays for.''

''Think how much Nova has improved since you came here. In spite of the fact that you switched cubers after I hired you.''

''I didn't.''

''You did.''

''Not since we came here.''

''No. The cuber before the Gambler. The first time I heard you in—where was it? That place that looked like a morgue, with coffins for tables.''

''Oh. The Marble House.''

''Yes. The cuber with the heart-pins all over her hair.''

The Magician nodded, his face growing reminiscent. ''The cuber with the face of gold . . . She played with us for two years, until you hired us.''

''Why did you let her go?''

''I couldn't keep her. She was too good . . . Last I heard, she was doing a Sector tour with Alien Shoe.'' He swallowed beer, still remembering. ''She was young, too young to be that good. By the time I met her, she'd played in bands all over South Suncoast Sector. She came north on impulse, she said. She walked in off the street, sat in with us, and I wouldn't let her go. She was the best cuber I'd ever played with . . . Now I think Nova might be good enough for her.

But—'' He stopped the thought abruptly, drank more beer instead. Sidney finished the sentence for him.

"But you're only a club band.''

"I'm not complaining,'' the Magician said mildly. "What other club owner would put up with my playing all night, and then pour me beer for breakfast?''

"Think nothing of it,'' Sidney said graciously. "But if you could consider making a habit of this, I'll sell tickets.''

The walls flickered around them at the changing hour. The chartreuse heated to a vibrant orange that caused them both to duck over their beers.

"Lord,'' Sidney said painfully. "I had no idea what goes on here at this time of the morning.''

The Magician swallowed most of the second beer, then stretched, pleasantly groggy. "I'd better check the stage, make sure everything is off.''

"Take your body-wires off,'' Sidney suggested; the Magician felt the neck-ring then, and freed himself, methodically rolling wire as he crossed the floor.

He covered the piano. The Nebraskan, his lanky, drawling sound man, had put everything else to rest. He stood a moment, frowning at the clutter, expecting to see something, but not remembering what. He touched the piano, reassured by a familiar curve. Then he leaped down from the stage, joined Sidney, who was washing their glasses. Sidney wiped them, put them in place, then glanced fondly over his domain, readied for another night.

"But first,'' he murmured, reminding himself, "a message from the Underworld.''

The Magician stared at him, felt the hair lift at the nape of his neck. He saw it again: the twisted rings, light and dark, journeying soundlessly in and out of the Earth's shadow. The intimation shuddered lightly through him: a psychic quake. Then it was over, past, and he could speak.

"The Underworld,'' he whispered. "That's what I was doing while I played.''

"What?''

"Watching it.''

T W O

Jason Klyos glared at his reflection on the bathroom wall. Eleven years in this floating pretzel and you're still trapped in the same damn mirror. When are you going to break out of here, Klyos? When? He touched a com-light beside the mirror and ordered, "Coffee. Hot and fast."

"Yes, sir."

He leaned closer to the mirror, studied the capillaries in his eyes. His dark hair was receding year by year like a slow tide. Up here, it didn't matter. Up here—

The com signaled, two gentle, musical tones. He slapped at it irritably. "What? Speak."

"Sir, Jeri Halpren."

Jase grunted, wondering what he had done to deserve

Jeri's voice before he had had his coffee. Jeri Halpren was the Underworld's FWG-appointed Rehabilitations Director; he had fake hair, fake teeth and he snapped awake in the morning full of missionary zeal, which he strove to impart to Jase before his own brain had crawled out of dreams. I remember, he thought. I've been putting him off. Three meetings delayed. Something to do with . . . art? The face in the mirror looked martyred, as if its owner had stepped into something noxious.

"Sir," Jeri Halpren said reproachfully. "You promised you'd see me this morning. I know you don't like to be bothered with Rehab matters, but you told me yesterday to schedule this call. It's on the roster for ten hundred hours—"

"What call?"

"I told you—"

"No, you didn't." He held his hand underwater, ran it over his face. For no reason at all the face of a girl he had known twenty-five years before crossed his mind. He smelled the soap and sunlight in her hair, and found himself smiling. "Oh. Yes, I do." All those protein-head scientists are wrong, he thought. Time isn't a circle or a straight line. It's a smell bottle. You catch a whiff here, a whiff there . . . "Yes," he said, interrupting Jeri. "Yes, yes, yes. I'll authorize the call. Who is it I'm supposed to talk to? Oh, never mind, tell me later. I'm in the bathroom." He cut off Jeri's flurry of protests and immediately the com sounded again. "Hell's bells," he fumed. "Can't you wait until I reach the office?"

"Sir—"

The door alarm buzzed, then lit, going through its triple ID scan.

"Voice ID 246-859-7. Johnson, Samuel Nyler. Status—"

"Sir, it's your coffee!"

"Come in!" Jase bellowed, and the locks snapped back at the sound of his voice. He took a deep breath, smelling Time again: wind, and a house with a door that didn't talk back. Johnson, Samuel Nyler, bleary-eyed and immaculate, set the coffee tray on the table. Fresh coffee. Not black plastic dispensed from a vein in the wall. That's all it amounts to, he thought. That and the privilege of introducing myself to artistic geniuses. Of the two niggardly rewards he much preferred the coffee.

"Sir," the com on the table said. It was his Deputy Chief, Nils Nilson. He was just going off duty; his voice sounded tired. Jase liked him, so he toned his own voice down a few decibels. Nils' great dream in life was Jase's job; Jase's dream was to give it to him. But the wheels on Earth that turned over spacers' fortunes were oiled by the endless perversity of the FWG bureaucracy. Because Jase wanted Earth, they'd keep him in space forever. Because Nilson would do an excellent job of running the Underworld, they'd find someone who couldn't, to replace the mummified Jase.

"What is it, Nils?"

"I'm sorry, sir. There's a Dr. A. Fiori calling from New Horizon. He won't talk to anyone but you."

"Oh, for—what does he—tell him to go to hell." He gulped coffee. The com chuckled. "All right. Tell him I'll talk to him. When I've reached the office. Not before. Who is he anyway?"

"Equipment salesman, I think."

"What does he want?"

"A lifer."

"Tell him to stand on his head."

"I'll tell him," Nils said, yawning.

The room was silent. Jase drank his coffee warily. He daydreamed a moment. Bacon and hot biscuits. Lose thirty pounds when I get back to Earth. If. Maybe even a face-job. Nose not so bad. Change eyes *brn* to *grn*. Hair. Fifty-six, Chief of the Underworld. Lots of credit, nowhere to spend it up here. Request Sundown Sector. Beaches. Sun. Or Archipelago Sector. Warm blue water. Maybe I'll just resign . . . But he knew he never would, just as he knew the Underworld would never release him. Perversity.

In the office half an hour later, he read the shift reports on his console screen, while Nils, at his own desk, completed the night log. Their office was in the Hub of the Underworld, the circular fortress at the center of the rings, connected to them by two spokes: one for transport; the other holding water lines, generators, the main greenhouse. The Hub spun to its own gravitational needs. It housed the vast central computer, communications, a small armory, the chief officers' quarters, its own kitchens, greenhouse and generator. It even contained a tiny dock, with one smallcraft always in readiness. In fifty years, the smallcraft had been replaced twelve times but never used.

The office, for a few moments, was soundless. The grey carpet was spotless. There was no dust even between the console keys. The air smelled strange. Jase, distracted, found himself taking short, tentative sniffs. What odor was it?

Ward 14BL. No incidents.

Ward 15AD. No incidents.

Ward 14CL. Accident report, Ward Officer P. C. Lawson. Prisoner D186521C1: superficial hand burns from contact with cell shield. Treated Infirmary Ward F. Returned to cell 5:47 GTE.

Nothing. The recycled, purified air smelled of nothing. "Christ," he muttered, and Nils' fingers stilled on his noiseless keyboard.

"Sir?"

"Nothing." He tapped at his own keyboard, scanned a list of security officers and dock guards for the next shift. Then a report on incoming cruisers and their prisoners. Then he okayed a request for two cruisers in the L1 vicinity, and his meal-menu for the next day. Then he read Nils' report. Nothing. Nothing.

"Good. Good." He wanted to say: "I'm so bored I could eat carpet." But in the face of Nils' frustrations it seemed cruel. So he said instead, "I'm going to try another transfer request."

Nils' habitually serious expression relaxed. "Where to this time?"

"I don't know. The south pole." He pushed the message-key. *Halpren,* the screen said. Again: *Halpren.* Then: *FWGBI.* "Who called from *FWGBI?*"

"Darrel Collins."

"Mm. He wants us to throw some lifer into solitary and stick pins under his nails for information, I bet. Or it's a court-gambit with some temp."

"You could ask him," Nils said mildly, and Jase smiled.

"I could. I will."

Nilson, his own shift finished, didn't move. For a moment the air was tranquil. No lights burned in it, no voices caused tremors. Jase moved to the front of his desk, sat on it. Nils lounged back in his air-chair, sipping a vitamin-shake. He was a lean, rangy, red-haired man whose brain was focused on the Underworld twenty-four hours a day. He didn't understand Jase's lack of enthusiasm, but his respect was genuine, and Jase trusted him more than any other man he knew.

"The south pole . . ." Nils murmured. "Penguins. Tourists."

"Beats me why you like this place so much."

Nils shrugged. "It's not all administrative. We're the Command Station for all the off-world patrol stations. I guess I like pushing buttons, sending cruisers out, getting them back with lawbreakers, sending them back to Earth, reading the trial reports, getting prisoners back again, putting them where they belong— When I was a kid I had the cleanest desk in school. There wasn't a speck of dust on my rock collection. There were no fuzz balls under my bed."

"Is there a point to this?"

"You asked. I like things tidy. All the bad guys in their cells, and me without dust, grime or blood on my hands. I had enough of that Earthside."

Jase grunted. "If I didn't know better, I'd send you to New Horizon for observation."

Nils tapped his temple. "That's just it. It's patrol work by the brain. Battling the forces of evil by computer."

"A game."

"I always did like those old video war-games. If I had your job—" He stopped, shaking his head. "I'll never have your job."

"I'd give it to you for breakfast if it were my choice."

"I know." He swallowed the last of his shake, brooding without rancor. "I watch you. You know that? I watch you a lot. To see why you're sitting there and I'm here. You know what I think it is?"

"Some idiot in L. E. Central."

"No. Well, maybe that too. But it's something I don't have. A feel for when to cut through the rules. An instinct that tells you how to get to the heart of things. You used it as a patroller, but you can't use it here, that's why you can't stand the job. But that's why you got the job. Because this place could easily be run by someone with a microchip for a brain; it could almost be run by robots. But it's the Underworld, the only isolated, self-sufficient, armed and orbiting prison colony, and those bureaucrats on Earth needed to put somebody human up here to talk to."

Jase considered him almost surprisedly. Then he shook his head. "It's neat, but I don't see it that way. I see it as the perversity of Fate. I like wind, Fate gives me purified air. I like action, I get a desk. I like people, I get thousands upon thousands of people I only know by number. I like solving crimes, I get the criminals, tried and sentenced. I like Earth, I get . . . well, maybe you're right. Maybe if I start sounding like a computer, they'll take my transfer requests seriously . . ."

His voice trailed away; he gazed at the carpet, not seeing it. For a moment, the silence seemed to have mass. He felt a curious sense of dislocation, as if a fresh breeze had stirred under his nose, or a patch of sunlight had just faded in the windowless room. Something absolutely familiar that shouldn't have been where it was. A name surfaced in his head. He remembered his early years as a patroller, when a name, a chance word, a hair on a sleeve came into sharp and unexpected focus: a small detail that linked everything else he knew about a crime into an unbreakable chain. That was when he began cutting rules. At that moment of unassailable intuition. But why now? And—

"Who the hell is Fiori?"

Nils rose, stretching. "You know. That doctor from New Horizon. I told him you'd call him before you even sat down."

"You did."

"A little PR between outworlders."

"Oh, him. He wants a body?"

"A particular one. It's in with your messages." He tossed his cup down the wall-chute. "I'm off."

"Sweet dreams."

Jase found Dr. Fiori's name among the dozen people on his message roster who required his immediate attention. The message itself was peculiar.

Request permission study prisoner Q92814HD2, use of experimental equipment patients New Horizon. Dr. A. Fiori. Project: Guinea Pig.

Trying to make sense of that, he pulled the records of prisoner Q92814HD2. A bald, thin-faced woman with startling eyes gazed out of the screen at him and he grunted. Terra Viridian. The list of her crimes against the FWG was endless. For murder by laser under broad daylight of 1509 civilians and FWG services personnel . . . for desertion . . . for raising a laser-rifle against her Commanding Officer . . . for firing said weapon against . . . against . . . An image from a newscast of the massacre flashed across Jase's mind; his brain, for the instant, filled with light . . . the fire-seared skeleton of the stockade, the desert burning beneath the hot eye of the sun, bodies engulfed by light as if a solar flare had stretched millions of miles across space to kiss the desert and withdraw . . . For attempting to transform, under the broiling, blue noon sky, everything she saw into light, she was consigned for all her days, without appeal, until her final breath, to the Dark Ring of the Underworld.

She had walked away from the massacre and boarded a commuter shuttle to Suncoast Sector. For three weeks rumor had her everywhere in the world at once: running weapons to a secret rebel space station at the same time she toiled up a mountain in Dragon Sector to join a monastery for her sins. Then, in south Suncoast Sector, two patrollers arrested a vagrant rummaging through a jammed recycling bin for something to eat. They brought her in when she fought, charged her with resisting arrest, possession of an illegal weapon. Then they found out who she was.

Terra Viridian. The illegal weapon was the bent steak knife that had been jamming the recycling bin . . .

She had been in the Underworld for seven years. No incidents, no accidents. No communication from anyone outside the Underworld. She ate her meals, therefore she was still alive. Jase stared at the screen, remembering her sensational trial. The Madwoman versus the Free World Government. He had been disgusted when they sent her to the Underworld. She was so far out of her mind, she'd warped into a different universe. A woman who had no idea where she was had no business being in the Underworld. But Desert Sector was threatening to secede from the FWG, taking its oil, mines and commerce with it, so the FWG declared Terra Viridian sane and criminally responsible for her actions. She sat in silence in the Dark Ring, alone with her visions, as little disturbance to anyone as if she were buried. And now some Dr. A. Fiori wanted to fiddle with her brain, make her realize exactly where she was. For the next fifty or a hundred years. The Dark Ring. No appeal.

He touched a com-light. "Outchannel. Klyos."

"Voice ID 3. Identified."

"Link New Horizon. Jason Klyos to speak to Dr. A. Fiori."

New Horizon hovered appropriately in the shadow of the moon, a quiet place, privately funded and FWG supported, for the study of the criminally insane. "On-screen," the com said a few moments later. "Dr. Fiori."

"Chief Klyos," he said. "Thank you for getting back to me." A middle-aged man who ignored the latest fashion in faces, he looked as if he had been up for days. His thinning hair was tousled and there were shadows under his eyes. His smile seemed determinedly cheerful. He rattled on without breathing, apparently, while Jase tried to pick out the salient points. He interrupted finally, to break the flow.

"Under no conditions may the prisoner leave the Underworld."

"I know, dammit. It doesn't matter—here or there she's probably incurable. We'll transport the equipment there."

"You will, will you? Where are you planning to put it? In my bedroom?"

Dr. Fiori paused, puzzled. "Well, no. But it's not that—surely you can spare a space the size of a cell."

"Dr. Fiori, the Underworld is not a research center. People are sent here to be punished, not experimented with. I question the legality of this whole idea."

"Legality—" Dr. Fiori gave an incredulous laugh. "She's crazy. She shouldn't even be in the Underworld."

"She was tried and sentenced according to FWG law. The law didn't say anything about experimentation."

"Chief Klyos, we'll treat her as carefully as one of our own patients."

"Then why aren't you using one of your own patients?" He caught Dr. Fiori with his mouth open, searching for words, and added ponderously, "Dr. Fiori, this conversation is being recorded for the Underworld log. I have no private conversations. All conversations concerning prisoners may be used as evidence for whatever purpose in a court of law."

Dr. Fiori finally remembered to close his mouth. "Is that a threat?" he asked confusedly. "Have I done something wrong?"

Jase leaned back in his chair. "No. I'm telling you something you didn't know. We have specific instructions about how to treat prisoners here. The FWG doesn't like those rules broken. The FWG doesn't like much of anything to happen here that it hasn't thought up first. Now. You want to use one of our life prisoners for a biocomputer still in experimental stages. I'm basically a simple man. Can you tell me in simple language what it does?"

"Well." The glib flow of words gave way to a careful concentration. "It translates the chemical, neurological and electrical impulses of the brain into images on a screen. We named it the Dream Machine. Look. Suppose I show you a loaf of bread. Nothing is distracting you, nothing else is demanding a response from you but that loaf of bread. The Dream Machine makes a recording of your response. It shows you thousands of images and records your responses to them. Then, when you think or dream, the Dream Machine can match the patterns your brain produces with the images it has already stored, and it translates your brain activity back into images. Does that sound harmful?''

"It sounds fascinating."

Dr. Fiori's voice lost its faint wariness. "Language is of course hopelessly imprecise. You and I can't even imagine the same loaf of bread. But we can't refine the Dream Machine further to help our patients without using a patient. And at New Horizon, which, while it has some government support, is not an FWG institution—''

"You're concerned about lawsuits."

"Absolutely."

His frankness surprised a smile from Jase. "So. You want to use a lifer with no legal status on earth. I'd be willing to bet many of the Dark Ring prisoners are borderline candidates for New Horizon. Why her?''

"She—I remember her trial. She used a private language that was remarkably rich in symbols, imagery. She's perfect. And she has no family.''

"According to her status-sheet, she does have a sister on earth. With no record herself, and no known address. In seven years, nobody has tried to communicate with the prisoner. No letters, calls, no requests for visitors' passes. Not even a Christmas card from her lawyers. Nothing.''

"She's a derelict. Nobody cares about her. She could be used to help other patients. Perhaps even cured.''

"I hope not," Jase said bluntly. "For her sake. Incurable, cured, she'll never leave the Dark Ring." He paused. The tired face on the screen waited hopefully. "Well. If it were up to me, I'd say leave her alone. A crazy woman killed, a crazy woman was convicted—that's the woman who should take the punishment. But it's not up to me. I can't give you permission."

"Oh."

"I don't have the authority to make a decision like that. Another point. If you do get permission, we can probably find space for your equipment. But staff quarters will be limited and I can't let you use our computer."

"The Dream Machine is self-sufficient. But," Dr. Fiori added rather plaintively, "who do I go to now?"

"Let me think . . . Someone in FWGBI. Ah." He smiled thinly. "Ask Darrel Collins. He'll know whom you should talk to. I'll let him know you'll be in contact with him. I think he's about to owe me a favor."

He muttered at Dr. Fiori's thanks impatiently, and placed his next call to the Free World Government Bureau of Investigation. As he suspected, the investigator did want to owe him a favor. He requested lodgings for himself and three lawyers, and an hour's private conversation in a closed room with one Harl Tak, LR, 49 yrs, no commuted sentence, ringleader of a silver sand connection. Jase gave him a dock-pass code, and Dr. Fiori's name, and found, as Collins' face vanished, that a dozen com-lights were flashing at him.

Half an hour later, he looked up to find Jeri Halpren standing in front of his desk.

"Oh," he said without enthusiasm.

"It's ten o'clock."

"I've got—"

"You promised," Jeri said inflexibly. "The call's on the roster. It's going through now." He blinked once, nervously, and added, "Do you want to know who you'll be talking to?"

Jase swallowed an expletive. "I wouldn't mind."

"Sidney Halleck." He paused. After a moment Jase sighed.

"Who?"

Jeri stopped smiling. "Sidney Halleck." He leaned on Jase's desk then, and began to babble. "He's the authority on Environmental Auditory Influences, recommended by the FWG Bureau of Arts as well as by the FWG Institute of Social Institutions. He's a musicologist, composer, inventor, he's got the world's largest collection of musical instruments, and he designed the Constellation Club in Suncoast Sector, which he owns—''

"He owns Suncoast Sector?"

"No. The Constellation Club. People fly to it from all over the world. Twenty bands nightly and its own private smallcraft dock—"

"What the hell," Jase said blankly, "do you want me to talk to a musician for?"

Jeri stopped. He took a deep breath and swallowed. "Musician." He took another breath. Then he tapped his ear. "Sounds." For a moment Jase wondered if his tongue had gotten tangled up. Then he became coldly articulate. "I'm your Director of Rehabilitations. For prisoners to be rehabilitated into Earth society. There are noises on Earth. There are no noises up here."

There's you, Jase thought.

"Sidney Halleck has done studies for FWG committees on the effect of background noise on workers under all kinds of conditions. It's his theory that a lack of familiar, natural sound is as debilitating as too much, too varied an input of sound. It's my theory that the abrupt change from the nearly complete silence of the Underworld to the aural chaos on—"

"The what?"

Jeri sighed. "Racket on Earth might contribute to the sense of isolation and social withdrawal that ex-prisoners go through. The Underworld is only fifty years old. Most ex-prisoners were sent off-Earth for good reason, and they were here for an average of thirty years. We're still getting the first wave of analyses of our Rehab program."

Jase grunted. "I've never found it quiet around here. What do you want me to do? Send some prisoners down to his nightclub?"

"Please," Jeri said stiffly. "Just be polite to him. Ask him if he'll take a few moments to speak to me."

"All right," Jase said, "all right, all right. Sidney Halleck." He was intrigued in spite of himself. "It almost makes sense. Do you know any experts on air?"

"Air?"

"Familiar, natural smells or the lack of them?" The call registered on-screen. A big, benevolent face turned toward him inquiringly, and in the instant he felt his own harsh, professional gaze. Sidney Halleck wore his life on his face —an unfashionable thing to do on Earth—and it seemed to Jase a life of intelligence, humor and goodwill.

"Mr. Halleck."

"Chief Klyos?" Sidney said. His deep, calm voice sounded bewildered but courteous. "What can I do for you?"

"I don't know anything about music, but I'm told it's an honor to meet you."

"Did you ever sing a nursery rhyme? Then you know something about music."

"No."

"Oh."

"Mr. Halleck," Jase said carefully, trying to remember Jeri's babbling. "You've been recommended to us by the FWG Bureau of Arts as well as by the FWG Institute of— ah—Social Institutions. May I ask you to talk for a few minutes to our Director of Rehabilitations, Dr. Jeri Halpren? He's experimenting with a new program for inmates due to be sent back into Earth society. May I transfer you to him?"

"Of course," Sidney Halleck said bemusedly. "I'm at a loss to know how I can help him; I know nothing about prisons, but—"

"He'll explain." He glanced at Jeri, who was staring at him in grateful disbelief. He kept his voice courteous with an effort. "Thank you very much, Mr. Halleck. It's been a pleasure to—oh." He stopped, surprised. "I'll be damned."

"I beg your pardon?"

"I just remembered a nursery rhyme."

Sidney smiled cheerfully. "The brain is a marvelous junkyard."

"Isn't it, though?"

"Which rhyme was it?"

"Ah—tarts. 'The Queen of Hearts, she made some tarts, all on a summer's day . . .' But, Mr. Halleck, there's no music to that one."

"Strictly speaking, no," Sidney said apologetically. "You're right. But there is rhythm, and if you define music as a succession or pattern of sound intervals set to a predictable or varied rhythm, then you're halfway there with 'The Queen of Hearts,' right? Whereas something like 'All around the Mulberry Bush—' "

"Oh, yeah—'the monkey chased the weasel'—"

"Actually has its own melody. You remember?"

"What the hell was that next line?" They were both silent, thinking. Then Jase became aware of a turmoil of emotion at his elbow. He glanced at Jeri. "Ah—my Rehab Director is getting restless. Mr. Halleck—"

"Please. Sidney."

"Sidney. If you decide to visit the Underworld, I'll look forward to talking to you again."

"I hope I can be of some help. Good day, Chief Klyos."

Jase turned the com over to Jeri and rose to get away from Jeri's irritating nasal. What was that line? The monkey chased the weasel . . . And who was the Queen of Hearts? He stared at the question blankly, until the sheer nonsense of it, of him standing entranced in the Hub of the Underworld wondering about the identity of a nursery-rhyme character, overcame him.

But, he thought stubbornly, they all meant something else. All those rhymes. Didn't they? Politics, plague, fire, life and death . . . He resisted the urge to interrupt Jeri's conversation, then yielded to it the moment Jeri broke contact and said, "He's coming." His smile beamed against the force of Jeri's irritation and dwindled. "Now what did I do?"

"I wanted to ask him something. I wanted to ask him—" He waved a hand. "Ah, forget it. Ridiculous."

But he heard it again, teasing his brain as he resumed his work. The monkey chased the weasel . . . Only he was chasing the Queen of Hearts too. And—pop!

They all disappeared.

He scowled severely, blocking the bizarre image, and concentrated on the monotonous, crucial habits of the Underworld.

T H R E E

The Magician was flat on his back beneath the control panel of the *Flying Wail* when Aaron Fisher ascended the ramp and rapped his knuckles on the open hatch. There being no response from the body beneath the panel, he stepped across the threshold into the smallcraft. A gentle, ancient mingling of horns and trumpets sounded at the step. The Magician put down his laser-welder and rolled out too abruptly, banging his head.

"Ouch, damn it to molten—Aaron." He got to his feet, smiling, extending one hand and rubbing his head with the other.

"You okay?"

"I'll live." He spun the commander's chair around,

casting an eye on Aaron's rumpled uniform. "Have a seat. Or are you here on business?"

Aaron shook his head tiredly. "I'm on my way home."

"Coffee?"

"Yes. No. Have you got a cold beer?"

"Coming up." He lingered a moment, still absently rubbing his head, his expression peculiar. "I hope you enjoyed the concert the other night."

Aaron grinned briefly, amazedly at the memory. "When did you finally stop?"

"Six in the morning. Sidney was still there."

"What were you on? Just out of professional curiosity."

"Nothing. I finally decided one of my body-wires must have triggered something in my brain, because the music wouldn't turn off. But I've been experimenting with them here, and nothing's happened."

Aaron's smile faded. "Be careful," he said, and the Magician's eyes changed, focused with unconscious scrutiny on the patroller. Aaron's face moved fractionally away, into the warm morning light falling through the open hatch across his chair. The light was soothing, not yet bright-hot; the air over the dock, which would smell later of asphalt, exhaust, chemicals, carried now a cool hint of the sea. Still feeling the curious, searching gaze he turned again to challenge it. But the Magician had disappeared; Aaron heard the cooler swish open in the tiny kitchen. He eased back in the seat and stared uncharacteristically at nothing.

He was a tall man, slender and hard, with a face that was at once amiable and aggressive. He wore an old-fashioned growth of dark hair on his upper lip, and made no attempt to eradicate the restless lines and hollows he had earned. His eyes took color from their surroundings. At the moment, within the grey and silver interior of the *Flying Wail*, they were shadowed.

He said, as the Magician returned with beer, "You changed your door bell."

"Handel's *Water Music*." He swiveled the navigator's chair and sat. Aaron nodded toward the welder.

"Problems?"

"Just the com-system. The receiver's old."

"This is an old cruiser. I took my off-world training flights in this model, thirteen years ago. Ugly, but reliable. The Underworld changes models every four or five years; this was one of the best."

"It's so ugly," the Magician said fondly, "I got it for a song." He stretched out against the worn leather, propped his bare feet on the toolbox. For a moment he seemed to daydream, his face looking blurred and somehow boneless, his eyes intent on his coffee as if he were watching landscapes float across it. He asked abruptly, "What happened last night?"

"A sniper."

"Who died?"

"A pat—" He stopped and drank beer. Then he eyed the Magician, his expression quizzical, defensive. The Magician was still gazing absently into his cup, but the lines of his face had become more pronounced. Aaron yielded, finished the word softly. "A patroller."

The Magician looked at him quickly. "Someone you knew?"

"Not too well. He was just transferred into the station; they put him with me for the night. I had to fly him in. He died on the way."

"You were shot at in the air?"

"The sniper was in a sol-car. Luckily the traffic was light." He lifted the beer bottle; it touched his lips and descended again. He added, as if the silence were suddenly threatening, "It was a laser-rifle." The Magician's voice rumbled wordlessly in his throat. Aaron opened a hand to the air, pushing at the memory. "The sniper didn't—the only thing on his status-sheet was docking fines. It wasn't a grudge; he wasn't on drugs, he did a normal day's work—there was nothing for him to get out of opening fire on us. I've been shot at by kids over nothing more than a pack of cigarettes they didn't feel like paying for. That makes me furious. But this—someone killing, someone killed for no reason anywhere under the stars, not the smallest reason—that gets to me like nothing else does.''

He lifted the beer again, drank this time. The Magician watched him almost curiously, as if he were hearing a chord that, with all his variegated musical background, he couldn't chart. He said, with feeling, "You were lucky you didn't get blown apart in midair."

"Luck . . . What does that mean, really?"

"You mean is chance truly a matter of chance?"

"That's a hackneyed question, isn't it?" He stirred, pulling away again, but his brows were drawn hard at some memory forming in the sunlight. "I could see—I could see time slow down. While I was under fire. Seconds elongated . . . Magic-Man, I swear I saw that laser-beam part the air inch by inch. The one that killed. I would never have seen it that way unless I knew it was going to hit. But how could I have known? I knew it was going to kill, and I knew it wasn't me about to die. How?"

"I've heard about things like that," the Magician said softly. "I've never understood them."

Aaron pulled his attention from the light. "I've seen it once or twice before. But it always surprises me. It makes me wonder . . . what other things I might know without knowing . . ."

"Or, while you're so busy looking for other things, what you might be missing."

Aaron looked at him. The widening light spilled over his face, washed the expression and most of the color out of his eyes. He was silent a moment. The Magician heard his breath gather and stop before he spoke. "How do you do that?"

"Do what?"

"Know things—before I want you to know them."

"Do I?"

There was another silence. Then Aaron said dryly, "I say good morning and you ask me who died."

"Oh, that." He shrugged a little and tapped at his ear. "I pay attention to sounds. It was in your voice."

Aaron shook his head. "I wasn't even talking then. And you were staring at your coffee. I'm paid to notice things. You picked it right out of the air. It's not the first time."

The Magician smiled. "Why? You have some deep, dark secret you're afraid I'll discover accidentally? You might as well tell me, then, since—" His face changed as Aaron shifted. He frowned at his cold coffee, listening to the silence between them. But it was empty; it gave him no cue. He said finally, "It just happens, sometimes. That's all. How long have we known each other?"

"I don't know. Four, five years. Since they came up with that program to put patrollers on foot during part of their shifts. I walked into the Constellation Club and there you were, playing Bach and turning orange."

The Magician grinned. "If I was orange, it wasn't Bach. Five years. If one of my band members died, and I walked up to you the next morning and said it's a fine day, what the hell would you say to me?"

He shook his head, unconvinced. "There's more—"

"Okay. Sure it's more complicated than that. But it's not that important, and it wouldn't be bothering you unless you had something—" He was on his feet suddenly, his back to Aaron. "This coffee tastes like lube oil. Hang on a moment. Besides," he added above his noises in the kitchen, "I never pay much attention to it myself. I hate cluttering up my life with what's in other people's heads. I'm interested in music and money. In that order." He reappeared with a fresh cup. "Maybe in that order."

"You like money," Aaron said. The warm light had awakened some of the color in his face; the grit of sleeplessness in his eyes became more bearable. "You'd sell your soul—if you had one—for music."

The Magician sat down. He contemplated the worn, patched interior of the *Flying Wail* with complacent pride. "If I have a soul," he said, "we're sitting in it."

Aaron smiled. In his mind, the sniper's fire ripped the dark air as if it were fabric, but his body no longer moved at the memory. It would streak across his final waking thought, he knew, but for now the Magician's company kept it at bay. "Are you playing tonight?" he asked. "My schedule changes so much I never can keep yours straight."

The Magician nodded. "It's poker night at the Constellation Club."

"Come again?"

"I'm trying to teach Sidney Halleck how to play poker during breaks once a week when he's not off somewhere lecturing."

"Sidney wants to play poker? Why?"

The Magician shrugged. "He had five minutes when his brain had nothing to do, so he got interested in cards. If I'd been playing a zither instead of poker, he would have gotten interested in that."

"What's a zither?"

"It's like an autoharp."

"Oh," Aaron said blankly.

The Magician sipped coffee and added, "Come to think of it, Sidney has a zither. That's where I saw one: in his collection. He must own the log somebody hollowed out a million years ago to make the first drum."

"What is—"

"It's a flat soundbox with a lot of strings. As obsolete as the krummhorn. Sidney said he found his in an attic."

"Most of us would have trouble finding an attic these days."

"Sidney's a magnet. He says he thinks about what he wants and it finds him."

"He must be a hell of a poker player."

The Magician gave a grunt of laughter. "He's terrible. There's nothing the cards can give him that he wants."

"He thinks about what he wants . . . and it finds him?"

"That's what he said. You know Sidney. The rest of us want fame, money, power—Sidney wants a nine-hundred-year-old instrument that sounds like a tree frog. Life gives him that, plus fame, money, power—"

"Is there a moral here somewhere?"

"I wish I knew."

"Why? What do you want that you haven't got?"

"A change," the Magician said simply. "We've been playing the Constellation Club for five years. Bands like Cygnus and Alien Shoe are doing off-world tours on nothing but three chords and their face-jobs. I wouldn't mind a few orchids and orbiting hotels, not to mention money. Then maybe I'd have a smallcraft with a receiver that works." He gave the disemboweled panel a dour look. Aaron set his empty beer bottle down and stretched. "Let me know if you need—" A yawn smothered the rest of the sentence. He blinked vaguely at the dancing light. "God," he said with gratitude. "I might actually sleep."

"You want another beer?"

Aaron shook his head. "I've got to go." Still he lingered, listening, he realized finally, to the overtones of music constantly trembling beyond the silence within the *Flying Wail*. He turned to make a request, and found the Magician already in motion.

He had swiveled his chair; his fingers played a pattern on the rows of lights beside the control panel. The panel opened to reveal an old-fashioned black-and-white keyboard. The Magician touched a few keys gently. A reflector over the main porthole turned slowly to intercept light.

Aaron smiled, both at the lovely synchronicity between mechanics and music, and the Magician's unabashed satisfaction in his handiwork. The Magician disengaged the keyboard from the ship's power and glanced at Aaron, acknowledging his thoughts. Then all his attention drained out of the world around him. His face grew detached, gently contemplative. His hands strayed randomly over the keys, slowly fashioned the sounds into something complex, elegant and, Aaron guessed, a few centuries older than the FWG. For a moment the numb weariness in his brain eased, and even the squat, battered patrol-cruiser took on dignity under the Magician's vision.

He was still playing when Aaron left.

* * *

When Aaron woke in the late afternoon, the sky was roiling white with summer fog.

He watched it as he dressed. He lived high above the city, in one of the huge FWG ghettos. They marched among smaller constructs like alien spiders; their intersecting arches buttressed one another against earthquake, and their free form took up space instead of land. Aaron had a small room close to the top of an arch. It contained nothing much besides a bed and an FWG-issue computer. It faced west; on hot evenings he could watch the horizon blaze with odd colors as the sun sank behind the haze the sea-factories expelled. Suncoast Sector was three hundred miles wide and a thousand miles long. The north section Aaron lived in was haunted by a stubborn ghost of pre-FWG history. In a hundred years it had grown extremely elusive. But even Aaron, whose imagination was negligible, could sense it now and then in the sigh of the tide, the silent fog drifting through old streets running always to the sea.

The fog was feathering now through the immense arches of the ghettos. He watched it mindlessly, his eyes reflecting its paleness. He turned abruptly, a brisk, finely tuned movement away from the fog, negating with his body the subtle, chilly silence drifting into his head.

He had three hours before his night shift started. He took an elevator to the street and got into an empty magne-car that carried him to the parking dock where he kept his sol-car. He eased himself up into the milky sky. He liked flying fast; he had raced felons and drunk drivers to turnaround and brought them down under luminous moons, skies giddy with stars. But the fog's blank face looming out from the sea turned the long summer evening into an amorphous blur of white and shadow. Air traffic moved cautiously around him, slow blobs of indistinct light. He rose high above them and the world he inhabited vanished.

A single foghorn bellowed like a dinosaur in the mists. It was obsolete; an endless argument between Sector bureaucracy and FWG bureaucracy kept it sounding. It was said to forecast ghost ships, lives rising out of the brine of earlier times. It cried warnings at Aaron that grew fainter and fainter, though no less imperative, as he flew west. He landed finally on a promontory and got out. The breakwaters in front of the sea-factories and purifying-plants had calmed the tides, but the ocean could still braid a bitter whip of wind and spume. Aaron stood a moment in the cold, steeled against it and enjoying it. He strained his eyes for rotting sails, rusty hulls. But all the ghosts stayed hidden beneath the surface of the sea.

He turned, made his way to a hatch in the earth, and disappeared underground. The cliff edge seemed to him a ridiculous place to build a nuclear shelter, but a hundred years ago there must have been more earth between the shelter and the sea. A few more rainy seasons and the remaining wedge of cliff, bomb shelter and all, would slide soggily into the sea. But for now, it suited his needs.

A secondary shield opened to his voice, and triggered the ceiling lights. As he stepped inside, he saw the message-light flashing on his console. He took a sandwich out of the freezer, put it in the microwave, then read the messages.

There were two reports: one from Eastcoast Sector, and one from the asteroid colonies. He took the colony message first.

He sat silently, studying the list of recent applicants for various colony jobs. Seven had made the long journey from Earth, eighty had been refused. The reasons for refusal were theoretically private information, but in the FWG's eyes, a citizen who demanded privacy was probably up to something. Aaron had disguised his own deep instinct for privacy with the uniform of an FWG employee. No one questioned him and he had access to endless amounts of confidential information.

Age, physical description, work experience, family background, medical and psychological profiles: he ran through the records of eighty-seven strangers, then sat back with a sigh. Nothing. She wasn't in the mining colonies, nor had she applied to go there. His sandwich had grown cold again in the microwave, but at least it was thawed. He ate it mechanically.

Then he talked to Raymond Takuda, Sector Head of Eastcoast Patrollers.

"Aaron, give it up," Takuda groaned. His face was lined, hard and polished as a walnut after fifty years of patrol work. "You've been on that conspiracy theory for years without a nibble."

"I can't give it up," Aaron lied. "I'm still on assignment. Besides, she's still missing."

"Maybe she had a sex change. Maybe she's dead."

"I've checked hospital and morgue records all over the world."

Takuda grunted, looking interested in spite of himself. "No traces? That's highly inefficient of us, to lose a private citizen."

"You didn't find anything."

"She's not in any Eastcoast Detention Centers, she hasn't been arrested, she hasn't registered to vote in Sector elections, or been hospitalized at FWG expense, or got a docking or a speeding fine, she hasn't even got a registered vehicle or a credit account at this end of the world. Maybe she drowned or fell off a mountain."

"Maybe."

"Sometimes when you've torn your hair out trying to find something, you find it right under your nose—you're just not seeing it."

"Is that the best you can give me?"

"Are you obsessed?"

Aaron paused a moment, to give the question the consideration it warranted. "Maybe," he said slowly. "I hadn't thought about it. It's just—I guess I'm obsessed about how anyone could do that. Just walk out of sight. She's the sister of a mass murderer. The question of conspiracy, given the political climate of Desert Sector at the time, is certainly valid. Even if she's totally innocent, if she can disappear like this, so can other people. I want to know how she's doing it."

The walnut-lines merged as Takuda grimaced. "You're right. I don't like that, either. But, Aaron, we were given that Conspiracy to Disturb, Undermine or Destroy as a blind to absolve the FWGBI of any intent to use a madwoman as a scapegoat. Everybody knows that."

Aaron smiled. "They will now."

"Ah, nobody cares anymore. Yours is the only Sector still working on it."

"It looks better that way. Besides—" He shrugged. "Who knows? It might be true. We still can't find her. And I'm beginning to wonder who we'll find with her if we do."

"There's that," Takuda agreed softly. "There is indeed that. Have you checked with Sundown Sector? Maybe she's involved with the National Regression Coalition."

"That's a possibility. No, I haven't checked it."

"Well, I'll let you know if we come across anything. As you say, it's an interesting problem."

"Thanks. I appreciate it."

He had to get to work himself, then. Yet he sat gazing at the blank screen, a man trained to movement, alertness, decision, still as a shadow in an old bomb shelter inside the Earth, while seconds and minutes on the chronometer wound silently into the past. Memory traced a face lightly, briefly on the screen; he remembered, as if remembering a missing hand, what it was to feel.

He stirred, murmuring. His voice sounded eerie in the underground bubble. He moved then, quickly, restlessly, wanting familiar patterns of action, the beginnings and endings of small incidents, human voices.

As he walked into the Constellation Club, the walls around him kindled to a fiery rose. Midnight, by Sidney Halleck's frivolous timepiece. He stood a moment in the shadows near one of the house security guards, otherwise known as Sidney's bouncers. Eighteen of the twenty stages

were enclosed within silken falls of light. People wandered
in and out of the light, glowing, for a moment, like dragonflies
in the cascades of color. Eighteen bands were playing at once
under Sidney's roof, but the sound itself was caught and
transformed within the curtains of light. The only music to
be heard above the noise from the dozen bars was Sidney's
house band, Historical Curiosity, decorously playing chamber
music in a corner.

The place seemed untroubled. Aaron, who had been on
his feet for four hours, called in a shift break. He borrowed
a glittering receiver-belt from the bouncer and pressed a colored light at random. A robot band called IQ was running
through the popular tunes of the hour behind the blue curtain.
He touched other lights, got alpha music on the green stage,
electronic music on the yellow, and, behind orange, something that sounded like a battle between recycling bins. He
located Nova, finally, behind purple light.

Quasar was belting out a song about making love on an
asteroid passing too near the sun. The lyrics made Aaron
wince. But music shirred from the Scholar's rod-harp like a
solar wind, and the Magician was creating a wild, tangled
counterpoint out of his head with his body-wires. The Gambler's cubing made the air pulse like a war zone; Aaron
wondered, not for the first time, where anyone who resembled
a walking bundle of twigs hid so much strength. He returned
the receiver-belt, and made his way across the floor. He was
stopped, greeted several times; when he was halfway across
the vast club, the purple light in the distance vanished.

He located the Magician at a table in a corner, toweling
sweat and makeup off his face while Sidney dealt. Sidney,
his serene, bulky face ferocious in concentration, saw him
coming and beamed.

"Aaron. How are you?"

The Magician raised his smudged face out of the towel,
smiling. "Pull up a seat," he said, and Aaron chuckled.

"Thanks, I'd like to keep my job."

"It's not really gambling."

"Why not?" Sidney asked, affronted. A deep, throbbing

run of notes sounded from an unlit stage on the other side of the floor; the sound was faint but the Magician's ear turned curiously toward it.

"What was that?"

"A pre-FWG guitar: an electric bass. Someone in Thames Sector found it and wrote to me about it. I bought it from her unseen. It's in beautiful condition."

"Who's playing it?"

"Michael Mole of the Starcatchers. He loved the sound." He added cheerfully at the Magician's quizzical expression, "I can't play it well myself, and you've seen my house full of instruments. I have everything from a nineteen-foot grand piano to a didjeridoo—"

"A didjeri—what?"

"So what should I do? Put it into a museum? The Mole took to it as if he had come into the world playing it. As if it were the ghost of the music he'd been waiting to hear. Music is meant to be given away."

"Up to a point."

"No. Impose no limits and you'll encounter no limits." He appealed to Aaron, who was lounging against the wall behind him, wondering when Sidney was going to pick up his cards. "Isn't that true, Aaron?"

"Except for the FWG drinking laws and your own credit."

"Unless," Sidney said complacently, "you own the bar." He tossed a two-credit chip on the table between them and inquired of the patiently waiting Magician, "Are you in this game?"

The Magician shoved his own chip forward. "It's customary," he commented, "to look at your cards before you bet."

"I'm gambling," Sidney explained. He discarded, to Aaron's eye at random, and swallowed beer. The Magician drew one. His face was at its leanest, its most clinical; Aaron could almost hear his brain working with ruthless precision to take Sidney's money. Sidney ran his fingers down his nose and sipped beer again, his attention drawn fondly to his brilliant, smoothly running creation. The Magician's eyes lifted, first to Sidney's absent face, and then to Aaron, who met his gaze expressionlessly.

The Magician's head bent, all the reptilian intensity suddenly fled from his face. He laid his cards down, his voice struggling against laughter. "You're an awful poker player, Sidney."

"What did I do?" Sidney demanded. "What did I do? You were reading my mind."

The Magician looked surprised. "It's your body language. Every time you get a terrible hand you run your fingers down your nose and sip beer. When you get a good hand, you don't move and I can feel you concentrate. It distracts me so much I'm having a hard time taking your money."

Sidney was silent. He spread out his cards with a sigh, and the Magician looked at them and laughed.

"So," Sidney said good-humoredly, "even your merciless streak has its limits."

"Apparently so." He gathered the cards. Then his head turned toward the stage lights behind him.

Aaron said, "They're still off."

"One more hand?"

"I'll try to concentrate less audibly." Sidney turned to add something to Aaron; his wrist receiver beeped before he could speak. He propped his head on his fist, listening. Aaron scanned the crowd, found the problem in an entrance not far from them.

A man dressed in the rotting fabrics of the immense, eerie wasteland of the Sector dump had wandered into the club. He looked bewildered by his surroundings. The silvery glow in his eyes told Aaron what drug he needed. Aaron signaled the street patrol; a moment later they saw grey uniforms at the edge of the light spilling out of the door as Sidney's bouncers talked the wanderer back into the street. Sidney leaned back in his chair.

"Thank you, Aaron."

"It's odd he strayed so far . . . They think the world beyond the dump is dangerous."

The Magician, about to deal, looked up incredulously from the cards. "You have talked to them?"

"I've been in there a couple of times . . . It's a weird place. They have their trails, their territories, their hiding places from people like me, from the world. You walk their paths around mountains, through valleys of junk, all the debris of another century . . . I've seen derelict planes there, even old cruise ships stranded on their sides. You rarely see anyone; you see a movement, a shadow, maybe a kid who hasn't learned to hide fast enough. It's always silent, dead silent, and you know you're watched . . ."

"How did you get someone to talk to you?"

"Not everyone is afraid. Some are just eccentric old-timers who live in the dump because it's more peaceful than the city. They don't mind hearing news about the rest of the world."

"How," Sidney asked simply, "did you find the courage to go in there?"

"I was looking for someone."

"Did you find him?"

"Her." He resisted an impulse to shift under the Magician's curious gaze. "No."

"The outcasts of this century in the graveyard of the last," Sidney said thoughtfully. "I wonder what music they play . . ." He caught the Magician's smile. "No, I'm serious. Imagine what instruments they might invent, what music would occur to them in such isolation . . . Speaking of isolation, that reminds me: How would you like a free trip to the Underworld?"

The Magician's smile vanished. All the expression in his face disappeared; he looked, Aaron thought, as if he had just become his own effigy. Then he was back among them, his voice dry, slightly shaken.

"Is there a return ticket?"

"Did I phrase it that badly?" Sidney wondered.

"Well, no, but why do you want to send me to the Underworld? I thought you liked my music."

"I do. That's the point. Some creative soul up there

realized that the near-total silence on the Underworld might have a debilitating effect on prisoners who will serve their terms and be reabsorbed into Earth society. We have to live with them: that's the thrust of their Rehab program. To some extent we can determine what it is we want to live with.'' His fingers strayed through the deck of cards as if gathering information from them. ''They're up there in that twisted doughnut, spinning around a vacuum. On Earth a prisoner might hear wind. Rain. A cricket. Water flowing. A sound barrier broken. Air traffic. In Corcrow Prison they hear the sea and the factory generators. All the small sounds of the daily life of the society they're excluded from and will go back to . . . to live within the continuity of Earth-time, with both feet somewhere near the ground . . .''

The Magician made an acquiescent rumble. ''I can't argue with that,'' he said mildly. ''But why—''

''Why you? The Rehab Director wants me to go up and listen to their silence. He also wants me to suggest an experimental music program, among other things. I thought of Nova immediately. You're colorful, you're too disciplined to get into trouble in the Underworld, and you know what I think of your music. It's time you got some publicity. You'd do one concert in the Underworld, and if your band agrees, I'll hand the matter over to the Suncoast Agency and they'll arrange an off-world tour for you.''

The Magician's face was flushed under the smudges of magenta. Once again he was at loss for words. Aaron grinned.

''You said you needed a change, Magic-Man.''

''Will you do it?''

''An off-world tour? With your backing? Sidney, that's—that's—''

''There won't be much time to prepare: less than a month. But you'll have a captive audience up there, in more places than the Underworld.'' He chuckled indulgently at his own joke. ''Think about it. Talk to your band.''

''They'll go. I'll have to get the *Flying Wail* into shape.''

''The Agency could provide a smallcraft.''

''No. I like using my own equipment. I haven't taken

the *Flying Wail* off-Earth in five years . . . Sidney, that's—thank you.''

"You're getting too good for this place," Sidney said, "and you're welcome." His big hands swept the clutter of cards back into order. "Now. One more hand. Something easy.''

"Wild Star. It's quick and easy. Seven-card draw, jokers wild, draw comes back up— How do you expect me to maintain a poker face with an offer like that?''

"It's my strategy," Sidney said gravely. An inner clock geared to the restless, tidal movements of the night made Aaron shrug himself away from the wall. He lingered, though, to watch Sidney pick up his cards.

In the next second he remembered to breathe. He willed his bones loose once more against the wall and sent thought-messages to Sidney: Don't blink. Don't let your voice change. Pretend it's a handful of nothing . . . Sidney shoved a chip into the center of the table. The Magician added five more.

Sidney matched it. The Magician raised his eyes. "So you do have something . . . or are you learning to bluff?''

Someone was standing behind the Magician: a blur of red, a mask. Sidney drew a card for the Magician, faceup: the ace of spades. The Magician eyed it and added to the chips. Sidney matched his bet and upturned a final card.

Aaron's eyes were drawn then, almost against his will, by the face behind the Magician. Long, rose-red hair dotted with black heart-pins. An elegant face, painted gold. Wide, straight shoulders. Grey eyes met Aaron's, unsmiling, opaque, secret. Then Sidney glanced up at her and she smiled.

"The Queen of Hearts," Sidney said surprisedly.

The Magician murmured absently in agreement, and Aaron looked down at the card Sidney had drawn: her face again stylized, enigmatic. He resisted an impulse to tell Sidney to bet the entire Constellation Club.

"The Ace," the Magician said, "bets five.''

"Six," Sidney said wildly.

"Call.''

Sidney laid his cards down one by one. Ten, Jack, Queen,

King, Ace of Hearts, and the two wild cards, the jokers, the jesters.

"Fool's Run."

The Magician whistled without sound. Then he leaned back in his chair and laughed, scattering a worthless collection of spades and diamonds. "Your game, Sidney. Rack in the chips."

Aaron lifted his eyes again, feeling oddly dislocated in time and space, as if something, somewhere in an alternate universe, had ended or were about to begin. But the Magician had slid the Queen of Hearts back into the deck and she was gone.

F O U R

Sidney Halleck and Dr. Fiori arrived at the Underworld on the same morning. Chief Klyos, in a sour mood because his transfer request to Southcap Sector had been turned down without even a comment, had Sidney taken to the Hub quarters for visiting officials, where Jeri Halpren was waiting. Then he dealt with Dr. Fiori. The doctor had brought three assistants: two men and a very pretty, very bored young woman whose face changed only when she saw the small, spartan infirmary ward which Jase had allotted to them to live in. The Dream Machine was still drifting along the Underworld's orbit, to be scooped up later by the dock arms. Meanwhile, Dr. Fiori said, after a brisk glance at the room where the equipment would be set up, he would like to meet the prisoner.

Jase raised an eyebrow at the verb, but said only, "Come back to my office with me, Dr. Fiori. You'll be logged in officially as a guest of the Hub, and then I'll send for half a dozen security guards to escort you to the prisoner. Ms. Barton, Mr. Ames and Mr. Ng, if you'll wait here a few minutes, someone will come to show you the cafeteria and the rec room, which will be about the only places not off limits to you without my express permission. Enjoy your stay."

Dr. Fiori was silent as they walked down the still, grey-carpeted, curving corridor toward the transport spoke. Jase set his palm into the ID slot beside the round door. It opened like the eye of a kaleidoscope to reveal the long transport tunnel, the magnetic track disappearing toward the Hub, and the niches along the walkway where the robot-guards, armed with laser-rifles, stood at intervals, motionless, blindly watching. They walked down the ramp to the first car. Dr. Fiori said mildly, "You seem a little hostile."

Jase swallowed several replies. "I'll feel better when you start realizing where you are. The woman you want to meet is responsible for the deaths of over fifteen hundred people. I'm responsible for you. She's dangerous and I don't know how she'll react to you. At the same time, I don't want you to hurt her."

Dr. Fiori stared at him. The robot-guard, gold and metallic grey, began to blur along the walls as the car sped toward the Hub. "Why do you care?" he asked finally.

"I don't."

"Well, then, what—"

"There's something," Jase said grumpily, "about all this that makes me very uneasy. She's been down in the Dark Ring as quiet as a spider in space for seven years. Why did she suddenly attract your attention? It makes me uneasy because sometimes I have a hunch that things rarely happen by chance. They happen because events tug each other, because people's loves and hates and desires are constantly overlapping, because unfinished business, no matter how forgotten it is, is always asking to be finished. She shouldn't be down there. But, since we put her down there, we should have the sense to leave her alone." He swung himself out as the car halted, and gave both his handprint and his name to the ID scanner. It acknowledged him with a series of quick, musical tones, and the Hub gate opened. He added, "At least, that's what I think. You're the doctor."

Dr. Fiori followed him into the Hub, past the long, curving, smoky wall at the heart of the Hub behind which the central computer silently monitored everything from the robot-guard to the plumbing. Jase's office faced the main door to the computer room. He was used to the brilliant colored lights which substituted for a view above the main console, but Dr. Fiori gazed at them a moment before he answered.

"You have ambiguous views about the prisoner."

Jase sighed. "I have ambiguous views about just about everything, Dr. Fiori. And you know what? I'm too old to care." He gestured at the com. "Just give it your name and a vague idea of what you're doing here. Your voice pattern is important. It's for the Hub records, in the event you're caught here during an emergency." He glanced up to see Dr. Fiori smiling. "What's funny?"

"Nothing." He brushed at his untidy hair. "I'm a little tired. I keep saying trite things, you keep giving me sensible answers. I think that if you're concerned about the Dream Machine or me or the prisoner, you should come and watch me work."

Jase was silent, surprised. "Maybe I will," he said, and was again surprised, this time at himself.

Terra Viridian sat in a corner of her cell, one of a vast honeycomb of cells in the enormous walls of the Dark Ring. Dr. Fiori, surrounded by guards on the escalator to the top cells, saw the ring-wall with its individual, delicately glistening cell-shields, and was reminded bizarrely of insects with trembling, translucent wings about to swarm. Terra, on the other side of the shield, no longer even saw it; it was simply a backdrop for her visions.

Blurred, thick, vertical lines behind a misty, flickering flow of light . . . The cell-shield vanished; the thick lines became human: guards carrying rifles. She saw them disinterestedly; they belonged to another vision, another dimension. Her mind made them insubstantial, strips of color that could be peeled away from the air and discarded.

"Terra. Terra Viridian."

She heard her name as from another galaxy, across dust clouds and black, starless backwashes of space. In an unknown place something rested. She felt the vague confines of her body.

She said tiredly, without blinking, "Yes."

"I am Dr. Arturo Fiori. I am going to try to help you. Do you understand?"

"Yes," she said indifferently. Her eyes, enormous, vision drugged, gazed at the cluster of faces. They all might have been speaking, or none of them; it was not important. Stars replaced their faces. The red sun.

They came back, or else they had never gone. A food tray had appeared in front of her. Someone had eaten a little of the food. And then someone had rested, suspended in a timeless silence, within an amethyst mist.

"Please come with me."

She expected another shower, or a period of pacing in a circle. But they led her into unfamiliar places that protruded insistently into her thoughts. Dr. Fiori was speaking to her. Force fields winked out at her approach, elevator doors opened. She went up or down or sideways through the Underworld, trying to ignore Dr. Fiori, who was talking about loaves of bread. Bread was not in the vision. Nor were yawning doors, so much light, so much movement any part of her other daily life. Terra's life. Her breathing quickened; she could feel her heartbeat. She blinked rapidly, nervously, but the dark walls loomed; she could not find the vision.

"A language without words," Dr. Fiori said, and she said instantly, "Yes," stopping so abruptly that a rifle prodded her back. "Yes." Expression came into her eyes. She saw the doctor finally, a rumpled, dark-haired man shorter than she, and in the same moment she remembered that she herself existed within this silent, endlessly curved world. She had fingers, a mouth, a name. How had she gotten here?

"The sky is red," she said, remembering.

"Warped," a guard murmured. "Warped right out of the galaxy."

"Please," Dr. Fiori said. The rifle tapped her shoulder. "Go."

She whirled suddenly, terrified by the long walk, the strange freedom. "Are you going to kill me?" The guards had melded into a circle around her, their rifles raised. Dr. Fiori pushed through them to stand in the circle with her. For a second he was terrified, but not of her; she saw that, she felt it, holding him in her cloudy gaze. His voice was gentle.

"No one is going to hurt you. I want to try to understand you."

She held him motionless a moment longer. Then his face flattened, became a photograph, a cartoon. An oval. His mind held no understanding, only vaguenesses. She said wearily, "No."

"Trust me."

He took her arm. The human touch jerked her back to dangerous shores: loneliness, time passing toward a blank future, memories of other touches. She pulled away from him, panicked again, and began to walk mechanically. The long grey carpet turned into a twisted path through the stars, and then into the crystal sand. She turned away from the world into silence.

Jase was watching her on one of the monitor screens in the computer room. Cameras followed her every movement from her cell to the Dark Ring infirmary. She looked alien, he thought. A head taller than Fiori; a spacer, he remembered, bald and thin as an insect, with huge, secret, insect eyes. He watched closely, tense. If anything happened to Fiori, and word got out that Terra Viridian was doing anything but sitting in the Dark Ring waiting to die, it was his ass in the Big Dipper, and he didn't want a transfer that far. She had stopped once, turned, and had half a dozen rifles aimed at her so quickly he thought she was dead. She had moved fast, without warning. "Terra Viridian Killed On Rampage In Underworld." But Dr. Fiori was fast too, breaking in among the guards, talking nonstop. Jase breathed when they moved again: the mad murderer, the babbling, surprisingly courageous doctor, the six guards trained to kill.

His shift was nearly over; he was looking forward to supper and a beer with Sidney Halleck, one bright spot in the day. It had been lousy: Jeri Halpren annoying him before breakfast about some visiting nightclub band. the transfer refusal, Terra Viridian unburied, like something in an old movie, wandering wraithlike and ominous around the Underworld, a patrol-cruiser malfunction near the moon during a speed-chase. There was another crater in the moon now. Messages had flashed back and forth for hours, from Artemis, from FWGBI: Have the bodies been found? Yes. No. There was nothing left to find. How did it happen? Whose fault? Who were they? Who is next of kin? Where— Meanwhile, the smallcraft that the cruiser had been pursuing ran out of fuel and was drifting somewhere beyond the backside of the moon, sending erratic and drunken messages for help.

Nils should have caught this one, Jase thought. He'd have appreciated it.

Terra was in the Infirmary Ward. Jase turned away from the screen, relinquishing his responsibility to will them all alive. He rubbed his eyes tiredly and was rewarded, when he dropped his hands, with a vision of Jeri Halpren entering his office.

He made a noise and crossed the hall. Jeri was grinning. We should connect those teeth to a generator, Jase thought wearily. He sat down and let Jeri talk for a few moments, until a salient point struck him.

"You keep saying 'Sidney Halleck said this,' and 'Sidney Halleck suggested that—' I wouldn't mind hearing from Mr. Halleck himself what he said."

Jeri's smile eased faintly. "Well. You could call him when he gets back home in four days."

"What?"

"He had to leave this evening. He had some conference to attend tomorrow in Rainforest Sector. I tried to call you before he left," Jeri added nervously, "but I couldn't get through to you, and you always chew me out when I walk in on an emergency." Jase sighed. "He said he was sorry he missed you."

"So am I."

"One of his bands is coming to play here."

Jase scowled at him. "You keep saying that too."

"With your permission, of course."

"I don't care. It's your program. I just don't want to even know they've been here until they're gone. Music. Nightclub bands. This is a—"

"There is historical precedent," Jeri said warily but firmly. "Sidney Halleck said so."

Jase leaned back in his chair. "Thanks," he said sourly. Lights flashed at him, responding to his sudden relaxation; he leaned forward again, wondering who—the moon, the lost smallcraft, Earth, Dr. Fiori and Terra, or the unknown—was calling out of crisis, chaos and urgent necessity to deprive him of his beer this time.

"Terra. Can you hear me? Terra."

She was sitting in a bubble. It was warm, pliant, suspended in shadows above the floor. She lifted a hand, touched it wonderingly. The translucent wall stretched to her touch, then flowed back into shape.

"Terra."

A young woman in a red jumpsuit was speaking softly into a computer. Terra stared at the red, swaying toward it as if it were a flame. "Project: Guinea Pig. Dr. A. Fiori. Assistants: Reina Barton. Nathaniel Ng. Pietro Ames. Subject: Terra Viridian. Female. Age 28. Prisoner, Dark Ring of the Underworld. Status-sheet follows. Legal permission for use of Underworld prisoner in experimental bio-computer program given by Dr. Grace Czerny, FWGBI, Department of Psychobiology. Family: one sister, whereabouts unknown."

She looked at the doctor, who was standing beside the bubble. He nodded, smiling.

"Go ahead, Reina. Let's begin."

A screen above the console glowed. Colors washed across it, merged to form new colors that swirled together again into different shades. Terra, who had seen no colors outside of her own mind for seven years, watched, her lips parted. She put one hand on her head suddenly, felt a cap on it. But with the fuchsias and blues and golds fusing in front of her, the thin filaments running out of her head seemed unimportant.

"Terra. What do you see?"

"Colors. Novas."

"Terra." His voice was slower now, very calm. "I want you to do something very simple for me. All the things I will ask you to do for the next few days will be very simple."

"Nothing is simple."

"The beginning is very simple. Will you try?"

She moved her eyes from the screen, looked directly at him. "Override," she said clearly. Black lightning leaped through the red sky, struck a patch of the purple sand that melted and ran to meet the incoming tide. The colors on the screen dissolved into static. Someone whistled.

"How did she do that? Dr. Fiori, she called that one—"

"Sh. Terra. Concentrate on the colors. Remember them. Let them come back."

She thought of them and they returned: colors beautiful enough to drink, to smell, to wear.

"Good, good . . . Keep concentrating . . ." His voice faded; the colors danced together, fell apart, swirled into a memory, as sudden and astonishing to her as any of her visions. The greenhouses on the tiny, misshapen moon where she had been born . . . the warm, damp air, the smell of an alien earth, all the colors that grew out of that Earth as easily as wishes, as freely as dust and ice and magma grew out of all the worlds she knew then . . .

"Terra. Tell me what you see."

"A rose," she whispered.

FIVE

"Where," the Magician demanded surprisedly, "is that light coming from?"

The members of Nova looked at one another, and then at him. In the midst of the Constellation Club, with its stages flooded with light and its walls, at that hour, glowing a soft amethyst mist, the question seemed absurd. The Nebraskan stroked his pale, drooping mustache and glanced around obligingly. The Scholar, his black face split by a silver lightning bolt, narrowed his eyes incredulously.

"Would you care to elucidate?"

"I don't see anything," the Gambler said vaguely. Propped against the stage, he looked as if his long, wraithlike body would collapse into a formless pile if the stage suddenly disappeared. "Except. You know. The usual."

"Elucidate," Quasar said, sampling each syllable as if it were edible. She gave the Magician a sidelong smile, revealing scarlet teeth. "*Moi*, I will help you elucidate, Magic-Man. Just tell me where."

"It's not from our stage," the Nebraskan said. "What does it look like?"

"What?"

"The light," the Nebraskan said bewilderedly. "You just said—"

"Oh." He shook his head slightly, blinking. "I just saw something out of the corner of my eye. Or thought I did. I don't see it now."

"I don't, either," the Gambler said helpfully.

"Tell me about this thing: to elucidate. Is it legal, or is it subterranean?"

"Underground," the Scholar murmured. "If that's the word you're looking for."

Quasar waved fingernails that matched the hues of her short, rainbow hair. "*La même chose*—it's the same. Underground, subterranean—"

"One has political connotations, the other is from an ancient, pre-FWG language called Latin. Sub: under. Terra: earth. Underearth, underground—"

"Can we get down to business?" the Magician pleaded, "before the break is—"

"Anyway, the opposite of legal is not subterranean, but—"

"Underworld," the Gambler suggested. The Magician folded his arms and raised his voice.

"Which is why I called this meeting, if anyone happens to remember that this is a meeting."

"Well, what?" the Scholar asked affably. "We're here, we're listening. Sidney give us a raise?"

"Sidney's giving us an off-world tour, beginning at the Underworld."

They were silent, staring at him again, their vivid, painted faces still as masks hanging in the air around him. Then the Nebraskan grinned, and the Gambler made a sudden move to keep himself from sliding onto the floor.

"The Underworld," the Scholar breathed. "Magic-Man—"

"We'll play one night there, then go on to the moon, to Rimrock and Moonshadow, then to Helios—"

"The sun?" the Gambler asked bewilderedly.

"The space-city."

"Hot damn," the Nebraskan said. Quasar, expressionless, lit a cigarette and blew smoke in a jet stream over the Magician's head.

"Prison," she said brittlely. She added something succinct and untranslatable in old-world. "Magic-Man—"

"It's just one concert," he said again, quickly, watching her hand shake as she drew on the cigarette. "We'll only be there overnight."

"But what do they want with music in the Underworld?" the Scholar asked amazedly. "Especially ours?"

"They're starting a new Rehab program." He smiled dryly. "They're trying to bring more noise into the Underworld. Sidney recommended us. The Suncoast Agency is setting up the rest of the tour for us." He nodded at the Scholar's whistle. "It's too good to turn down. If we can get some publicity, maybe we can return to a full Sector tour."

The Gambler had come to life, standing almost straight. He looked horrified. "Fly?"

The Magician closed his eyes and opened them. "That's the general idea."

"Space?"

"It's ubiquitous," the Scholar said gravely.

"No."

"No what?"

"No way. Magic-Man, I can't. I don't have any balance."

"I'm not asking you to walk a tightrope to the Underworld. What do you mean you can't? You're going. Going without you is not among the options.''

"Here.'' The Gambler tapped at his ear. "I don't have any balance here. I get sick. Throw up. Even in tall buildings. Everywhere.''

The Magician gazed at him remotely, as if he had just dropped a pint of beer into the piano. "There are cures for that,'' he said distinctly.

"I can't—"

"You can't back out on me now, is what you can't do. You've been playing my music for five years. It might be the only thing inside whatever it is you call a brain, but you know it like you know air, and if you think Nova is going on an off-world tour with some cuber off the streets we've rehearsed with for three weeks, you are thinking with your head up your backside. You're going, and that's all—"

"I can't.'' He swayed back from the Magician's wrath, his pale, gangly arms draped along the stage. Only his shoulders, wide and straight from cubing, suggested any muscle beneath his bodysuit. "I don't even fly a sol-car. Magic-Man, I have to stay on the ground. I don't like air under me. At all. Ever. Me''—he put a palm to his lips and then to the floor at his feet—"Earth. We like each other. There's nothing I can do. I knew you would get famous on me someday.''

"What?''

"I left my last band because of that. They started to do tours. Fly. I knew it would happen to Nova.'' He sighed. "The best bands are always leaving me.'' He added, his fingers gripping the stage as if he might float away, "I'm sorry.''

The Magician regarded him expressionlessly a moment longer. He turned his gaze to the Scholar. "How's your balance?'' he asked with dangerous calm.

"Fine,'' the Scholar said hastily. "Me.'' He kissed the air. "Space. I'm with you, Magic-Man.''

The Magician looked at Quasar, who was puffing rapidly. "We can't go without the Gambler," she said nonchalantly, but she didn't meet his eyes.

"We're going."

"But—"

"The Gambler will either go with us or find a replacement. As good as he is."

"As good?" the Gambler said doubtfully. The Magician withdrew his eyes from Quasar long enough to glare.

"And you'll find one fast." He turned back to Quasar, all his attention focused on her, for while her delicately raised eyebrows suggested indifference, her eyes were dark, expressionless, and the movements of her cigarette too abrupt. She would not put her reluctance into words, and yet it was there between them, tangible as the haze of smoke around her.

"It's the prisoners we'll play to," he said, for she objected to authority instinctively and without compunction. "The Light-Ringers. Not the patrollers." And then he saw it: her edgy, nervous movements confined in too small a space, her eyes straining to see through an artificial darkness.

He drew breath noiselessly; she looked at him then, smiling a little, wicked smile at her own terror.

"If you want this, Magic-Man," she said, casting caution back to him. He made no move to intercept it.

"I want it," he said. He also wanted to take her hand, kiss her cheek in gratitude. He didn't move, but in some strange way the air around him transmitted his impulse: she looked surprised, the smile suddenly young.

"Good!" the Nebraskan said, oblivious to obstacles. "When are we leaving?"

"Three—less than three weeks."

"You taking the *Flying Wail*?"

"Of course."

"Does it still fly?" the Scholar asked.

"Of course it flies," the Magician said indignantly. "It merely has a small problem communicating."

"How big a small problem?"

"I'll fix it."

"Last time you had a small problem, the refrigeration

system broke down, and we spent two weeks touring with no cold beer.''

"Beer," the Nebraskan murmured. "Break's half over."

"We'll meet tomorrow night, get the details straight, decide what we're going to play. If," he added icily, "we have a cuber among us."

The Nebraskan fondled his mustache. "We could drug him for the flight," he suggested. The Gambler, galvanized, pushed himself away from the stage in the direction of the nearest bar, the Magician's brooding gaze between his shoulder blades.

The Scholar shook his head. "How will we play without him? He plays those cubes like he's inside our heads, hearing our music before we do."

The Magician didn't answer. Still frowning, he heard the rambling, chaotic noises in the club ebb to a distance, like a tide. A faint throb of cubing caught his ear, or the ghost of cubing from a different time.

He moved finally, it seemed to him toward the music. "Let's get a beer while we have time. Don't worry," he added to the astonished Scholar. "We'll have a cuber."

Aaron, off duty, was sipping Scotch at one of the quieter bars: a broad, half oval of mahogany and brass that reminded him vaguely of old sailing ships. He was running through lists in his mind: lists of factory workers, private hospital personnel, army recruits, lists of names that could be lies, of lives that could be faked, all except for one incongruity, one careless detail at the moment of interface. Among 5.2 billion people scattered from Earth to the asteroids, how could he find someone who didn't want to be found? She was picking rice in Dragon Sector, she was feeding birds and albino tigers in a zoo, she was leading Rim-Tours around the coast of Sundown Sector. She was studying for the priesthood. He mused over that one. But even they had credit numbers, ID cards, tax records. She had changed her name, but she couldn't falsify every single record of her past, and there had to be that one moment when the two, past and future, overlapped into their complex identity. He stared into his Scotch, almost too tired of thinking to think. Why should I care? After seven years? What am I going to do with her if I find her? Shoot her because her crazy sister killed my—I want to find her. I need something from her. I need.

He stilled his thoughts and was immediately enveloped in memory. He tasted the ghost of a kiss. She was dressed in khaki, the last time. She kissed me good-bye and turned, damn near hitting me with her rifle as she went to board the troop-cruiser. Three months later she called me. She was pregnant, she was laughing, they were letting her come home early . . . She said I had a pirate's face, she never wanted me to change it. She threw a frying pan at me once. Her eyes were so black you could fly in them . . .

Something hit his boots. He crawled out of the time-tunnel back to the present, back to Sidney's Wonderland. He looked down bewilderedly. Half a dozen roses were scattered at his feet. He glanced behind him, saw a figure swathed in a cocoon of gold sequins, all but for one bare arm still gracefully completing the arc of its toss. Even the eyelashes glittered gold. The dark eyes smiled, but there was no telling what sex the slender arm belonged to. Aaron, distrusting ambiguities, let the roses lie.

"Whatever happened to the art of gentle conversation?" Sidney Halleck murmured beside him. "It went out with the bassoon." He bent, scooped the roses off the floor and dropped them onto the bar. Aaron touched one. Sleek, shiny black acrylic, they were all perfect and they would never die.

"Sometimes it's easier not to talk . . . No confusion, no embarrassment, no hurt . . . and no tomorrow."

"Really?"

"That's the rule of the rose. One night, no questions, no complications—"

"No names?"

He shrugged. "It doesn't matter; no one would believe you even if you gave your real name. That's the simplest lie of all."

"Is it?" He picked up the roses, let them fall gently. Aaron felt the amiable expression on his face suddenly strained.

"And," he added lightly, "no thorns. Nothing to hurt with."

"I see thorns," Sidney said. Aaron looked at him. The powerful, kindly face made him smile suddenly, tiredly.

"So do I. But if I catch a rose, I take it for what it's worth, and sometimes it's worth clinging with one finger to the edge of life for one more day—" He stopped, startled at himself, and picked up his glass. Sidney motioned for a beer.

"I understand," he said mildly. "I'm just critical because they clog my vacuums." He smiled as Quasar, in black leather from head to foot, the heels on her boots impossibly high, strode across the floor toward them. Then he blushed as she flung her arms around him and left a rainbow stain of color on his lips. She turned on her heel to face Aaron, dragged deeply at her cigarette and threw it at his feet. He ground it out, his expression unruffled, as she spun away. Sidney wiped his mouth, looking as if one of his pop robot-bands had just broken into opera.

"Impulsive," Aaron commented. The rest of Nova scattered around the bar, the Magician at his elbow.

"I think," Sidney said, emerging from behind his napkin, "it might actually catch on. A social dinosaur emerging back into fashion, outlasting even the roses."

"What's he talking about?" the Magician asked Aaron.

"Kissing."

"But as a social gesture, the cigarette was bewildering. Does that mean she likes you or she doesn't like you?"

"It means she wants to set my boots on fire."

"She'll more likely set my club on fire one of these days." He added to the Magician, "Will Nova go to the Underworld?"

The Magician nodded a trifle grimly. "One way or another. The Gambler gets space-sick, and Quasar—does she have a record, Aaron?"

"Yes," Aaron said. Then he put down his glass, flushing slightly. "How did you know—"

"You told me once you even did a status-check on me, when we first met. What kind of a record? Will they give her an off-world passport? Will they let her in the Underworld? Will they let her out again?"

Aaron nodded. "She had a pretty wild youth in Lumière Sector. She lived underground, in the old sewer and train tunnels. They charged her with a lot of things, but the only things ever proven against her were property damage and disturbing the peace."

"She was in prison."

"For a couple of months. That was so long ago it shouldn't be a problem. As long as she doesn't create problems herself. She doesn't like patrollers."

"I think she likes you," the Magician said, with an unusual flash of insight. "It's that she likes you that she doesn't like."

"Come again?"

"Never mind. It was a brilliant thought but fleeting. Thinking about people scrambles my circuitry. Have you ever been to the Underworld?"

"Once. I was doing some investigating in their Records Department. They don't give Earth-access. It's an amazing place. Quiet as a morgue and as efficient as death."

"I had a pleasant conversation with the Chief of the Underworld," Sidney commented. "We talked about nursery rhymes."

"Klyos?" Aaron said amazedly. "Nursery rhymes?"

"Have you met him?"

"No. I've heard rumors, including one that he's human."

"Is that strange?"

"In a prison that size, with that potential for disaster, yes." He shook his head. "Nursery rhymes. How did you get the Underworld Chief even to admit he might have been born?"

"He didn't go that far," Sidney said. The Magician's head turned toward Nova's stage an instant before the curtain-light spiraled down around it, then up again, signaling a two-minute warning. The Nebraskan was looking at his watch.

"Break's over," he called cheerfully. "Back to the salt mines."

The Magician put his glass down. "You staying awhile, Aaron?"

Aaron shook his head, draining his Scotch. "Not tonight. Too noisy. I'll drop by the *Flying Wail* soon, see how you're doing with that receiver."

"Thanks." He made a movement to turn, then didn't. "You all right?"

"Yes," Aaron said, feeling his face stiffen. "Thanks. Just tired."

He watched the Magician cross the floor, lost sight of him in the crowds, then found him again, taking his place on the stage. A cataract of purple fell; Nova dissolved into light, and Aaron caught his breath at the sudden, powerful and absurd vision of the light as an alien thing that had just reached down and hidden them forever somewhere within the secret worlds and mysterious, overlapping times beyond the Earth.

His fingers were digging into the muscles of his arms. He dropped his hands, wondering at himself. Too many dead-end messages in the bomb shelter? Too little sleep, too many dreams in a lonely bed? He found Sidney watching him gravely. He smiled wryly and picked up a black rose.

"Maybe I should use one of these."

"Talk to Quasar," Sidney suggested.

"No. I prefer anonymity, these days." He brooded at the room through narrowed, critical eyes, then shrugged, feeling boredom pull at his bones like gravity. He faked a yawn, wanting to go sit in the silent shelter, make more lists, search out new leads. "Tired tonight. I've been working overtime."

"Aaron, is something bother—"

"I'm fine, I just—" He stopped, alarmed at his own response to an unexpected voice-tone. He drew away from the bar, away from Sidney's puzzled, generous impulse. "Sometimes it's too much trouble. I'm just tired, thanks. Good night."

He eased quickly through the tangle of faces, perfumes, metallic fabrics, body paints, voices; he murmured greetings, steadied a drunk, sidestepped lovers and robot waiters. He reached the door finally and was halfway into the night when he realized he was holding something. It bit his thumb. His hand jerked and he breathed in a light, elusive scent. He stopped, blinking.

Someone had given him a living rose.

SIX

"**O**kay," Dr. Fiori said, wiping bloodshot eyes with his fingers. "Okay, okay, okay. We can never be certain. We can never know that what we're seeing is precisely what she's thinking. But you have to admit it's hard to say 'roast beef' and think of an elephant simultaneously."

"Then why," Reina asked, "is she giving you a red sun?"

"I asked for red."

"Why not a fire?"

"Because she's crazy."

"Then how . . ." She paused, confused, her mouth open. Terra, curled in the curve of her bubble-chamber, heard their words disinterestedly. Dr. Fiori sighed.

"I'm sorry. That was a stupid answer. Of course her responses will be somewhat distorted on the screen, and we can't know how distorted. But I asked for red and she thought red. The Dream Machine showed that she thought red. That's what's important. The Dream Machine picked up her brain responses for the word *red* and recorded them. It is working."

They both looked up at the prisoner, the young woman at the console in her sleek silver uniform, with her curious eyes and her painted mouth still open, and the rumpled doctor who had driven his hair up in spikes with his fingers.

"There's nothing wrong with her that I can find," Dr. Fiori added. "No lesions, no chemical imbalances, no growths, no peculiarity in the communication between the two sides of her brain. She should be perfectly healthy. The only aberration any of the tests have located is what I suppose we might call a 'brainstorm.' An excitation of electrical impulses with no apparent purpose or result. I've never seen anything quite like it . . . But these come at intervals; between them, there's no reason why she is not aware and lucid. Instead she seems addicted to these 'brainstorms' and the images they apparently create. Why? Perhaps, when we see the images, we'll begin to understand her." He smiled reassuringly, almost affectionately at Terra. To his surprise she spoke, with a dogged, weary patience,

"This is not in the vision."

Reina glanced at a smaller screen, which showed constantly changing cross sections of Terra's brain in vivid colors. "She's alert. No interference."

"Terra," Dr. Fiori said gently. "Terra Viridian."

"What?"

"How do you feel?"

"I am sane."

He was briefly silent. "Your perceptions of reality are distorted. We're going to analyze that, try to help you to see more clearly. Do you know where you are?"

"I am not here."

"You are in an Infirmary Ward in the Underworld. The same place you've been for the past five days. I'm finished showing you pictures. Now it's your turn. I'll ask you many questions; I want you to show me your thoughts, your dreams. If you do this, you'll be helping yourself, and you may help other sick people at the same time. Do you understand?"

She gazed at him, her eyes enormous, haggard. "I see," she whispered.

"Do you understand?"

"You must understand. The vision is all. The vision. The vision is the knowledge. The vision is life."

"What vision?"

"Caterpillars."

"What?"

"Initiation."

"Your words aren't making sense to me."

"Form. To take form. Something needs to take form."

"What needs to take form?"

"Something . . . in the mind."

"In your mind?"

"Yes."

"What?"

"I don't know. There is only the vision. The Dark Ring is nothing, no place. The vision is everything."

"So. You know where you are."

"No. I only know the vision."

Her head dropped wearily against the bubble-wall. An image appeared in the eye of the Dream Machine: a strange, distorted oval in grainy, pale purple sand.

Dr. Fiori pulled at his hair absently, chewing over the language she was creating. "Sand. Sand in Desert Sector? Are you recording this? Audio and visual?"

"Yes, Doctor."

"It's going to get complicated."

"Yes, sir. What is the oval?"

"Somebody's head? A memory of her killing, perhaps, distorted into a safe symbol." He watched the changing screen. "Now what?"

"It seems to be a wall."

"Or a cliff ? It's rising out of the sand."

"But it's solid black."

"A wall, then, I guess."

"It's too lumpy," his assistant objected, gazing, like the doctor and Terra, in fascination at the screen.

"It's a wall of the military station, distorted in memory. Something needs to take form . . . It's her memory that needs to take form. The truth she's terrified of. Trying to hide from it is making her crazy."

"But she was crazy before she shot all those people, or else why would she kill them? Unless she wasn't crazy, and she deserves to be here."

"Then something even more terrible happened before that. . . . Terra. Can you hear me? What is the first thing you remember? The very first thing in your life?" The screen changed. They were silent. "Water?"

"An ocean?"

"She's a spacer," Dr. Fiori said puzzledly. "There's no ocean on Mars."

"It's not the right color. Doctor, maybe you'd better test her colors again."

"Sh. Terra. Think back. You were born on a tiny moon circling a planet with no seas. What do you remember? What's that?"

"Static."

"From what? Is it the system?"

She touched lights. "No, it's her. Sort of—a brainstorm, I guess." They watched the screen. "Electric blue against black. It's pretty . . ."

"Okay. Let's try another question. Terra. What is it that needs to take form? What is it? Can you show us?"

She spoke from behind him, startling him again, for he had been talking to the screen. "I need to take form." Her voice was very thin, far away. "I need."

"What form?"

She was silent; the screen went dark. Dr. Fiori sat down.

"All right," he said softly, patiently. "Let's try something else."

An hour later he was pacing. Terra sat against the bubble-wall, watching him indifferently under half-closed eyes. The image on the screen had barely changed in ten minutes. "What is it?" he demanded. "Did I not ask you the right question? All right. Never mind. Your mind is your locked, secret room; I can't batter my way into it. I must persuade it open with the right key. I have a million keys, a million words, but only one word is right . . ." He stopped in front of the screen, stared at the black wall, the shadowy red background. It was fading. "Now what? Reina, what's she doing?"

His assistant blinked. She checked the monitor screen. "Falling asleep. So am I. What did you say, Doctor?"

"Nothing," he said penitently. "I'm sorry."

She frowned. "We've all been at it fourteen hours. She'll get sick at this rate; she's already thin as a stick. We'll all start hallucinating."

He dropped reluctantly into a chair. "All right. Call the guards. I want her back here in nine hours. Tell Ng I want him in your chair in nine hours."

"Okay, yes, Doctor." She shut down the Dream Machine and stretched.

"I wonder if we could rig up some way of taping her dreams . . ."

"I'll come back myself," Reina said suddenly. "There's nothing much else to do in the Underworld. Nat and Pietro have a card game going in the cafeteria with some of the guards. I'd rather watch this."

He smiled. "All right."

"It's interesting. I just keep wondering . . . something about the colors she sees."

"What?"

She gazed at the blank screen, still frowning. "There are no cliffs in that Sector. And why is the sky red?"

A handful of colored, viscous drops slowly elongating as they fell. A horizontal line, dark above, light below. Something flickering, out of focus, against a yellow surface.

A lightning bolt or a crooked bone frozen in cloudy red. A cave full of colored teeth, a mouthful of jewels. The bent oval . . .

The prisoner sat once more in the bubble, creating images. Jase had been drawn to watch; he leaned against a wall, his arms folded, eyeing the screen coldly. Dr. Fiori, looking a little less exhausted, swiveled on a stool like a top, monitoring Terra and her incomprehensible thoughts.

"That," Jase said finally, of something that flowed and rippled itself down into a disturbed surface, "is the weirdest thing I've ever seen. Dr. Fiori, are you sure this machine is working right?"

"I tested it," Dr. Fiori said. He tapped his head absently. "My own thoughts. Minor variations . . ."

"Does it bother her if I talk?"

"Look at her. She hardly knows you're here. You're not in the vision."

"The vision," Jase repeated softly. Life, it seemed to him, was a clutter of visions. Your own, someone else's, all demanding attention, all interfacing with or rebounding from another stubborn mingling of aspiration and experience. I have a vision of not working here, he thought, that is bumping against someone else's vision of me working here. My vision nudges his, his nudges mine . . . While we wait to see whose vision is stronger, the work gets done. When your vision is so strong you can't see the world any longer, when you see nothing but what's in your own head, that's when you go crazy. He pondered his own thoughts, and added, Or you change the world.

He studied the prisoner, huddled limply against herself, too lost in her own mind even to blink. She can't even change her socks.

Then she was looking back at him, her eyes direct, smoky, and he felt the skin move on the back of his neck. Shifting his eyes, he saw a man's face on the screen, dark browed, heavy eyed, grim, on the plump side, its individuality lost in the translation from Terra's eyes to machine, but his own face.

I'm damned, he marveled. It works.

"Terra," said Dr. Fiori gently, "can you tell us about the images you've just shown us? What do they mean?"

"They mean . . ." Her voice faded tiredly, returned. "What they are."

"But what are they?"

"They are what exists."

"Where?"

She swallowed. Her hands fluttered slightly in the shadows. "They are the messages. They are the doorways."

"Doorways to what?"

"To the change."

"Who will change? You?"

"Yes. I."

Hopeless, Jase thought. But Dr. Fiori seemed pleased. "When did the images begin?"

"On that day," Terra said.

"On what day?" He paused, added softly, "That day in the desert?"

Her fists clenched; her head swung back and forth. "No. No. No—"

"Terra."

"No."

" Terra."

"That was in the vision."

"It was—" He paused again, his mouth open, groping. Reina glanced at him, her brows raised in her poised, polished face. Jase thought, It's a game to her. Terra isn't human to her, she's a puzzle broken into pieces. Nothing like this could ever happen to someone named Reina in a silver jumpsuit, as long as she puts her lipstick on straight and never uses words like *initiation* in a sentence.

He said aloud, "Premeditated?" Dr. Fiori glanced at him vaguely, as if a chair had spoken.

"Terra. What day, then? What day did the visions begin on?"

"The day the oranges turned red."

"The day the— Terra, can you show me? What else

happened on that day? What were you seeing? Think. Remember. What happened when the oranges turned red? Why did they turn red? Show us."

Oranges in a blue bowl. Their reflection in a chrome table. The hem of a white curtain above them. A hand, reaching for an orange. A red shadow spilled over them.

"It began," Terra said simply.

"You must see," Dr. Fiori said in the cafeteria, over a cup of bouillon. "She is groping for a way out of her craziness. She's inventing her own symbolic language of change, but she's afraid to use it, follow it through. She's afraid to remember what drove her crazy in the first place. What happened on the day the oranges turned red."

"So it wasn't the massacre itself," Jase said politely.

"I don't think so. Although," he admitted, "it's difficult to conceive of a more traumatic event than that. Something outraged her sense of reality, her sense of balance in the world."

"Are you saying something happened to her that would justify her actions in Desert Sector?"

"No, no," Dr. Fiori said quickly. "I'm not looking for justifications. I'm primarily interested in the language she's using, and if it will lead her out of her trauma." He sipped bouillon, and added, "Terrible things happen to all of us. Most of us find ways to assimilate experience, to adjust to it. We don't turn bowls of oranges red in our minds. We— You don't care," he said accusingly, and Jase, still feeling the polite expression on his face, let it sag finally.

"I guess not," he said slowly. "She lost me with the oranges. Up to then, I could see a little of what you're seeing: that the strange images might have protected her from something. But if all this began because of a bowl of oranges, then I think it doesn't matter where she is—the Dark Ring, New Horizon—she's simply loony, and you'll never—" He stopped himself, gesturing. "What do I know? You're the doctor. I think your machine is incredible, but you're wasting your time with her."

"Maybe," Dr. Fiori said, steaming his face over the hot cup. "Why are you so judgmental about a bowl of oranges?"

Jase leaned back in his chair. "She massacred those people because an orange turned red. That leaves me cold. I can't have any feeling for her as a human being. I can't care anything more about her."

"You did care, then."

He shook his head. "I never cared. She got what she deserved here—less than she deserved. And yet—"

"And yet."

"She's not criminal. There's no malice, no gain, no anger, no human reason for her to have done what she did. You can't have feelings for someone that alien. Except maybe fear."

"Of her? Or of yourself?"

Jase eyed the doctor. The best defense against questions like that, he had decided long ago, was to answer them. "I think," he said finally, "that peoples' minds are like houses. Full of bedrooms, cellars, attics, closets, kitchens, elegant living rooms, gardens . . . Full of doors. By the time you've reached my age, you've pretty much opened all the doors. You know what closets the monsters are kept in, what ugly thought lives down in the basement, what bloody impulse is behind the attic door. You know, by this time, what they're worth to you. I'm comfortable in my own house. If someone rings the door bell, I let them in."

Dr. Fiori put his cup down, smiling. "I didn't think I'd like you," he said, "when I first talked to you."

"Well," Jase said uncomfortably. "You never know."

"I think you shouldn't judge her too quickly at this point. Bowls of oranges don't make people crazy. There's nothing wrong with her brain. It's she who's making herself crazy. And she'll tell us why. She can't speak. Words are terrifying to her. Or too precise, too imprecise, who knows? Or else we have never invented the words to say what she has seen. So she tells her story in a language that is silent, in hope that someone can learn to hear."

S E V E N

The Magician sat alone in the Constellation Club, listening. Sounds suggested other sounds in his head; the silence surrounding him slowly became layered and textured with music. The walls were indigo. Between three and four in the morning the world was as still as it ever got. He could even hear the mournful, distant moan of the last foghorn warning, warning. His fingers found the two bass notes on the keyboard between which the note of the foghorn hid; he touched the notes softly, played them against the foghorn, still listening.

His right hand strayed up the treble, a ripple of mist against the brooding bass. In his mind, he heard the rod-harp's brilliant, restless voice, the thunder of the cubes. The moon-white face of the mist looming against the indigo sky, the welter and crash of tide, the foghorn crying in its private, urgent voice of things invisible, secret, unexpected, that might or might not be within the mist . . .

A step in the mist dispersed it. Startled, he spun on the piano stool. The dark walls built around him once again. The silence within them was empty. The rod-harp, the cubes on the stage, covered against the dust, had sounded only in his head.

Aaron, in uniform, paused midstep. "Sorry," he said. "I saw the outer door unlocked. Thought I'd check . . . You're here late."

The Magician nodded, rising to stretch his legs. "We had a band meeting after hours. I stayed later to tune the piano. I got sidetracked, I guess . . . It's quiet here at nights. Quieter even than the smallcraft dock."

"Did I interrupt genius?"

The Magician grinned. "Hardly. I was just listening to the foghorn."

Aaron crossed the floor, dropped down onto the stage ramp. "It's a peaceful night," he commented. "About once a year we get a night like this. No full moon, no brawls, no speeders, no family fights. The muggers and snipers, even the street gangs stay home. You're the most dangerous man I've seen."

"Demented but harmless," the Magician murmured. Aaron watched him sound a key, lean into the strings to make a minute adjustment.

"Are you ready for the tour?"

"Outside of the receiver, which has gone berserk, a jammed reflector shield, an unidentified thunk in the plumbing, an ex-con for a singer and a catatonic cuber, we're ready."

"Is the Gambler going?"

"He says no. We may have to kidnap him."

Aaron grunted. "You must know someone."

The Magician shook his head, tuned another note. "No one good enough. We're going, though."

"How? Without a cuber?"

A low G answered him, soft, repetitive. Aaron listened, but the minuscule change in pitch eluded him. He leaned back tiredly on his elbows. A dispatch in his ear made him tense again; the message wasn't for him. His body stirred anyway, then subsided. He needed a break, and within the indigo silence, he could almost hear music, last night's, the next night's, drifting, waiting, on the edge of time.

He caught himself yawning; the Magician stopped sounding an A-flat.

"You look like you haven't been sleeping," he commented. Aaron shrugged a little.

"I keep dreaming." The Magician's attention had an impersonal quality; he added, as if to himself, "Sometimes I go through cycles of bad dreams . . . You ever been married?"

"Once." He chuckled for some reason. "We parted friends. You?"

"Once." He waited through another note. The Magician's face was quiet, absorbed. Then the note stopped sounding. Within the silence, all the music suddenly stopped.

Aaron lifted his head, found the Magician staring at him. His breath stopped; he felt the hair on the nape of his neck stir. For a moment a ghost, unbidden, stood between them. The Magician, his face pale, his eyes wide, seemed to see her, seemed to have picked out of the innermost place in Aaron's brain some sense of his torment. Aaron, frozen under his gaze, waited like a doomed man for him to bring her back with language.

But it had been little more than an intimation of grief. The Magician's eyes turned again to the key under his hand.

"An accident?"

Aaron swallowed. "Yes."

"I'm sorry. So you've been dreaming about it?"

"It comes back now and then."

"You never mentioned it."

"No." There was a hard warning in his voice; the Magician's head bowed over his work. The B-flat sounded once, twice. Aaron sighed. He spoke again and it stilled. "It—

I've always had a hard time talking about things like that.
Maybe that's why I have to dream about it.''

"Probably. Sorry I brought it up."

"You didn't," Aaron said helplessly. "You just pulled
it out of my head. You just—''

The Magician looked at him again, trying to remember.
The key still moved under his hand. His face had lost color
and its calmness; his eyes were narrowed slightly, as at a
chill wind. "It was in your voice."

Aaron shook his head doggedly. "It was in the silence
after my voice."

The B-flat sounded once more. Then the Magician lifted
his hand, touched his eyes with his fingers. He came over to
the stage edge, dropped down beside Aaron.

"I don't know. Maybe."

"Did you grow up doing that?"

"I don't remember being obnoxious with it. I hardly
pay attention to it. Sometimes I know things, that's all. Everyone does. You do."

"I don't pull things out of your head."

"That's because I don't store much there besides music," the Magician said, so reasonably that Aaron smiled.
"Right now I'm storing the sound of the B-flat. I was listening
to it, to the vibrations of it in the air when you spoke; maybe
I accidentally picked up some overtones in you too." He
paused, listening once more, or taking a sounding of the
silence. Aaron resisted an impulse to shift away from him.
His eyes on a far door, he blocked the Magician from his
sight, let his silence block the Magician from his mind.

He didn't hear the Magician move; the B-flat sounded
again, gentle, remote. He felt himself breathe again, the blood
flush back into his face. He wanted to speak, then, for even
he could feel the chill he had left in the air. Ghosts, he
remembered, emanate cold. He turned, not knowing if words
would get past the stiffness in his throat. But the Magician
had ducked back down into the piano, leaving Aaron his
privacy. Aaron turned back again, stared at the unlocked

door, and for a moment it seemed just another entry into nowhere, into a world roamed by ghosts, all searching for the nonexistent doorway back into the past.

The door opened.

He froze on the ramp, ambushed, despite all his training, by an ambiguity. A woman appeared in the shadows; he watched her, not moving, not breathing. She glanced at the stage, at the Magician lost inside the piano, tightening and refining the small, single sound he was making. She closed the door gently behind her. She moved out of the shadows and Aaron breathed again.

She wore a rumpled, silvery jumpsuit. The bulging bag over her shoulder was about to overflow with odd things: black lace, red satin, the rhinestone-studded heel of a shoe, a pair of rose-colored cube-sticks. Her face winked in the light, glitter from her hair caught in the lustrous mask of paint that was so smoothly and richly gold, Aaron had a sudden desire to touch it, see if it was as warming as it looked. Her hair, long, wild, crimson as the color on a playing card, nudged at his memory. She saw him then; her quick steps missed a beat, lagged. Her head turned toward him; her eyes, wide set, deep, opaque grey, gazed back at him. I know those eyes, he thought, his body tense again, memory struggling to surface in his head. I know them. Seconds passed, it seemed, or whole hours between her steps, while he dragged the memory out of him, out of her. Her eyes changed, shadowed as under a change of light, and he finally glimpsed it in her, the place he recognized: the haunted world he lived in.

Then she shut him out, left him staring at a mask. Her pace quickened again; she turned her head toward the Magician, beginning to smile as he groped for another key. The smile became a laugh, husky, exuberant, and he pulled himself out of the piano, his head snapping toward her.

"Heart-Lady!"

That's it, Aaron thought, remembering Sidney's poker hand. Fool's Run.

She laughed again as the Magician leaped down from

the stage, and threw her arms around him. Things fell: a cube-stick, a heart-pin from her hair. She was a spacer, Aaron realized. Long-boned and slender, the kind of body made to drift.

"Magic-Man, you're still here! After all these years! Can't you tear yourself away from Sidney Halleck's pianos?"

"He keeps finding me new ones." He held her away to look at her. "What in the world are you doing wandering around here at four in the morning? Last I heard you were touring with the Ramjets."

"I couldn't come any sooner," she said vaguely. "The Ramjets— Oh, I left them a month ago."

"Why?"

She shrugged; another heart-pin fell. "I got bored."

"In the middle of a full-Sector tour?"

"Well, yes, but I stayed to the end of the tour. Magic-Man, you look—you look—" She threw up her hands, laughing again, touched his shoulders. "You're a sight for my eyes, like coming home or something. I missed you playing Bach. Nobody else plays a piano. Oh, a few bands do, but not that. Not like you. Anyway. I saw you, but I didn't have time to—I'm playing down the street. I know I haven't heard your music for a while, but I've played everything. Everything. Even"—she glanced at Aaron, still smiling—"Primal Mind Reds. Not Full Primal, nobody died, but it was still spectacular. Lots of noise, though. I didn't last long; I got tired of broken instruments. I wouldn't let them touch my cubes, though, and since it was me, they didn't make me—"

"You played PMR?" the Magician said incredulously. Aaron, fascinated by the gentle swirl of words, wondered if she were on something. Then he thought, No. The Magician looks used to this.

"Well, I wanted to play every kind of music."

"PMR is not—"

"Magic-Man, we can argue about that later, over a barrel of beer. Or do you still drink Scotch? Anyway, if you want to, you can come and hear me play before you say yes or no, and I won't be offended if—after all, it's been what? Five years since I've played with you? And after all—''

"Yes or no to what?" the Magician asked, finally bewildered.

"Me. I ran into the Gambler the other night at the Starshot, where I played this last week. He was sort of attached to the bar as if it were his mother, looking like a jittery scarecrow. You know how he looks . . . He can't drink at all, must have something to do with his balance. Anyway, he told me about your tour to the Underworld, so I said if he could sub for me at the Starshot, sure I'll go. On your off-world tour." She touched a heart-pin. "To the Underworld."

The Magician was so still for a second that Aaron wondered if he had died standing up. Then the air around him flushed a sudden red, as if his heartbeat had bled color into it. Aaron's body tensed, a word starting and stopping in his throat. Before he could move, the aura was gone. The woman, suddenly wordless herself, felt the air behind the Magician's back.

"Magic-Man? Are you still connected?"

The Magician, oblivious, lifted his hands, held her lightly, as if she might turn to smoke between his fingers. "You? You'll come?"

She was silent. A little, affectionate smile changed her eyes again. "If you want me, Magic-Man. I'd love to play with you again. I miss your music."

"If I want you. God," he said reverently. "I threatened the Gambler with his life if he didn't come up with a replacement. I never thought he'd come up with you." He kissed her cheek swiftly. "Thank you." He caught sight of Aaron, grinning behind her. He loosed her, led her over to the ramp, and Aaron dropped down to the floor.

"This is Aaron Fisher, a good friend of mine. Aaron, this is the best cuber in fourteen Sectors: the Queen of Hearts."

The hand she held out was slender, long-jointed; she had a cuber's muscular grip. Her eyes, on Aaron's face, were smiling, again opaque. "I'm not musical," Aaron said. "I recognize elevator tunes. But I've heard your name."

"Well, I've been in so many bands, so many places . . . though not," she said thoughtfully, "in elevators. No. I'm sure not. Was the Magician giving you a concert? Is that why you were stretched out on the ramp?"

Aaron smiled. "I just came in to see who had left the door unlocked." The face paint, even that close, was flawless; again he resisted a desire to touch it. He heard himself say inanely, "That's quite a compliment, Magic-Man, the best cuber in fourteen Sectors leaving everything to play with you."

She shook her head; heart-pins slid and clung; a black crinoline collar dropped out of her bag. She picked it up absently, drew it like a garter up one arm. "I've played everywhere all right, in the asteroids, in the floating sea-hotels, in clubs so tiny I could hardly lift my cube-sticks without knocking out a stage light. I've done three full-Sector tours, each with a different band. You'd think no one would let me come near them, I always leave. But I leave them better than they were, and people say I bring luck with me. The Queen of Hearts, the Lucky Lady." She laughed softly, without a hint of bitterness. "I don't know if that's true. So I've been everywhere, played everything. And nothing has ever stuck in my mind like the Magician's music. So I came back." She paused; they waited, in a charmed silence. "Here." Her eyes changed unexpectedly, grew wide, glittering slightly. She bent quickly to retrieve the cube-sticks. "Here."

A shoe dropped out of her bag. Aaron fielded it; when he straightened, she was barricaded again behind the smile. She swung the shoe loosely between finger and thumb; the rhinestones glittered wildly.

"You still play Bach, Magic-Man?"

"Oh, yes."

"And the *Flying Wail*?" The rhinestones were suddenly still; her face, behind the smile, was very still. "Do you still have it?"

"We'll be touring in it," the Magician said, and the lights gyrated again in her hand. "We'll be rehearsing after hours every night here for the next two weeks. Can you make it?"

"Of course."

"Tell the Nebraskan where your cubes are and he'll help you move them. I'll call the Agency tomorrow about an off-world passport for you—no, I can't call until I get that bloody receiver fixed—"

"I'll get the passport," she said quickly. "Magic-Man, you need help with repairs? I used to tinker with my dad's shuttle when I was a kid. I'll take a look at your receiver. Oh, and I can navigate, too, in space. I learned that on one tour or another. I think it was with Cygnus." She laughed at the Magician's expression. "Well, I was bored."

"Heart-Lady, you're a godsend."

"Maybe. Maybe it's you, though . . ." She tucked the shoe back into her bag, her face hidden behind the long, rippling, rose-colored hair.

Aaron asked curiously, "Where were you born?"

She shook her hair back, looked at him. One hand went up, settled a pin. She said slowly, "I remember you now. The Magician and Sidney Halleck were playing poker. You were watching behind Sidney's shoulder."

He nodded. "Sidney dealt you into his poker hand."

Fingers still troubling the pin, she seemed suddenly aware of him: his height and weight, the timbre of his voice, the hint of choices made in the lines of his face, the shadow of morning stubble along his jaw. He watched himself change in her eyes to something more than a piece of backdrop in the Magician's world. She started to say something, stopped. Then she said it, sounding tentative, surprised.

"Will you come and hear me play?"

He smiled. He felt tired, then pleasantly so, and knew that for some reason he could not yet fathom, he would sleep that day without dreams.

"I'd love to."

* * *

He came the next night, and the night after, and all the nights after that, snatching moments out of his street patrolling to slip inside the doors of the Constellation Club at two, three or four in the morning, to watch her. Sometimes he had a chance to speak to her, sometimes not. On his nights off he sat through their full rehearsals, at the bar beside Sidney Halleck, while the cleaning crew whirled soundlessly around the vast floor, vacuuming, polishing. Though he had little ear for distinguishing one cuber from another, the powerful, controlled rhythms of her cubing shook him sometimes as if something deep inside the earth beneath them were shifting, speaking. Surrounded by the hot, glowing cubes, her face remote in concentration, washed in gold and the inner fires of the cubes, she brought a word out of Aaron's memory that he had forgotten he ever knew.

"She looks like a sorceress . . ."

Sidney, sipping beer beside him, smiled. "Maybe she is. She appeared out of nowhere and granted the Magician's wish. Did you do a status-check on her?"

"No," Aaron said, startled. "Why should I?"

"You always do."

Aaron was silent. Was that where the mystery lay? he wondered. Somewhere in the stat-sheets of the FWG? His own haunting was reduced to a single, barren phrase: Wife . . . deceased. It said nothing. The glimpse he had had of a fellow traveler in the sad frozen wasteland he knew so well might be explained by a word or two in FWG files, if he could even recognize them. Or, by FWG standards, it might not even have been worth a word.

"This time," he said softly, his face turned away from Sidney, "I want to ask."

She seemed drawn to him, chattering her way amicably across the floor during breaks to drift beside him, like a boat out of a storm finding a quiet harbor. She told him many things. They had walked familiar streets, seen the same noisy, smoky bars, the same rich and drunken clubs, heard the same snatches of music through open doors when the summer fog stayed out to sea and the full moon hung like a blood-orange in the sky. And yet she told him nothing.

"How come you never answer a direct question?" he asked her recklessly one night. She only laughed.

"Like what?"

"What's your name? Where were you born? Do you ever take that paint off your face?"

"No," she said. Then, "Well, sometimes. But never, ever in front of anyone. Do you know the Magician's name?"

"Yes. But I'm sworn to secrecy."

"Well, I don't. I never asked him. It's not important. It's like the Nebraskan. I asked him once where Nebraska was, when it was Nebraska, and he said it was somewhere in Eastcoast Sector. You'd think he was born there, in what was pre-FWG Nebraska, wouldn't you? But he got his long mustache and his drawl out of old videos, and the place he thought Nebraska was, was West Virginia. Something gets lost, though, don't you think, if you know that? Something very small but important. In its way."

"Where were you born?"

"The Moon." She added, after a moment, "I was named after it."

"Oh."

"So." She shrugged a shoulder, bare except for a sheen of sweat that made all coherent thought suddenly vanish from his head. "You asked a question. I answered."

He looked for her subconsciously, as he looked for trouble in the restless city; every throb of cubes he heard seemed to come from her. No matter what else occupied him—sky patrolling, dispatches, reports, street brawls or wild chases —he would find himself inevitably walking into the Constellation Club during the hours when Nova would be there. I'm addicted, he thought helplessly. A junkie for a cuber with a face of gold. She demanded nothing from him; dwelling in his mind, she never interfered with his work. She was simply there in his thoughts, because he wanted her there, until the moments when he could walk into the club and watch her eyes search the lights and shadows until she found him and stopped searching.

He missed their final rehearsal. Accidents and painstaking reports held him away until, near dawn, he came wearily into the club. Sidney was still there, at that lost hour unclaimed by night or morning. Aaron joined him. On the stage the Magician, turning green, shook the keyboard with one last chord. A run of light spattered down the rod-harp. The Queen of Hearts framed her face with her cube-sticks and brought them down with a crash. The stage went black. There was a beat of silence. Then out of the darkness came a single, sweet phrase of Bach.

Aaron and Sidney clapped. The Nebraskan turned the stage lights back on. Quasar dropped down on the ramp, shook her hair wildly, throwing glitter into the air.

"*Merde,*" she said huskily. "What time is it?"

The Nebraskan's answer turned into a yawn. The Magician glanced at his wrist, but his mind seemed still enveloped in colors and nothing registered. Sidney said, "It's four-thirty. Good morning, Aaron. Who ripped your pockets?"

"*Merde,*" Quasar said again. She turned, flashed a manic grin full of silver glitter at the Queen of Hearts. "That was some cubing."

The Queen of Hearts started to lean against a wall, then remembered there was no wall. Her eyes had found Aaron beyond the light. He breathed in soundlessly, for, as when he had first seen her, he felt mercifully adrift of both past and future. That was the addiction, he realized: that freedom from memory, from himself. That was how she drew him back, to stand at the borders of the hidden country behind her eyes. She didn't smile; her eyes, above the luminous, cooling cubes, turned a shade darker.

The Magician jumped down off the stage, headed for the bar. "How was it?" he asked Sidney. "Good enough for the Underworld?"

"You'll probably cause a permanent disruption of its sound waves."

"I gather that's what they want." He reached behind Aaron for a bar towel. "What happened to your pants?"

"I didn't run fast enough," Aaron said absently, watching the Queen of Hearts descend from the stage. The Magician glanced at him curiously. He hid the sudden smile tugging at his mouth behind the towel. Sidney, an amiable sorcerer in his own realm, moved behind the bar to pour beer.

The Queen of Hearts joined them. She did not look at Aaron, but she stood close to him, and he realized with a shock how soon she would be leaving. Her question, asked of the universe in general, was directed at him. "Did you enjoy it?" She looked at him finally. In the smoky, jeweled shadows her eyes were the color of the air.

"I loved it," Aaron said.

She smiled. "You weren't even here."

"I was," Sidney said. "You were wonderful."

The Scholar draped himself over the bar. "I am dead and on my way to the Underworld. Heart-Lady, you worked us so hard, I thought my rod-harp was going to shatter."

"Me," she said. "That was you making me work." She lifted her hair off her neck, wound it on top of her head with her fingers. "Times like this I want to canonize whoever invented sweat-proof face paint."

"Did the Agency get hold of you?" Sidney asked the Magician.

The Magician shook his head over his beer. "Why?"

"They told me today that your concert at Helios will be picked up by satellite and broadcast over NSBC."

The Nebraskan's mouth dropped. "You're kidding! Us?" He pounded the Magician's back. "We're going on the air!"

The Magician shook spilled beer off his fingers. "Nova's a club band. How on Earth did you get the media to pay attention to us?"

"Human interest. The first band to play the Underworld, the effect on off-world prisoners, et cetera. They'll do a story about the Rehab program, but they couldn't get permission to bring a film crew to the Underworld, so they'll film you on Helios."

"Sidney, you're a genius."

"I know," Sidney said unabashedly. Aaron turned to the Queen of Hearts, wanting to see her eyes again. But she was no longer at his elbow. He glanced around bewilderedly and found her back on the stage, walking aimlessly around her cubes. He wondered at her odd silence, the sudden distance she put between them. He made a move toward her, subsided against the bar, then knew the unexpected hollow of loss at words left unspoken, action only contemplated. He felt the Magician's attention like a searchlight sweeping over him. The old, familiar impulse to guard his actions, to hide his life, kept him a moment longer at the bar, sipping his beer, acknowledging nothing.

Then he thought, Ah, to hell with it.

He put his beer down and crossed the floor, went up the ramp to where the Queen of Hearts stood staring at her cubes. Almost cold, they still flared darkly now and then from within, like cooling stars.

Standing beside her, uncertain, he said the first thing that came into his head. "Did you get the receiver fixed yet?"

She shook her head abruptly, almost fiercely, as if she were answering a question he hadn't asked. Heart-pins slid; she caught at them. He helped her. His fingers brushed her cheek once, and her face followed his touch, seeking. She met his eyes, suddenly shaken, vulnerable. He took her hand, opened it, filled it with hearts.

"No," she said. She drew breath. "It's more complicated than I thought."

"I have access to patrol-cruiser information, repair manuals for cruisers sold to the public. You could get it through the Library Bank, but this way you won't have to pay the user's fee. The Magician will appreciate that."

She smiled a little; it didn't reach her eyes. "I don't want—It's too late. I mean early. You're still working."

"I get a breakfast break in thirty minutes. Wait for me here."

"Aaron—" She stopped, shook her head again. But she didn't withdraw her hand, didn't move. He reached into one untorn pocket, opened her other hand and dropped a rose, faded to a dusty burgundy and still lightly scented, into her palm. She gazed at it; he saw her swallow.

"It came into my hand one night out of nowhere. I brought it for you." She was still silent; he added, feeling suddenly uncertain, inane, "It's just a dead rose. I know. There's no user's fee. It meant something to me, that's all."

She looked at him; without words she finally told him something. Around them, the dark walls began to swirl with light.

EIGHT

They flew high above the
city, talking, while a
huge, milky cat's-eye
of a moon stared at them
above the sea, and the
eastern sky shaded
slowly into pearl.

"Cubing," she said. Her low voice was husky with
sleeplessness. "Just cubing. I fell in love with them when I
was thirteen."

"On the moon."

She gazed at it puzzledly a moment, as if it had intruded
unexpectedly on the wrong side of morning. "The moon.
Yes. I played my mother's music tapes until they broke. I
practiced riffs and patterns with pencils, forks, saucepan lids.
I went into the greenhouse where my mother worked, and
turned empty plant pots upside down and beat on them. I

wanted power over the cubes. I wanted them to stir alive to my playing, feel them warm themselves to me, begin to smolder, change color . . . I was obsessed, in love. In a dream. I thought that if I had a set of cubes I would be happy for the rest of my life. Playing music, on my private corner of the moon.''

"But you left the moon," Aaron said softly.

Her head bowed; he couldn't see the gold mask behind her hair. "They died. My parents. In an accident, four years later. FWG welfare rules said we were too young to stay by ourselves—"

"We—"

Her head lifted; she swept her hair back with both hands, frowning at the full moon. "It's so hard lined," she said wonderingly. "So pure. It looks like the eye of God out there, without a shadow or a subtlety on it. Close up, there are shadows . . . Me. And my sister. She's on Rimrock, now; she married a geologist. So we were sent to Earth. To Suncoast Sector. Which, I discovered, had a set of cubes on every other corner. It was like falling down a long dark tunnel into some kind of disreputable Paradise . . ."

"A bar on every corner," Aaron said. "And a set of cubes in every other bar."

She nodded, laughing. Glitter shook through the air. Aaron took his eyes off the web of lights along the dark coast, drawn to the illusion of light, of warmth on her face. Brief lines gathered, then vanished under her eyes as she smiled. Twenty-five, he guessed, then asked her.

"Twenty-eight."

"That seems young to be turning your back on Sector tours."

She shrugged. "There's fame and fortune. And then there's the Magic-Man's music." She peered out of the window, down at the ghostly surf. Glancing at her, surprised, Aaron was left looking at the gold in her earlobe, and the long curve of her neck.

"So you came to Earth."

"To get an education." She settled back in her seat; one

corner of her mouth crooked upward. "According to FWG regulations for Wards of the State. We had our parents' credit, insurance, compensatory credit. And we were orphans, in a world we'd never seen before. We got educated. I started playing in bars when I was still in school. I was tall; I painted my face, went out at nights, and no one ever knew I was underage."

"You painted it gold? Like it is now?"

For some reason, her face stilled. The gold became once again a mask. "No. This came later. The night I met the Magician."

Aaron paused, his mouth opened, half a dozen questions occurring to him at once. "Why that night?"

"It was the first time I'd ever heard Bach . . . I was walking down the street at midnight, and someone opened a door and this sound came out that I'd never heard before, so I followed it and found the Magician. I sat in with his band, played cubes for two hours, and he asked me to stay. So I stayed."

"Were you lovers?" The question seemed to come out of nowhere, startling him, as if the scanner had spoken. He flushed, then grinned sheepishly at her laughter. "I'm sorry. It's none of my business."

"No. I suppose we might have been, but I needed him for other things."

"What things?"

She made a vague gesture, frowning again; her eyes, gazing at the vast, dark grey sweep of sea, reflected it, seemed at once as familiar and as enigmatic. "Him," she said finally, "and his music—they're the place I come back to. When I go out into the world, learn to play PMR, take a bite of fame, see a million strangers whose names I'll never know, even though they all, every one of them, know mine—there's still a safe place to come home to. That's what I need the Magic-Man for. To keep that safe place for me, the private piece of moon, where no one is a stranger, and the music never changes."

He was silent, thinking of the bomb shelter, the safe

place where no life could get at him. Then he thought, What hurt you? But she was questioning him.

"Were you always a patroller?"

"I've been one for ten years."

"Do you live with someone?"

"No."

"Why not?"

They were nearing the coast; he slowed the sol-car, angled it down. For a moment a glib reply was on his tongue. Then, listening to himself with astonishment, he said, "I loved a woman once. She got killed, seven years ago. I've lived alone since then."

"How did she die?" He shut the cabin lights off as the sun rose behind them. Light seared the sea; her face was in shadow. Her voice was very soft, almost hollow. Aaron saw the circle of red lights he had installed over the shelter and dropped toward them.

"How?"

He had stepped into the station headquarters, whistling; the morning air smelled of spring. A fellow patroller, sipping coffee while he watched a newscast, had turned his head abruptly.

"Hey, Fisher. Isn't your wife stationed over in Desert Sector?"

A sudden, cold sweat broke out on his face; he felt physically sick. The Queen of Hearts' face lifted. The changeless gold mask, the still eyes were oddly calming. But he couldn't tell her; he couldn't put it into the past tense.

"Just a freak accident."

They landed. Aaron checked in with the patrol station, then led the Queen of Hearts down beneath the earth. He heated soup and sandwiches, then tracked down the mechanics' diagrams in the Library Bank for patrol-cruisers of the vintage of the *Flying Wail*. She studied them, chewing a rose-colored nail, and made notes. He handed her a sandwich.

"Here. It should be better than nail polish."

She looked at her fingers blankly, then took the sandwich, still gazing at the screen.

"It's not complete," she said abruptly.

"Why?"

"Inside the *Flying Wail*'s receiver, there are two seals about the size of a fingernail, with the Underworld logo on them. I couldn't figure out what they were for. There are no seals at all on this diagram."

"Oh. Simple," Aaron said with his mouth full. "Every time the Underworld sells its cruisers to the public, it adjusts the frequency capabilities of the receivers so that an ordinary citizen can't pick up patroller or Underworld business. The seals are just a proof that the receiver has been altered for public consumption."

"Why would they—"

"Keeps the air clear for emergencies. And there are a lot of things—docking procedures, patrol codes, other highly restricted information—carried over the UF. The Underworld Frequency."

She bit into the sandwich, chewed slowly, still transfixed by the diagrams. "Which receiver am I looking at? Before or after the seals?"

"It's an altered receiver. The Underworld doesn't like the public even to know that the UF exists. So, not wanting a thousand questions about the seals—which aren't easy to spot, unless you're really digging—they didn't put them in the diagram."

She looked up, surprised. "How do you know all this?"

"I like knowing things. Coffee?"

"Please. And this place—" She glanced around her at the expensive equipment, the privacy and dustless order of the place. He paused, not knowing what lie or truth he might tell her when she asked. But she only said, "This is the place where you come to learn them . . ."

Aaron moved to the sink, washed cups. He glanced at her once; she was gazing at her reflection in the darkening screen, or the vague reflection of his own movements.

He turned back to the cups. Her hands lifted to the noiseless keyboard, typed.

Research: Underworld.

Letters ran across the screen, across her face.

A space-prison, satellite of Earth. Designed by H. Kent Claus. Funded by the Free World Government for the purpose of transporting life prisoners and potentially dangerous nonlife prisoners off-Earth. Completed: 29 FWG. Capacity: 500,000. Further information restricted. Apply to FWG Security Bureau for permission and codes.

Architectural design of Underworld.

Restricted.

Docking procedures.

Heavily restricted. Apply to Chief Administrator of the Underworld: Klyos, Jason, for information.

She cleared the screen. Aaron crossed the room, handed her coffee.

"Thank you."

"Finished?"

"Yes." She tilted her head on the back of the chair and smiled at him, and he wanted to take her out of the silent, windless, sunless place into the brine-filled dawn. Her smile froze suddenly. She touched him very lightly, for the first time. "I won't get you into trouble, will I? Using your computer?"

"I like trouble," he said.

He flew her back to the inner city. She was waiting for him when he came off duty, in the rumpled, light-speckled shadows of his bed. Moved, he did not trust himself to speak. He sat down on the bed, tired, sweating, and lifted the palm of her hand to his mouth. She leaned forward, slid her gold cheek across his stubble, turning her head until their mouths touched. He gripped her other hand, drew her arms wide, outflung to the light. She pulled him down, down, into a gold and ivory river of forgetfulness.

He heard his voice from a distance, or maybe only in his head, murmuring. Light streaked across his eyes. He heard gulls crying outside the window. Later, he found a thigh under his cheek. He was covering a breast with one hand, holding a foot with the other. He raised the foot curiously, as if he had forgotten what it was, and kissed the instep. Someone said something.

"What?" He lifted his head, blinking. Her face, barbaric gold, startled him. She looked at him silently for a long time, her eyes heavy, unreadable. Then she gathered the pieces of herself back from his hold, and putting her arms around his neck, she kissed him gently.

"You forgot it was me," she said, "didn't you? You were remembering . . ."

He held her face between his hands, gazed at her in amazement. "You aren't going to kick me out of bed for that?"

"I need you too much." Her hands were roaming; her voice sank to a whisper. "I need you, I want you, Aaron Fisher . . ."

"Who are you?"

"The Queen of Hearts."

"Who are you?"

"A cuber. A hardworking woman you gave a rose to."

"Who are you?"

Her whispering slid down his belly, licked at his groin like fire. "Don't ask me, never ask, that's the question you should never ask . . ." He cried out. Then he drew her against him, muscle to muscle, bone to bone, as if the stubborn boundaries between them were as inconsequential as air.

He woke slowly, saw her wake with a change of breathing, a flicker of eyelash. Her face was all but hidden by arms and hair; there was only a curve of brow, an eye. He slid his hand beneath her armpit to her cheek and watched the eye smile.

He pulled her on top of him; she lowered her head, circled his head with her arms. In that safe place they kissed until they could not breathe, and the ghosts who knew them were left outside, looking for them in vain.

She sat on top of him, looking down at him. His hands rested on her thighs. He stirred, started to say something, then was silent, smiling up at her. She traced his mouth and ear with her fingers. She sat quietly again, her hands on his chest, her head bowed, reflecting his smile.

When he woke again, he was alone. It was two in the afternoon. The hot light lay in slabs on the floor. For the first time he realized how dusty his windows were. The white walls were bare. The regulation ghetto carpet looked like a bleak grey desert. I should fix this place up, he thought, surprising himself. For years he had lived sparsely, wanting little more than the fastest sol-car, the finest equipment for the shelter. He swung himself upright, sat blinking at his feet, realizing slowly how much of herself the Queen of Hearts had left behind to linger in his lonely room, in his heart.

Something was staring at him. He turned his head, saw his message-light burning. He reached across the bed, touched it, yawning.

He remembered amazedly as he answered the Magician's call, that the *Flying Wail* was due to take off.

"Magic-Man?" he said as the Magician's screen cleared. "You still here?"

"Aaron," the Magician said vaguely.

Aaron reminded him, "You called me."

"Oh." He chuckled. "This tour is already getting to me. I called a couple of hours ago, looking for my cuber. She's here, now."

"Is she?" He rubbed his eyes sleepily, trying to think, while the Magician waited patiently. "You about to leave?"

"We're waiting to be towed into the launch lineup."

He was silent again, not thinking, letting feeling come. It came as simply as the rose had, out of his pocket. "I want to say good-bye."

He flew his sol-car to the dock, found the Queen of Hearts sitting on the ramp of the *Flying Wail*, her chin in her hands. The rest of the band was inside; he heard the engines warming.

She rose without a word, put her arms around him. Her smells were different—soap, scent, fresh face paint—but the dark warmth was still there. He raised his head finally, opened his eyes to the brightness of her hair. "Well," he said, "good-bye." Her mask was flawless: the face card in gold, red, sunlit grey, the Queen of Hearts, the lady who traveled from hand to winning hand.

"Good-bye."

Neither of them moved. She took her arms from around him finally; he felt their reluctance, saw the sudden emptiness in her eyes. He swallowed, his breathing quick, knowing he was about to step into a whirling mist that might be hiding solid earth or a long fall into nowhere. He heard himself say, "I'm such a coward. I want to see you again."

"Yes," she whispered, and he saw then the smile she had been born with. Then she drew back, her eyes dark, startled, her face stylized, elegant, hiding a bewildering conflict.

"I'll call you." Her voice shook. "When I get back. If. When. Aaron—"

"If—"

"If you still want me—"

"Why—"

"I just want you to know something. Before—"

"Before what?"

She sighed, closing her eyes, trying to see in the dark. "I want you to know that you'll be on my mind. Like the cubes. Like the Magician's music. Always. Say good-bye."

"Good-bye," he said, completely confused. She kissed him and turned. And then the memory struck him, full-force and full of terror, as the hatch opened and closed again behind her. He wanted to scream at her, to batter at the hatch with his fists. I have said good-bye before! He stood rigidly, his mouth dry, urgently separating past and present, and praying to the Cosmos that it was possible, while she, with the dark vision in her eyes, took her place beside the Magician to chart their path to the Underworld.

The Underworld computer had routinely recorded the request for its most tenaciously held secrets and presented the record to Jase's bleary eyes that morning. He gazed at it, sipping coffee. Kids, he thought. Schoolwork. But he didn't consign it to the files; he sat staring at it until Nils, about to leave, came to look over his shoulder.

"Kids," he said. Jase made an ambiguous noise in his throat. He raised one hand slowly, tapped lightly at the screen.

"Track it down for me, will you?"

"Why?" Nils said bewilderedly. "It's not worth—"

"Please."

Nils sat down again, worked over his keyboard, looking as close to muttering under his breath as he ever got. "You're just jumpy because of Terra Viridian," he said. "Somebody in a Library Bank, playing around out of curiosity . . ."

"Maybe," Jase said.

"Your intuitions are working overtime."

"I know, and so are you. Want to bet on it?"

Nils stopped tracking down the request through a pyramid of codes and stared at him. His fingers moved again. "Suncoast Sector, Public Library Bank 5 fielded the question . . . How much?" His head ducked down over his work. "Private terminal . . . All bets off . . . ID code . . ." A flush ran over his face to his red hair. Jase leaned forward. "You did it again," Nils said incredulously.

"Who?"

"Aaron Fisher. ID 2146WOSS. Suncoast Patroller Class A1A." He looked at Jase, fingers poised. "So now? What? Call it idle curiosity?"

Jase shook his head. "A patroller that good learned all he needed to know about the Underworld years ago." His voice felt tight in his throat, with anger, with frustration, for he could sense something coming, like some dark planet careening out of its orbit, but its coming was silent, and darker than the night it fell through. Nils was watching him, puzzled, uneasy.

"Why would a first-class patroller try to milk the Underworld for docking procedures?"

"Get his records," Jase said. "Get his superior and get him up here. We'll ask him."

P A R T
TWO
THE UNDER-WORLD

O N E

Thousands of miles above the Earth, the *Flying Wail* reached the Underworld's orbit, made a musical statement to that effect, shut down its engines and began its serene glide to meet the Underworld. The Magician, uncharmed by weightlessness, clamped his boots to the floor grid, strapped himself in, and turned to the news on the video screen. The Nebraskan disappeared into the hold to see what might be floating. The Scholar lay on his side near the ceiling, his arms folded, his eyes closed, listening to a book. Quasar painted her nails grape with a paint-tube especially constructed for the well-groomed traveler in free-fall, and watched over the Magician's shoulder. The Queen of Hearts lowered the back of the navigator's chair and took a nap.

"She doesn't snore," Quasar commented after half an hour, causing the Magician's attention to gyrate wildly.

"What?"

"The Queen of Hearts. You all snore. She gives nothing away, even sleeping. Look at her. *Comme le chat*."

The Magician glanced at the Queen of Hearts in spite of himself. "Quasar—"

"*Merde*," Quasar said surprisedly. The Magician caught a tiny purple globule floating past his face.

"God damn it, Quasar."

Quasar chastised the paint-tube in old-world. "*Une chose dérangée*," she finished darkly. "I paid a hand and a foot for it."

"An arm and a leg."

"But why?"

"Quasar, I'm trying to watch this."

"You won't let me smoke. I'm nervous. I don't like space. It's too big, too empty. The sun is too lonely here. I want it ruling the sky, commanding attention among the clouds." She blew on her nails. The Magician smiled, his eyes on a newscaster in Sundown Sector.

"Just an old-fashioned girl, you are."

"There was also," Quasar said with unexpected relevance, "a National Regression Coalition in Lumière Sector. But it argued with itself until it fell apart. Paris. What kind of a name is that?"

"City of lovers, poets," the Scholar murmured. He touched the ceiling and drifted down to them, taking the book out of his ear. "What's going on among the Sundowners?"

"The FWG is threatening to move the troops in."

"*Plus ça change, plus c'est la même chose*," the Scholar said, causing Quasar to stare at him.

"Your accent," she said, recovering, "is terrible."

"My accent is Parisian, yours is sewer. *Comprends?* I don't like your nail polish either."

Quasar grinned a purple grin. "Come to the kitchen. I'll think of something you'll like."

"You're on," the Scholar said cheerfully. The Magician turned the sound up.

". . . Sources say that the FWG will continue its hardline policy to stamp out the NRC before its ideas have a chance to trouble other Sectors. Nationalism, Secretary of Defense Marie Juneau said today, created the weapons which inspired the formation of the Free World Government. Without the FWG there would have been global war. The National Regression Coalition, she said, wants nothing more than to return to the precarious world situation which caused the FWG forces to form and which compelled its historic takeover of the last world summit meeting. The FWG, the Secretary of Defense stated, prevailed then, will prevail today, and will not hesitate to carry out its policies.

"In other news today . . ."

"The iron boot heel," the Magician murmured.

"What else can it do?" the Scholar said. "The FWG, pain in the ass that it is, has actually managed to survive a hundred-odd years. We would have blown ourselves up without it."

"Maybe not."

"Maybe not, maybe we'd still be alive and bickering. But who wants to test that theory?"

"I don't," the Magician said. "I just wonder how long the FWG can keep its grip on the world. It's part democracy, part tyranny, part socialist, part plain parental, and it has kept itself alive so far by our memory of near annihilation. When the memory fades, will the bureaucracy still work?"

"Magic-Man," the Scholar said wryly, "every government in the world started that way."

"True." He turned the sound lower again, gazed at the screen. "They came down hard on something a few years ago, came down far out of proportion . . . What was it? One of the FWG's draftees. Terra Viridian."

"That lunatic in Desert Sector."

"She had sunstroke, massacred all those people, then gave the FWG a merry hell of a chase. They finally found her in Suncoast Sector in a garbage bin . . . She got the most inept trial in FWG history. A two-year-old could tell her circuits were burned, but the court declared her sane so they could legally throw her in the Dark Ring and placate—''

"Magic-Man," Quasar said nervously, "shut up. I don't want to hear about the Underworld. We play there and go. That's all I want to know."

The Magician looked at her. Beyond her, he saw the Queen of Hearts' sleeping face. The secrecy that Quasar had glimpsed in the lustrous, expressionless gold suddenly snagged at his attention: beneath the smoothly painted eyelids, the mind was awake and listening.

The Queen of Hearts opened her eyes a second later, blinking, seemingly oblivious of the Magician's attention. "Where are we?" She consulted the control panel, then ran her fingers tiredly, absently, through her hair again and again until it floated around her languorously, like kelp. They were all watching her then, charmed, even Quasar.

"Another hour," the Magician said.

She nodded, swallowing a yawn, her eyes on the star-screen. "I'd forgotten how beautiful it is up here," she murmured. "I haven't been in space since Cygnus did the off-world tour two years ago."

"When you learned to navigate," the Magician said. She seemed to hear an odd overtone in his voice; she turned to him, smiling, but she hesitated slightly before she answered, and he could not see past the smile in her eyes.

"When I learned to navigate in space. Yes. I got us this far, Magic-Man. I didn't forget what I learned, did I? It's like riding a bicycle. At least that's what they say; I've never ridden a bicycle in my life. But why is that, do you think, that some things you have to learn and relearn, and other things you never forget how to do? You might forget a language, but you don't forget how to add or subtract. Or sounds—you don't forget the difference between bird song and a human voice."

"I don't know," the Magician said, distracted by her amiable chatter. "Instinct?"

"Mathematics is not an instinct," the Scholar said witheringly.

"I was thinking more about bicycles. A sense of balance being connected with a survival instinct."

"What is—" Quasar began; the Scholar answered her question.

"Like breathing. You do it to live; you stop doing it, you die. But it's not something you think about doing one way or the other. As long as you live, you do it. Or your body does it. Like jerking your hand away from fire. Or running from something dangerous."

Quasar nodded, inspecting a streak on one of her nails. She pulled the polish-tube out of her pocket. "I have done that. But then I learned something strange. When you run, you run backward, you never reach the future. The past runs faster than you and waits for you to reach it. You have to walk out of danger, out of the past. Because you look back when you run, but you look to the future when you walk."

The Scholar and the Magician looked at each other. "I'd say that's a survival instinct," the Scholar said.

The Queen of Hearts gathered her hair out of the air, bundled it around itself at her neck. "How do you know that?" she asked Quasar. Her voice sounded husky, almost abrupt to the Magician's ear. Quasar retracted the nailbrush with an audible snap.

"I know." She eyed the chip of light ahead of them along the *Flying Wail*'s path. Then she smiled, her eyes dark, mocking. "Look at you. We were in your past. You came back to us. The Gambler found you and brought you back. Why?"

"Because the Magician's music had to be played."

"And that makes," the Scholar murmured, "the Magician as big a megalomaniac as the FWG."

"What?" the Magician said, startled. The *Flying Wail* sang delicately; he took his eyes off the screen and swiveled his chair to the controls, answering the cruiser's message on the keyboard. He settled back again; the Scholar broke the silence.

"Well?"

"Well, what?"

"Well, what did it say?"

"Oh. Just company. A smallcraft entered scanning range." He looked up suddenly. "What was that about me being a megalomaniac?"

"Quasar says your music is responsible for the synchronicity of the universe."

"Quasar used 'synchronicity' in a sentence?" His eyes widened as she uncapped the polish-tube again. "No! Don't do it! I take it back, I'm sorry—"

"I am not appeased."

"Come into the kitchen. No, better yet, the hold. The Nebraskan put all the Scotch back there."

"You drag me to a space-prison. And you refuse to let me smoke. And then you insult me. For that I will loose purple floating globs all over the *Flying Wail*." She had the Magician's full attention; half alarmed, half laughing, his hands up, open, placating, he pleaded without words; her smoldering gaze held a manic gleam. The Queen of Hearts lifted a hand languidly, slid the tube out of Quasar's hand.

"What is this? This is marvelous. I've never seen anything like it. Is it new? Do you have more colors? Do you have a shade that will match my hair?"

"Do you have a shade that will match my lightning bolt?" the Scholar asked meekly. Quasar, diverted, disarmed, glowered at him, then trained the force of her restlessness at the Queen of Hearts.

"I have a color that will match your mask."

The Queen of Hearts brushed her cheek vaguely. "My face paint."

"Your mask. I know these things. You never take it off, do you. Not even to make love."

"Quasar," the Magician said, even while his mind veered briefly to explore the possibility.

"You see the paint," Quasar said stubbornly. "But you don't see her eyes."

"Sure, I do," the Scholar said. "They're wide open in front of my face and they're smiling. It's just her stage-face. It means one of the best cubers in the world. People everywhere recognize it. It's a symbol."

"What's a symbol?"

"Her gold face. Something that means something. Something you react to without thinking. Like an instinct, but it's cultural rather than biological."

"Comment?"

"A physical object or design that represents an emotion, a belief, a ritual, a cultural experience—"

"What language are you speaking?" Quasar inquired icily. The Scholar sighed.

"Magic-Man—"

The Magician pulled a flap on the arm of the commander's chair. Gold floated into his palm. He held it up between finger and thumb: a small, perfect circle. The Scholar took it from him, smiling.

"A wedding ring. Where'd you get that?"

"It belonged to my great-great-grandmother. I actually wore it once. Now it's emergency fuel if I ever get stuck somewhere without credit." He added to Quasar, "That's a symbol: two virgins giving each other gold as a promise to love and make love only to each other for the rest of their lives."

Quasar's brows lifted in distaste. "You never did that, Magic-Man. Did you?" The Magician's mouth twitched. He sealed the ring away again. The Nebraskan drifted overhead like an angel.

"Did what?" he asked interestedly.

"I'm trying to explain to Quasar what a symbol is," the Scholar said.

"Why?"

"I forget."

"That's easy," the Nebraskan said, fingering a straying end of his mustache. "It's like a horseshoe. Nail a horseshoe over your door and it attracts good luck."

"That's a superstition, not a symbol."

"Okay, a rainbow, then. That's a symbol of good luck. Or a four-leaf clover."

"I was trying for something a little more profound."

The Nebraskan gave his mustache a final tug and reached down the neck of his bodysuit. A thread of silver snaked into the air. He pulled it over his head, sent it down toward the control panel. A thin chain of silver with a charm the shape of a triangle flowed past the Queen of Hearts' face. She lifted her hand, her fingers tangling in the silver, and the triangle turned slowly to transfix her with its eye.

"What is that?" The sharpness in her voice startled them. The Magician took the chain from her, frowning.

The Nebraskan said apologetically, "I saw it on some pre-FWG U.S.A. currency. The eye within the triangle. I liked it, so I had it cast in silver. I'm not sure what it is."

"It's the eye of God," the Magician said, as if recognizing a casual acquaintance. The Scholar reached for it; the Magician looked at the Queen of Hearts, his brows raised questioningly. She was laughing again, fingers making furrows in her hair, pulling it around her face until it was barely visible, and the Magician saw only one grey eye.

"Of course I've seen that before," she said. "Of course I have. I don't remember where, though."

"Me neither," the Scholar said. "That's funny. We've seen it, we don't know where it came from, yet we all recognize it, and it means something. Something without words, something from the past."

"Like a cross," the Nebraskan said.

"Or a star. Star of David, the pentangle of—"

"I met a man once who believed in that flak," Quasar interrupted. "He tried to tell me about someplace called heaven. Then he told me I was going to hell. I can't remember what I did to make him angry. Something. I don't like the past."

"Starlight is always in the past," the Magician murmured. The cruiser spoke again, a short arpeggio on a harpsichord; a com-light went on at the same time. He touched it and the air was filled instantly with static.

"Identify," a woman's voice said abrasively. "Imperative. Identify—"

The Magician winced at the noise. "Smallcraft ID 960PCS, the *Flying Wail*. From Suncoast Sec—"

"Name."

"What's your name?" he asked civilly. Quasar's fingernails clamped down on his arm.

"Patrollers."

He blinked, his face suddenly expressionless, and shifted a shield-angle over the window. They saw the long, bulky body between them and the Underworld, the flashing cruiser lights. He whispered rapidly, "God damn it, Quasar, if you've brought anything illegal aboard—"

"No, Magic-Man, I swear—"

"This is patrol-cruiser WG11F from the Underworld. Transmit navigational codes for all ports beyond Earth."

The Magician breathed something and glanced at the Queen of Hearts. She was upright, but her hands over the controls were clenched. "Heart-Lady." She took her eyes from the cruiser, stared at him without seeing him. "They want our itinerary."

"Oh." Her hands loosened abruptly; she began transmitting. "I'm sorry, Magic-Man, I'm sorry—"

"Stay calm." They heard cross-chatter under the static; he deciphered it incredulously. "You're intercepting what?"

"State your business in the Underworld."

"We're on a tour," he said bewilderedly. "The Nova Band. The Underworld, Helios, Rimrock, Moonshadow— we booked through the Suncoast Agency, we've got permissions, passports, docking dates and codes—"

"Hold."

He held, his mouth tight. He turned to Quasar, held her eyes. The Nebraskan said softly, "Quasar, they can search us when we dock, and if you've got something in the hold, just show me—"

"I didn't! I haven't!"

"Just what I always wanted," the Scholar muttered. "Private lodgings in the Underworld."

"Magic-Man, it's not me this time, I—"

"Quiet down. I don't have any idea what we're transmitting. Heart-Lady, did you notice anything funny when you—"

The patroller's voice interrupted him, a fraction less harsh. "Permission and entry code for *Flying Wail* on record. Why is your receiver open to the Underworld Frequency?"

"I didn't know it was," the Magician said blankly.

"Who owns the craft?"

"I do."

"Where did you acquire it?"

"From a used-smallcraft lot in Suncoast Sector. All its records were—"

"Beneath the control panel there is a serial number. Give me that, your license number and your ID number."

The Magician sighed noiselessly. There was a longer silence when he finished. They waited. A sudden thump came out of the bowels of the *Flying Wail,* and a trill of the harpsichord. The Magician jumped, slapped it silent.

"Roger Restak. ID 4069PC1114."

"Yes."

"All communications systems on patrol-cruisers sold to private citizens are adjusted to receive only legal frequencies. Why are you monitoring our codes?"

"I'm not! I had no idea—"

"ID numbers of all on board."

"They're already on record with the Underworld. Are we in trouble?"

The static sounded slightly more human. "It's possible that an error was made in your presale adjustments. Are you the first civilian owner?"

"No."

"The sales history will be verified. Roger Restak. Legal status: owner and commander of a suspect smallcraft, *Flying Wail.* You are not formally charged. You will proceed as scheduled to the Underworld. Any attempt to deviate from docking schedule will be regarded as a felonious act. Questions."

"No."

"*Sunbird*. Out."

The cruiser accelerated out of orbit, left them a clear vision of the Underworld. Quasar swallowed audibly.

"Magic-Man."

"You can smoke in the hold."

"Me too," the Nebraskan said, trailing after her.

"Not," the Scholar said, "a friendly place. Roger."

The Magician grimaced. "There is nothing secret from the FWG. Heart-Lady, did you check with the Library Bank about fixing that receiver? Was there any warning to private citizens about the Underworld Frequency?"

She shook her head. "No." Her hands were still trembling. She didn't look at him but at the looming space-prison, the great wheel of light and dark constantly turning under the sun's eye. "No," she whispered. The Magician reached out finally, touched her; again the expressionless gold, turning to him, disturbed him. "Magic-Man, I'm sorry."

"You keep saying that," he said, listening at last. "You didn't do anything. You couldn't have, if all you were doing was following the mechanics diagrams."

"There were two—there were two small copper seals with the Underworld logo on them. They weren't on the diagrams. So I thought—I thought they shouldn't be there. So I took them out."

The Magician made a sound. He touched a light at random, so gently nothing responded. "So," he said softly. "You probably activated a subsonic transmitter, as well as opened the UF. Too bad we weren't listening—"

"We are lucky," the Scholar said emphatically, "we weren't listening. They'll check our log-tape."

"I didn't—I didn't think of that . . . Magic-Man." She put her hand on his arm, held his eyes, her own eyes so distressed that he shook his head a little, mute, worried. "I didn't mean to get you into trouble."

"Will you calm down?" he pleaded. "You're making me jumpy. We're not in trouble."

"I'll tell them," she said, coming to a sudden, bewildering decision. "In the Underworld. I'll tell them." He shook his head again, sharply.

"No. Absolutely not."

"Then what will you do?"

"We're here to play music. When I leave, I'm leaving with a whole band, come hell or high water. It's not your fault. How are you supposed to know about frequencies that don't exist on record?"

"Then what will you do?" she said again. He smiled, gave her shoulder a quick pat.

"Let them hear what they want to hear. That's what I'm good at. Cheer up. It was an innocent mistake. Even if they don't believe my lies, they would never throw us into the Dark Ring for that."

"It was a mistake," she whispered. "It was a mistake to come."

He was silent, suddenly overwhelmed with her nebulous emotions and at a loss to comprehend them. The Scholar said gently. "We'll play and then leave. It's as simple as that."

She didn't answer. The *Flying Wail* spoke again, announcing their dock escort. The Magician lifted his head incredulously, hearing a note that he hadn't programmed into the cruiser. But, listening to it again in his head, he realized the false sound was not in the music, but in the Scholar's vision of their future.

TWO

In the Hub computer room, Jase watched the *Flying Wail* dock. The room was shadowy, nearly soundless; light from the lovely panoply of nebulae and galaxies, someone's dream of space, colored his face. He liked spending spare moments in there, in the brain of the Underworld, knowing that every second it was making countless decisions to keep the Underworld running smoothly, calmly, the way a body made decisions, inarticulate and precise, to keep itself alive. Usually, so much power at his elbow was soothing. But the computer wasn't invented yet that could be plagued with premonitions.

"Challenge."

"He was born with the gift of laughter, and a sense that the world was mad."

"Challenge."

"$E = mc^2$."

"Challenge."

"Flash Gordon."

"Entry code 6B. Channel 9. *Starcatcher*, escort *Flying Wail* to Station C. *Flying Wail*, follow instructions precisely to avoid destruction. Acknowledge."

"Acknowledged."

"Permission to enter the Underworld."

The immense outer lock swiveled open, closed again. The red web of warning lights around the two cruisers gradually turned gold. The cruisers settled.

Jase studied the *Flying Wail*. It was an outdated cruiser, a Moonflivver, bulky and clumsy looking; there were people who swore it was the best model the cruiser designers had ever come up with. No one came out of it. A tech crew was going through it first, checking the faulty receiver. He doubted if anyone on board had tampered with the system. They were musicians, come to play one evening in the Underworld, and be a memory by lunch the next day. They were Sidney Halleck's chosen band, not a handful of conspirators trying to use the Underworld's equipment to gain entry. They were guests, here in good faith . . . "So why," he demanded of the Hub computer, "am I standing around here in the dark waiting for all the alarms in the Underworld to go off ?"

Because, he answered himself silently, they've barely landed, and already there are too many coincidences.

"Chief Klyos."

He touched the com-light. "Here."

"Tech-Captain Rethro speaking, sir. We checked the *Flying Wail*'s receiver. The logo-seals are missing. I'd guess it got sent to Earth without being altered. An error on our part. Nothing from the UF showed up on their log."

"Fine," he said. "Fine. Let them loose, have a dock crew help them with their equipment. Is Halpren down there to meet them?"

"Yes, sir. Sir? Is the concert just for prisoners or can anybody go?"

"Ask Halpren. It's his baby. I'll tell him he can have all the security guards he can handle, as long as you're all off duty."

"Thank you, sir."

"One more thing." He paused, contemplating one final, niggardly detail.

"Sir?"

"Check the repair records on that cruiser before it was sent Earthside to be sold."

There was a tiny silence. "Yes, sir. You think—"

"And get someone to dig back into its resale history. No. I'm not thinking. I just want to know."

"Yes, sir."

"Out."

He crossed the corridor to his office. Nils was sitting at his desk, sipping coffee and looking bleary.

"What are you doing awake?" Jase asked.

"I assigned myself as security for the concert."

"You did." He raised a brow. "Maybe I'll ask Jeri to do a Rehab program for the staff."

"Are you being sarcastic, sir?"

"No," he said, surprised. "I complain so much, I forget other people might complain too. We're all up here with no escape. Maybe we can work something out with Helios, fish in their rivers or—"

"In return for what?"

Jase grinned. "I'll think of something." He sat down, glanced over their visitors' status-sheets, which Records had sent up for his inspection.

Nils said, "Sir?" The odd tone in his voice made Jase realize the peculiar quality of his own stillness. He breathed again, blinking, but nothing on the stat-sheet changed.

"I'll be damned," he whispered.

"What is it?"

"I don't know . . . Run down a Queen of Hearts, Suncoast Sector for me, will you?"

* * *

"How can she be doing that?" Dr. Fiori demanded of the ceiling.

"Doctor, maybe it's the machine."

"It's her."

Terra gazed at them without blinking. She hadn't moved in half an hour. The image on the screen had changed twice in half an hour. Neither time had it made much sense. The first image, they had decided, was the swollen, ponderous face of the planet that had loomed over Terra when she was a child. The second image was a seashell.

"It's a chambered nautilus shell," Reina said helpfully. Dr. Fiori flicked her words away.

"It's the same image the computer gave her for seashell."

"Maybe she's finally shot out of the galaxy."

"If you can't make meaningful suggestions—"

"I thought I was."

"She can't be doing that. How can she do that?"

"She's concentrating."

"On a seashell?"

"Doctor, maybe it's the machine."

"Sir," Nils said. "A report's coming on screen from Records."

"Go on."

"Says the mechanics sheet dated twelve years ago on cruiser UP29548YP indicates all repair work, including UF scrambling, was completed before it was sold to Earth." His eyes lifted puzzledly. "Did they make a mistake? Or did someone who bought it—"

"I won't know until I get the sales history."

"So you're taking this seriously."

"It's a hunch."

"About what, for God's sake?"

"I don't know yet. So who's the Queen of Hearts?"

Nils shook his head, his fingers moving on the keyboard. "She's the Queen of Hearts."

"Well, what—"

"That's it. Seven years ago she didn't exist."

Jase sighed. He said patiently, "Well, find out what name she changed it from."

"Sir," Nils said as patiently. "There's no record.'

"No record? She's in the band, she's not a seven-year-old child—"

"Then, sir, why don't you just ask her?"

They glared at each another a moment. Then Jase growled, "Ah, that's too easy. Humor me. Records has every status-sheet on every citizen who even trimmed his toenails crooked in the solar system. Try credit, taxes, traffic violations, anything. She's up here in the Underworld and we don't even know her name."

"Sir."

"What?"

"Why?"

Jase opened his mouth. Then he slid his fingers over his eyes and up over his hair. "Nils, if I told you exactly why, you'd recommend me for a brain scan."

Nils leaned back in his chair. "Really?" he said curiously. "Then you could get transferred and I might have your job?"

"Exactly."

"It's that warped."

"Uh-huh."

Nils whistled. "Okay, but I can't find her under the usual headings. She just doesn't exist beyond that date."

"All right." He moved to watch the screen over Nils' shoulder. "Take the earliest date she used that name. Pull up old news headlines, patrol activities in Suncoast Sector, special assignments, criminals at large—anything big . . ." He scanned the words flowing down the screen. He made a noise suddenly, and Nils' fingers stilled. "There. See what you get from that."

A blurred news photo appeared on the screen: a young woman, her face half turned from the photographer. Nils stared at her, then at Jase.

"Status."

They both read it silently.

"Update."

"None."

"Nothing?"

"Nothing," Nils said. He cleared his throat. "Past that date. Seven years, three weeks, two days ago . . ." He looked up at Jase incredulously. "How do you do that? How do you pull rabbits out of thin air like that? How did you know to—" His face turned abruptly back to the screen. "My God. That's Terra Viridian's twin sister. Here. Wandering around the Underworld."

The Queen of Hearts, she made some tarts . . . "Well," Jase said wearily, "there's no law against it yet."

"But how did you know? What made you go after it like that?"

Because, Jase thought, I was talking to a musical genius named Sidney Halleck about old nursery rhymes, and her name happened to pop into my head, and she was in a band Sidney happened to recommend, and now she happens to be in the Underworld, and damned if I know what's going to happen next.

"I'd explain," he said, "but you'd have me certified."

"Well, what do we do? We can't arrest her for that, but we can't ignore it. It might be just coincidence, but she came here in disguise, on a suspect smallcraft, which just happens to be an old Underworld—"

Jase nodded. "You're starting to see what I'm seeing." He was silent a moment, tapping noiselessly on Nils' desk with his knuckles, frowning at nothing. "At least we can let her know we know." He touched a com-light. "Klyos. Infirmary, Dr. Fiori."

On-screen, the doctor looked a trifle demented, as if he had been around Terra too long. "Yes," he said vaguely.

"Dr. Fiori, is your patient interested in visitors?"

"She's only interested in seashells at the moment."

"Oh. Well, her sister is one of the Underworld guests tonight. She turned up unexpectedly. She hasn't made any requests to see Terra, but I thought I should let you know in case you were interested.''

''I am, but I don't— What kind of relationship did she have with Terra?''

''How the hell would I know?''

''I guess you wouldn't.''

''They're twins, that's all I—''

''Twins!'' Dr. Fiori said explosively. ''Why wasn't that on record?''

Jase shrugged. ''It's on ours.''

''I had no— Does she want to see Terra?''

''I don't know. I intend to ask her.''

''It might jolt Terra's mind off the seashell.''

''Seashell?''

''She's stuck on one image. Do you have any idea how difficult it is to think about one thing for more than—''

''She's crazy. All right. I'll talk to Michele and—''

''Who?''

''Her sister. Michele Viridian.''

''Michele!'' Dr. Fiori shouted. ''Not seashell! Michele!'' Then he was still a moment, awed. ''Terra knows she's here.''

THREE

The Magician, following Jeri Halpren through the hall curving away from the dock, blinked away the sudden, fine sweat that had broken out on his face at his first step into the Underworld. Tired, he thought, but he knew that was not why the air and the changeless, muted light seemed to sparkle as if he were inhaling too much oxygen, or why the shadows of the robotguards seemed to stretch, black and taut, like warnings, beneath his feet. Jeri Halpren, an effusive and annoying man, was explaining the wonders of his Rehab program. Fortunately he required no response, since no one seemed inclined to give him one, not even Quasar, who eyed him incredulously, as if he were of a sex she hadn't yet come across. The Scholar made gentle, absent noises now and then. The

Nebraskan had stayed with the dock crew to help them unload. The Queen of Hearts was so uncharacteristically silent that the Magician had to look back once to see if she were still among them.

Jeri Halpren opened a door finally to a small, comfortable suite.

"VIP quarters," he said proudly. "It's an old twentieth-century design, complete with doorknobs and private locks. There is a twenty-four-hour cafeteria down the hall, and a rec room across from it. You are asked not to wander beyond that. Now I'll see that your sound man finds the hall suitable. I'll be back in an hour to show you where you'll play. Any questions?" He gave them another white beam of teeth and departed.

"Where's the Scotch?" the Magician asked, when the door had closed.

"You jittery?" the Scholar asked surprisedly. "Magic-Man, I thought you had nerves of piano wire."

The Magician had walked to the back wall, opened a curtain before he stopped to think. The room had no windows, just a simulation of a nebula forging stars like chips of sapphire against the black of space. Staring at it, he drew a silent breath.

"I'm not," he said steadily, for Quasar's sake. "I'm just thirsty."

"It's back in the luggage."

"Stupid place for it." He turned finally; Quasar, her eyes flicking to him, had scented his uneasiness. She was pacing a small, very contained oval between two couches; its exact dimensions fascinated and appalled the Magician. The Queen of Hearts had curled up in a corner of one of the couches. She seemed to be thinking nothing, seeing nothing; her peculiar silence wore at the Magician as much as Quasar's prison pacing. Only the Scholar, engulfing Quasar in one arm to stop her, seemed immune to his surroundings.

"Cheer up, people," he said. "We're in the Underworld. Land of hundred-eyed monsters and three-headed dogs, musicians, poets, and the river of forgetfulness."

"Tu es fou," Quasar said morosely. "Whoever heard of a three-headed dog?"

"Cerberus, Watchdog of the Underworld."

"What did he guard it from? He already was in hell."

"From the living."

"Fou." But the Scholar's muscular arm and his fantasy seemed to calm her. She regarded her nails. "Green, I think, for tonight . . . Lime."

The Magician, turning to find a memory in his path, stopped his own rambling. "Wasn't there some old story about a musician rescuing somebody from the Underworld? Do you remember? There was some catch to it . . ."

The Scholar loosed Quasar, dropped onto the couch beside the Queen of Hearts. He contemplated the swirling stars. "Some pre-FWG Greek . . . Orpheus. The woman he loved died and he followed her down to the Underworld. He played for the dead so beautifully that his wife was allowed to follow him out again. But he had to have faith. If he lost faith and looked back to see if she was following, she'd never be able to leave. The catch was: Don't look back."

"Well," the Queen of Hearts said after a moment. "What happened?" Her voice sounded as fragile and unexpected as a child's voice in the Underworld. "Did they escape?"

"Of course not," the Scholar said cheerfully. "He was so happy, his lady was so beautiful, he looked back. How else could it end? No one escapes from the Underworld."

The Magician shifted his stance to roam again, but didn't. "Are you sure?" he said puzzledly. "That's the way it ends?"

The Queen of Hearts gave a short laugh, as unfamiliar as her voice had been. "I believe it," she said. The Magician, listening for all the vague lilts and switchbacks of her conversation that he was used to, stood motionless, his eyes on her. She was staring upward, as if she could see past the ceiling of their small suite, into the enormous, winding maze of rings. "This place is so big," she whispered. "And there is only one way in."

The Magician remembered then what he had casually stored away, like a curious dream, in the back of his mind during the past hectic weeks: the vision he had had in Sidney Halleck's club, the premonition that a time was coming when the Underworld would be the focal point of all his thoughts, when no matter where he looked, what music he played, the Underworld would fill his eyes, his mind; its darkness would revolve not around the Earth, but around him.

And here he was.

His body gave a sudden blue flash of terror.

The Scholar's feet hit the floor audibly as he rose. There was a knock at the door; the Scholar, mute, breathing quickly, could only stare at the Magician. The knock sounded again.

"That'll be the Scotch," the Magician said faintly. Since no one else seemed capable of moving, he turned, noticing as he did so how the room seemed to lift gently and settle around him as if he were letting wind through the opening door. The luggage was nowhere in sight.

A man stood in the doorway. His dark hair was rumpled, his sleeves pushed up. He was of unremarkable height, slightly pudgy and might have been anyone—dock crew, maintenance man—but for his eyes. They seemed to take in the Magician's past along with the cut of his hair and the old stains on his flightsuit.

"I'm Jason Klyos, Chief of the Underworld." His eyes moved to the still faces beyond the Magician's shoulder. He found the one he wanted and spoke again, direct, impassive. "Michele Viridian?"

The Magician's mind went blank; he tried to remember what names they had all relinquished to a blurred past. Then his skin constricted. He stepped aside, not wanting to watch but watching the Queen of Hearts rise with dreamlike slowness from the couch. Her face seemed changeless as ever, he thought, reassured: It's nothing, a minor problem, a mix-up in their records . . . Then two wildly dissimilar matters connected in his brain.

Terra Viridian. The docking frequency.

His body, for the moment, seemed to have exhausted its blue impulse. He felt the sweat at his hairline again. He tried to swallow, but his throat was full of moondust. The

Queen of Hearts stood beside him, the cuber with the face of gold, guarding a woman whom no one even knew was still alive.

Chief Klyos' eyes changed slightly as he studied her. The Magician could feel her trembling.

"Ms. Viridian. You don't know this because no one could locate you to tell you about it, but there's a Dr. Fiori from New Horizon here working with your sister Terra in an experimental capacity—"

Her hands slid up her arms, closed. "Experimental?"

"It's harmless, painless; I've seen it. It's just a machine that records her—ah—visions. The FWGBI gave him permission. I told him you were here for the night. He asked me to bring you to see Terra. Do you want to?"

"Do I want—"

"To see your sister."

Her fingers opened, gripped again. "Yes," she whispered. "How—how is she?"

"About the same, I'd say." He was silent, still studying her; his voice suddenly shed its dry politeness. "How'd you do it?" he asked curiously. "How did you disappear like that?"

"People do things . . . they have to do." She paused to swallow. "Terra—we looked alike seven years ago. I needed privacy. From her."

He nodded, unsurprised. "I guess you did. I'd guess even the tree-people in Rainforest Sector knew what Terra Viridian looked like seven years ago." He turned to the Magician. "Are you the head of the band, Mr. Restak?"

The Magician recognized his name after a moment. "When we need a head."

"Did you know her name?"

"No one knew," the Queen of Hearts said with intensity. "No one."

Chief Klyos opened his mouth again, hesitated, glimpsing something. "So," he said very softly, "you never knew either, why she did it."

"If I had known, I wouldn't have had to hide." She

pulled away from his gaze, stared down at the carpet, her eyes wide, blind. The Magician watched her, incapable of movement. But she didn't cry: the mask held. Behind them, he heard Quasar light a cigarette; even she was wordless.

"Will you come with her, Mr. Restak?" For a moment the question made no sense; seeing Terra Viridian was not in any future he had ever envisioned. Chief Klyos was still speaking, running a hand through his hair. "Dr. Fiori couldn't say how Terra might react to her sister. But—damned if I know how—she seems to know you're here." He dropped his hand, said again to the Magician, "Will you come? I'd like someone to be with her."

He nodded briefly. "Yes." He turned, said to the Scholar with some semblance of efficiency, "Start setting up as soon as you can. I don't know how long we'll be."

The Scholar nodded, still mute. The Magician closed the door and followed his cuber into the Dark Ring of the Underworld.

He gave up after the first five minutes, trying to memorize their way back in case Michele Viridian's guerrilla tactics included a swift jailbreak. There were elevators, escalators, transporters, monitor screens everywhere, guards everywhere, including two that Chief Klyos had picked up along the way, and where there were no human guards: robots. After ten minutes he had no idea whether they were going up, down or sideways within the rings. The Queen of Hearts walked in front of him, beside Chief Klyos. She looked back once to see if the Magician were still behind her. He found a smile for her somewhere even as he remembered her with her stained jumpsuit and competent hands lying under his control panel and remorselessly putting the *Flying Wail* in jeopardy. They took another brief transport ride along the curving wall of the ring. Then there was another elevator, another hallway, another pair of guards, another doorway.

Infirmary, Ward D411.

The Ward was dim, full of odd shapes, and lively. A doctor began babbling at Michele while one of his three assistants cast a flickering green glance over the Magician.

She turned back to the console and screens in front of her. The screens were constantly monitoring different aspects of Terra in vivid color, except for one, which showed nothing but a seashell. As the Magician looked at it, it wavered. He turned, his skin prickling, aware then of the life the screens were monitoring in the shadows behind him. A huge bubble was suspended in a corner of the room. He stared at it, fascinated. The Queen of Hearts took a step toward it. Another.

Something rose within the globe: a naked, spidery form that pushed against the transparent wall until it lost shape, melted around the hands straining to reach out of it. The voice was child-thin, exhausted.

"Michele?"

The Magician felt his hands and face chill. The Queen of Hearts moved past him, her face paint smudged with sudden tears, and gripped the hands within the bubble. "Terra," she said. "Terra." Her voice shook badly. The Magician closed his eyes. But still he saw them, two women wearing each other's faces, both trapped by the past, helpless to help each other. He heard someone cry from a great distance, "Look at the Dream Machine!"

And then, behind his closed eyes, memories that were not his own—bright, precise and random—scattered like a pack of tossed cards through his head.

Michele's face or Terra's face, much younger; a tiny, misshapen moon dwarfed by the swollen red face of the planet; the navigational panel of a mining shuttle; the humid, drizzling air of a greenhouse; a bowl of oranges; a poem on a screen; black heart-pins; a red star; desert under a hot yellow star; a black wall rising against deeper black; the shadows of a line of soldiers marching across sand; an unfamiliar star pattern; a shield of dazzling, dangerous light; a child with short, pale hair drawing blue stars on her face; a bent steak knife; a bent oval on amethyst sand, beside a red-washed sea. . .

The images whirled like a film reel running too fast, then jammed, tore. The Magician's mind went blank.

He could see again, finally. People stood beside him, behind him, gazing at the screen. He still stared upward at the figure within the bubble. He saw Terra's face, misty behind the transparent walls. Michele had let go of her; the bubble had flowed back into shape. She was moving back from view, but as she shifted, she found his eyes.

The hair rose on the nape of his neck. He was too stunned even to tremble. You, Terra's eyes said. You. He closed his eyes again, felt icy sweat run down his back. But the memories were still there in his head: her memories. He knew where she was born, he knew the desert where she had killed, he knew the color of her hair when she was small. Spiderlike, she had spun a filament out of her need and caught him.

"No images," one of the doctor's male assistants said. "Did we lose her?"

"Michele," Dr. Fiori said gently. "Speak to her."

"Terra." Her voice caught raggedly. "Terra." She was trembling again. The Magician was rooted where Terra's eyes had touched him; she stood alone with Terra, isolated. Tears slipped down her face; she brushed at them now and then, absently. "Terra. Can you talk to me?"

They heard breath from within the bubble. "Michele?"

"I'm here."

"I am a solar wind, born out of fire."

Dr. Fiori murmured something. Michele said without turning, "It's from a poem. She wrote it when she was twelve. Terra. You're so thin. Don't you eat?"

"Which?"

"Which what?"

"Which I? I eat and I don't eat. Not at this time. Not until the end."

"What end?"

"The end of the vision."

A soft purple twilight dimmed the Magician's sight. He turned, half blind, panicking, and saw the screen colored with his vision. Someone looking at the screen said, "Again the amethyst mist . . . It means, but what could it possibly mean?" He breathed more easily. The light faded. He felt someone's eyes on him, found Chief Klyos staring at him from the doorway. He felt his dry mouth, his clenched fists. He might have tried to speak, but Terra tugged at him again, dragged his eyes back to her.

Her voice lost its remoteness. "Michele."

"What?"

"Listen to me. Listen."

A cliff face black as deep space. A dim, reddish sky beyond it. An oval bent back on itself, all colors or no color, lying on amethyst sand. A concave vision of a red star. The cliff. The oval. The red sun . . . The need, the primal, overpowering, overriding need . . . The vision.

He stopped himself from making a noise. His eyes felt frozen open. The thin face, the enormous eyes, seeing visions, seeing into his eyes, making him see . . .

Michele whispered, "I'm listening." It was a question. She still waited, the Magician realized, still listened for what had just been said . . . Terra's voice came again finally, half lost within the bubble.

"I'm so tired. So tired."

"Talk to her," Dr. Fiori murmured.

"She—"

"Talk to her. Make her remember."

"Terra." She paused, groping at the past. "Do you—do you remember when we came to Suncoast Sector? We saw grass under sunlight for the first time. And great gardens of flowers, growing outside of greenhouses. Do you remember?"

"Birds . . . mosquitoes . . ."

"Yes."

"Spiderwebs, strung in the morning light."

"Lemon trees. We didn't have words for all the things we saw."

"Words."

"We were sixteen. New to Earth. We were sad at first. But after a while we began to laugh again."

"You played music. Always, always . . . you dreamed

it, you loved it, you were haunted with it . . . It was your vision.''

"And you took care of us. You lied to the schools for me, you cooked, you even bought clothes for me . . ."

"You drove the sol-car. You fixed things. You had the dream.''

"You had—"

"I had no future."

"You—"

"I waited. For no future. For a place where they would cut off my hair.''

"It will grow—"

"Not here. Never, in the Dark Ring. And I will never leave.''

Michele started to speak. Then she put both hands over her mouth, hunched, raked by a noiseless grief. The Magician, shaken with pity, took a step toward her. A shape blossomed in his mind, halting him. It flattened like rain hitting pavement, then drew back into itself and scuttled away down the purple shore. Another followed. Another. A sound built in him. He closed his eyes but the shapes still bloomed. Terra, he pleaded. Terra. And, amazingly, they stopped.

"She's losing herself. Keep talking, Michele." Dr. Fiori's voice, soft, insistent. "Michele. Ask her about Desert Sector.''

"No." She shook her head sharply. "No."

"Ask her."

God, no, the Magician thought, horrified.

"Ask her. Be careful."

Michele turned, torn, agonized; he said again, "Be careful. Don't disturb her.''

"How?" She drew a shuddering breath. "How can I ask her that and not?"

"You know her."

"I don't know her! I never knew her!"

"Sh. Take it slowly. Try. For her sake."

She faced Terra again, her voice drained, barely audible. "Terra. Can you hear me?"

"Michele."

"I can hardly see your face. Aren't you cold in there?"

"Cold. There is no cold."

"Do you remem— Do you remember the last time we saw each other? Seven years ago?" There was a silence within the bubble. The Magician heard his heart hammering. I can walk out of here, he thought. I can keep walking. But his body held no more volition than a rock. And there was no place for him anywhere in the universe now beyond Terra's eyes, Terra's vision.

"Terra. Do you remember?"

"There is no time." The words were a whisper.

"You kissed me good-bye. You were in uniform."

"No."

"Terra, I tried—I tried to see you after that. I—they wouldn't—"

"I know."

The room was soundless.

"How could you know? They wouldn't let me see you, they said you were dangerous, they said—"

"Your face was not in the vision, but I knew you. The rest"—one thin arm gestured—"was nothing." She crumpled onto the floor of the bubble, held her knees tightly, her head shaking back and forth. "Faces. Voices. Questions. Noise. The vision."

"Terra. In Desert Sector. What happened?" Silence. "Terra. You said good-bye to me and you went there and you—and I never—I never—you never came back, you—"

The sun was dark, in the Magician's head, on the screen of the Dream Machine.

"You went to the desert, and—"

The vision was light.

The Magician's lips parted. Smothered, blinded in darkness, he hungered after light, dreamed light, envisioned light . . . He made light.

"Terra. You were—" Her voice broke; she covered her face. "I can't," she whispered. "I can't, I can't, I can't—"

"The vision," Dr. Fiori said. "Ask her what the vision is. Ask her, Michele."

"Terra. What—what is the vision? What are you seeing?"

Terra's face disappeared against her knees. Her breathing sounded ragged, exhausted. She swallowed, said finally, "Words. Questions. Words without sound."

"Words without sound . . ." She turned finally, bewilderedly, to face the Dream Machine. Something viscous, vaguely yellow, bubbled and spat in the Magician's mind. That stilled, faded into the twilight shoreline, where the oval lay, bent, colorless or of all colors, isolated and unchanging as a moon. The Magician wanted to release his motionless body to time, drown his mind in the cool purple.

"A word," Michele whispered, "without sound. But what does it mean?"

"The vision."

He saw the amethyst sand, grainy, translucent; he was in the sand; he was the sand. He saw nothing, heard nothing. Then the eye of God, the red sun, opened the darkness, and he felt an imperative like the drag of a tidal wave across the sand, revoking the past, transforming the boundaries of the world. He could not speak, he could not feel. There was only the hunger, inexorable and absolute, and with the hunger: the vision.

The vision was light. It fired across his mind from a hundred points; where the lifeless, empty darkness swallowed it, it streaked again, over and over, battling the long night until the dark curled away to reveal chaos and more light. The yellow sun against a fierce blue sky . . . It stared down upon a shifting landscape where blurred shapes were bewilderingly, hauntingly familiar before they too became transformed into light. The sand, pale, barren, ran suddenly hot, glazing into molten glass. Under the yellow stare even the oval melted.

It became a child's face, screaming silently in terror. And then the screaming was no longer silent.

Terra had risen; she was pounding against the bubble-wall, screaming the child's scream. The Magician, sagging on his feet, reached out blindly. He hit the edge of the Dream Machine, and then two people in the midst of some struggle.

"No. It's all right. She can't hurt herself."

"Let go of me!" That was his cuber, he remembered hazily, the Queen of Hearts.

Dr. Fiori answered her quickly, soothingly, "Okay, I'm letting go, now."

They broke apart; the Magician released them, balanced again and able to see. For a second he made Dr. Fiori veer from his relentless pursuit of Terra.

"Are you all right?" he asked, startled. "You look dead." He added, before the Magician could answer, "Can you stay longer? She's remembering. She's beginning to face reality. You saw how the symbol changed."

"Symbol." Michele, her face a weird smear of tears and colors, stared at him, trying to make sense of him.

"She's disguising her actions behind a screen of vague symbols which are safer for her to look at. You're helping her face truth."

She looked at him a moment longer, then at the shadows, the computer, the bald, whimpering prisoner, the assistants and guards, the segment of the vast, contorted ring around them. Tears slid again down her face. "For what?" she asked him. "Please tell me that. For what?"

FOUR

he Magician saw nothing, said nothing on the way back from the Infirmary, until, left at their quarters by the guards, he brought himself up against a door that would not open.

"The doorknob," Michele Viridian said faintly and turned it.

"Oh."

Their luggage was inside; the rest of the band was not. Somewhere, he assumed, a stage was being set up. He thought he was standing still; something within him was still. But he had crossed the room; a case was open; he was uncapping a bottle. There was another blank moment, tranquil, silent. Then he tasted Scotch in his throat. He lowered the bottle and shuddered suddenly, violently.

He turned. The Queen of Hearts was sitting on a couch, still crying, noiselessly and absently. Most of her face paint was on her hands. In the pallor of her skin, in her eyes, haunted, grey, seeing and not seeing, the Magician caught an eerie glimpse of Terra's face.

He drank again. Then he found a glass in the bathroom, filled it with Scotch and pushed it into Michele's hand.

"Drink that." He waited while she stared at it, then lifted it off her knee and took a swallow. She swept hair out of her eyes with her fingers, streaking it with gold. A heart-pin dropped; she gazed at the heart in her hand, a hard, glossy black acrylic, worth nothing. A memory that didn't belong to him slid into the Magician's mind: heart-pins scattered on long hair so pale it seemed to spark here and there with white fire.

He said, "Those heart-pins. They belonged to Terra."

She nodded. Then, her head still bowed over the pin, her eyes slanted up at him, like a child alerted and wary of something looming in the shadows. "Yes," she whispered. She was silent a moment; her face lifted cautiously toward the dark. "They shaved her head. Magic-Man, how could you look at her and see those heart-pins on her?"

He lifted the bottle again. He was still sweating; he felt the chill of it on his face, his back. "Why didn't you tell me about Terra?"

"I cou—I couldn't."

"What do you think I would have done? You never told anyone?"

"No."

"God, Heart-Lady." He balanced on the couch arm beside her, the bottle on his knee. "Michele." He touched her shoulder, and was overwhelmed by twin lonelinesses: one woman imprisoned in a vision, the other behind a mask. He said urgently, his mind filling again with Terra's eyes, Terra's power, "Tell me about her."

"There's so little to tell. There's nothing."

"Tell me where it began."

"I don't know!" Her eyes filled again. "I don't know."

"Tell me what you know, then. You weren't born on the moon. Not Earth's moon. Tell me."

She dragged a long breath; her voice shook. "Where we were born, there was a moon's tiny horizon. Space. Night. The planet's face. The red planet. There was a constant sound, always the same sound. The heartbeat. The generators. They never stopped. Like blood running. The first sound we heard. For me, it became the drum of the cubes. For her, it was always the heartbeat." Her voice faded; he touched her, pleading.

"Tell me what you remember. Anything. Everything. Tell me about the heart-pins."

"The heart-pins . . . Todd gave them to Terra . . . Magic-Man, we were born within the same minute. For years, when I looked into Terra's eyes, I saw myself. An extension of myself. For years there were no separations between us, not in thought, hardly in body. We knew everyone in the colony. All the eighteen other children, all the adults. They were our family, our world. The entire universe was winding, white-tiled corridors and tiny rooms, the throb of the generators, the familiar faces, the immense face of the planet over us, the first thing I ever dreamed about . . . We lived without thinking, without really being aware or convinced that we were two people, not one. For years. Until the separation. The first one."

"What?"

"We both went crazy together, that time. She fell in love with Todd MacNeal. I fell in love with music." She sipped Scotch again, sat silently, brushing at her face, a weary line between her brows. "It was the first time. That our thoughts didn't mirror each other's. It was the first time I watched my mother's music tapes and heard the sound of the generators—the sound of my world—behind every song I listened to. I wanted to make that sound. I dreamed the music, I dreamed cubing in my sleep. I beat on everything that would make a sound. I heard the cubes in everything I played. It was—it was—"

"A vision," the Magician said softly, and she nodded.

"A kind of madness . . . That seems to be what those years are for. Terra simply fell in love." She hesitated. The Magician swallowed Scotch from the bottle, waited.

"Terra."

"She—she was always sensitive, intuitive. I never noticed it so much until we started growing into different people. I never paid attention before to which of us did what. But now, she was the one who wrote poetry. She was the one to walk down a corridor like she was dancing down the Milky Way. Her hair seemed always windblown, always glinting with sunlight, even in the middle of a moon-factory. She saw us from the other side of the universe, the other side of time. I didn't see my face in her face any longer. I didn't see hunger in it, impatience, hopeless love. Her eyes weren't for me any longer. They were for Todd.

"I heard our parents talk about us at night. My mother said, 'What are we going to do with them? Michele and her saucepan lids, Terra trying to have her first love affair in a pharmaceutical factory on a chunk of rock so small you can hardly piss in private.' I remember thinking, So that's where Terra went. When I took my thoughts away from cubing, she wasn't there anymore; I hardly knew her. I missed her. But the cubing . . ." Her voice trembled again. "The cubing. The music. The vision was all. My mother would tell my father we had to go to Earth. My father would say we were happy here, we should stay here. My mother would say, 'Terra, maybe. But this moon is not big enough for Michele.' I didn't know what she meant, then. All I wanted was a set of cubes. And for us all to stay forever together on our private moon . . ."

"And Terra? What did Terra want?"

"Terra . . ." She paused, seeing nothing but Terra, warping time as she sat, returning to the past. Words came faster, all the words the Queen of Hearts had stored behind the mask for seven years. "Terra had what she wanted, all the magic of first love. She couldn't do anything wrong; all the natural rules suspended themselves for her. If she was late for dinner because of Todd, dinner would make itself late. When she cut time from the ed-com lab, that would be the day her terminal would decide to malfunction. Doors were never locked against her. If she was home late, our parents would be even later. She was inside the weave of magic that wove the world. She was—she was inside her vision. But this vision everyone understood. Everyone had had it, or thought they had it, or wanted it, or dreamed it, or mourned it. She turned that factory into a fairy tale, and then she walked into it herself. She turned beautiful. Todd grew taller; he spoke without blushing; his voice deepened. They both laughed a lot. They were using each other to grow, transforming each other. Maybe . . . When I think back, sometimes I think that's all she had needed to stay sane. To stay happy. If she could only have finished the fairy tale, if things had just come to a natural end. If she had married Todd, or grown up, away from him. If, one way or another, it could have been complete.''

''What happened?''

''She dreamed of fire . . .'' She sat still then, her face still, as the Magician had often seen it without noticing: the stillness that guarded Michele. He recognized it now. He touched her gently.

''A premonition?''

''A vision,'' she whispered. ''That was another of the separations. She was becoming psychic. I never was. She dreamed of fire and knew our parents were going to die . . .

''They had gone to the Surface on a cargo shuttle, to spend a couple of days in one of the resorts. I woke up and found Terra sitting on the floor in the kitchen. She wouldn't get up, she wouldn't go to ed-com, she wouldn't even talk. Not even to Todd when he came looking for her. So after ed-com, I sat down beside her on the floor and waited . . .

''The cargo shuttle had malfunctioned as it landed. Terra had dreamed the explosion.

''So. We were sent away from the colony. Away from our home, our world, everyone who had ever known our names. One day Terra was loved and in love. The next, she was flying through silence and darkness away from everything she had ever loved. We were born spacers. I could fly a mine shuttle as well as anyone. Terra could make anything grow. But we were fifteen. According to FWG regulations, we were too young to be hired in space.

"So we were sent to Earth."

"Eat," the Magician said. He had brought back sand-wiches and hot soup from the cafeteria. Michele picked at a crust; the Magician stirred his soup once. Neither of them ate.

"They wanted me to tape articles," Michele said, "after it happened. They wanted me to write a book. *Fire in the Desert*, by Terra Viridian's sister. They wanted me on talk shows. With my cubes and home videos of Mom and Dad and the little Viridians. This was even before she was tried.

"I had been out cubing. I came home late. I had new silver shoes on. I came home alone . . . I remember the shoes because I stepped out of them, making a sandwich, and that's where I left them, empty silver shoes standing at the kitchen counter, when I finally left the apartment and went five hundred miles up to north Suncoast Sector. For all I know, they're still there. I ran because I had turned on the newscast to watch while I ate, and suddenly there was her face. My face. Only her hair was quite short, since she was a draftee, and she wore khaki and ID tags. She'd mailed the same picture to me months before as a joke.

"They said she'd killed over a thousand people and escaped. They weren't sure, then, how many . . .

" 'This is not in the vision.' That's all she'd say when they found her. 'This is not in the vision . . .' " She touched a sandwich, then forgot why, gazing instead at the dust and stars in a fiery tangle on the back wall. "The vision . . . I kept thinking that after living twenty-one years with her I'd know what she was talking about. What vision? Did her mind just snap under the sun? Was it drugs? Or was there always a vision, something only she could see out of the corner of her eye, a shadow that followed only her, all the days while we were growing up? You'd think there would be something, like maybe she skinned cats in Suncoast Sector and boiled their bones, or she went out naked and preached about visions in the streets. You'd think there would be some hint, some clue. Wouldn't you?"

"Was there?"

"Nothing," she whispered. "Ever."

He let his breath out silently, noiselessly, he thought, but she heard him. She misinterpreted, her hand reached toward him, withdrawing.

"There was truly no warning, Magic-Man. We lived together when we got out of school. She worked at an employment agency counseling people about to leave Earth to work in space. I played the cubes in any band that would hire me. I cooked, kept the apartment clean. I fished the fork out of the recycler, hung the shelf, stopped the leak. The only odd thing about her life was that she never—she never looked ahead. She never thought about what she might be doing with herself for the next fifty years. She never brought the same man home more than twice. She'd let friends drift away. People liked her, they tried to get close to her. But she was so detached. It was as if she were made of glass. Nothing clung to her, nothing could trouble her. I was closest to her. But she never talked about the past, even to me. Never. Not about Todd, about our parents, about working in space —nothing. Ever since we were tiny, she had always told me her dreams. Now, when I asked her, she told me that on Earth she never dreamed . . ."

"You said she was psychic."

Michele nodded. Her eyes grew wide again, heavy with unshed tears. "I loved her, Magic-Man. I really thought she hadn't changed much, when we came to Earth. She always had been competent, sweet tempered . . . But now I can see what she was doing. She was hiding. Not only from the past, but from a future she must have seen coming . . . She said she never dreamed, but I think she must have just buried what she did dream, because it didn't bear looking at. Her future. The killings in Desert Sector, the Underworld, her loneliness and madness . . . If she caught glimpses of this in her future no wonder she said she—no wonder—''

The Magician put his hand on her shoulder, gripped it as he heard the long, jagged draw of her breath. ''Was she psychic in other ways? Besides dreaming?''

She straightened, reached for her glass. ''She always knew what I was going to wear in the morning, even before I knew. She could look at a message-light and know who had called us. She'd look at the light and say, 'It was for you—Will called.' She did that, the day she got drafted. She looked at the message-light when we walked in the door. Only this message had a strange feel to it. Because she said, 'I think it's for me.' As if she knew that this was the point where she would begin to change . . .

''So the next morning she went down to the Induction Center. And six weeks later she was in Gulfstream Sector, in training. And then, two months later she was at the airport, and I was saying good-bye to her just before she boarded the transport shuttle.

''That's when I saw her.'' She sat quietly a moment, her face still again, her shoulders slumped under the Magician's hand. ''I mean, saw what she had become. She didn't seem troubled; she was—what she always was. Patient, good-humored, detached. She looked beautiful, like a recruiting ad, like the kind of woman things are always happening to. I realized then what she had left behind her on the moon colony. I knew that everything she had ever wanted had already been given to her and torn away from her. There was no fire left in her from which to kindle events.

''She said—she said: 'It's just FWG technicality. I'll work in an office for a year, then I'll be home. Take care of yourself. Write to me. I'll miss you.' She kissed me good-bye and turned. A laser-rifle hung from her shoulder.

''I watched her trials.'' Her voice was nearly gone, husky, strengthless. ''I had gone south again, tried to see her after they caught her, but they said she was too dangerous. The journalists, the lawyers, all descended on me when I came back. They wanted me to tell them about Terra's secret, bizarre double life, to tell them that she hated our mother, she hated our father, that she had sabotaged the cargo shuttle that killed them, that she hated men, she abused young children, she— They wanted a reason. They wanted me to tell them anything except that a normal human being just like them could go berserk at a moment's notice and wind up on trial for murder.

"I couldn't tell them that. They wanted me at the trial, but I ran north again. I didn't know her anymore. I watched the trial alone inside the ghetto room I had taken . . . It wasn't Terra they tried. It was some thin, pale woman who spoke of visions, who said yes, she had killed but that it was not important. 'The vision is all.' It wasn't Terra.

"But she wore my face."

The Magician was silent, remembering a bar the size of a shoebox in north Suncoast Sector . . . a night seven years before, when a young woman with a gold face and Terra's black heart-pins in her hair had crossed his vision, dragged his attention away from the music under his hands . . .

"That night—that night I met you—"

She looked up at him, her eyes weary, stunned with pain. "Magic-Man, I was barely twenty-one. Of all the people I'd loved most, two were dead and one was mad. I hadn't—I hadn't planned to live very long. But I wanted to cube one more time. I disguised myself, and went looking for one last band. I heard your music." His lips moved soundlessly; his face was chilled again, white. "You named me, Magic-Man," she said softly. "And you gave me a reason to stay alive past dawn."

His hand slid from her shoulder. He rose, stiff, crossed the room until the wall stopped him. He stood staring at the web of stars, until they seemed to kindle and spark under his eyes. He said, "You came with us to take Terra out of here."

"Yes. You had the cruiser, I opened the Underworld Frequency to learn the docking procedures."

"Where were you planning to take her?"

"I don't know. Magic-Man, the moment I saw this place

I realized that I could no more get Terra out than I could jump over the sun. The Scholar was right. There's no way out of the Underworld. And then—and then I saw Terra. For years I thought that she could give me some answer, if I just asked her why. I thought she had just disguised herself, like I had, that somewhere in her the Terra I always knew still existed. She is still part of me, Magic-Man. Even though now I know there's no part of her I understand anymore. She's simply crazy. That's the final separation.''

The Magician opened his mouth and closed it. He reached out, touched a dying star. ''Michele.'' His voice sounded peculiar; so did her name. ''I never saw what was on the computer screen while we were with her. She put her vision into my mind.''

The silence behind him was so complete that he turned, wondering if she had disappeared, like an unobserved particle. She was still there, staring at him. ''Magic-Man,'' she whispered.

''The things she had to say: the red sun, the purple sand, the distorted oval weren't things that could be spoken. Not in language anyway. She gave them to me without words.''

''She went—'' He saw her shudder; Scotch splashed out of her glass. ''She went into your mind.''

''She had something she needed to say. I happened to be able to hear it.''

''What?'' She was on her feet, bewildered, incredulous. ''What could she possibly say to you? About killing all those people—''

''The sun was dark.''

''In the middle of the desert on a hot summer day!''

''The vision was light.''

''Magic-Man, only a crazy woman would stand under a blazing sun and think it was dark!'' She went to him then; he sensed her terror for him, her terror of hope. She caught his wrists in her powerful cuber's grip. ''Magic-Man. What is she thinking? Could you understand? Please. Please. Could you understand her at all?''

''Oh, God,'' he whispered. ''God help me, yes. You

saw what she told me. On the computer screen. But the computer couldn't feel.''

"Feel what?"

"The hunger. The absolute, overwhelming need.''

"For what?"

"To change. To complete the vision.''

"What vision?" She shook him, crying again. "What vision?"

"Her vision. Something else's vision. Whoever's vision it is, it must be finished.'' His voice had grown very calm, detached; from the expression on his face, in his eyes, he might have been listening to antique music. "There is no time within the vision. Time has not even begun yet . . . There is one imperative, and it is as absolute a need as breath: to complete the changing. Nothing else matters. Nothing else exists. Nothing but that drive toward time. Toward life.''

"Magic-Man.'' Tears slipped down her face again. She held him as if one of them were drowning. "You sound like Terra.''

FIVE

I n his office, Jase tapped out yet another transfer request. Tundra Sector, he'd heard, was a peaceful place if you didn't mind cold. Faster than he could type, more vividly than he could imagine freedom, the images he had seen on the Dream Machine rose between him and his typing. He gave up finally, leaned his head on his fingers. The silence in the Hub crept like a mist around him. Usually he was grateful for quiet. Now, in the waning of the day, all Terra's mad thoughts haunted his brain and the silence troubled him. He stared at the console screen, saw his own shadowy reflection, then the amethyst sand.

"What vision?"

His voice startled him. He scowled at his shadow. Dr. Fiori was right. She was disguising her thoughts; there was no mystery, just a crazy woman who couldn't face what she had done.

"Can't even get the color of the sun right," he muttered. He paused again, sat absolutely still in the silence. The red sun. The purple sand. The sea . . . "There's no sea in Desert Sector . . ."

The com-light flashed; he touched it. "Klyos."

"Nils, sir. That Suncoast patroller just arrived. Aaron Fisher. Do you want him now?"

"Not immediately. Let him sit and think awhile."

"He requested permission to go to the concert. Sir, I don't think he knows why he's here."

"He's under suspicion of conspiracy," Jase said grimly.

"On record?"

"No. On hunch. I don't want this on his record unless I make formal charges. He's not under arrest, but I didn't invite him up here for a concert either. Feed him and put him in the guards' dorm. That should keep him out of trouble."

"Should." He paused. "You talked to Michele Viridian. Is she—"

"She's hardly a hardened conspirator. She's not crazy enough to think she could get her sister out of here, though I suspect the thought crossed her mind."

"Is she like Terra?"

Jase sighed, remembering the hands straining toward Michele out of the bubble. He felt a sudden depression, like something damp and moldering in his chest. "No," he said, answering Nils' oblique question, "there's nothing in her to make you understand Terra. If anyone would want to. I wish to heaven Fiori had left her alone."

"Are you okay? Is something wrong?"

"Not yet."

There was another pause. "You want me up there?" Nils asked abruptly. Jase shook his head.

"No. Go listen to the music. Maybe I'll go too, before I start jumping at shadows."

"You don't jump at nothing," Nils said.

Later, Jase stood in the doorway of the D-Level Rec

Room, the only place big enough for a concert. The swimming pool was covered; the body equipment had been taken out. The walls were lined two deep with security guards, a good eighty percent of them volunteers. The prisoners sat on the floor, and on the sections of movable wall that had been laid over the pool. Their bald heads reflected odd colors under the eerie glow of the stage lights. They didn't talk much; they hardly moved, except here and there when someone would sneak a quick, incredulous glance at the roped-off area which was the stage.

It was worth a glance. The rod-harp, a fish skeleton of copper and glass, stretched across three-quarters of the stage. Behind it, big, translucent cubes were stacked like some alien sculpture. The gases in them were warming, slowly coloring. The Nebraskan was still working with the lights, flooding the air with purple, green, orange. The Magician had painted his face a nebula of swirling colors and was tuning, of all things, a battered old piano. He plunked a final note on it, ran his thumb down the keys in a brisk glissando that made heads move, flashing. The Nebraskan played an experimental rod. The copper spat electric blue toward a second rod; the glass emitted a high, fiery note. He darkened the stage.

The hall darkened a moment later. Even that brief blackness became strained. The murmurings of the guards ceased; Jase heard the creak of leather, the scrape of metal. Stupid, he thought, remembering the chains and bars still attached to the walls. Stupid, stupid—I'll have Jeri's hide for this. Then the place erupted with light.

The Queen of Hearts shook rose-red hair away from a face molded out of pure gold and brought her cube-sticks down. The cube she struck fumed crimson. She built a heartbeat out of crimson and indigo, fire and night, that shattered the Underworld silence like glass. Quasar, her hair shimmering the colors of the rainbow, leaped onstage with a street yell that must have come straight out of the sewers of Lumière Sector. The Magician, incandescent, began a duet between the piano and his body-wires. At the soundboard, the Nebraskan, his lank hair and mustache the color of pearl in the light, monitored the sounds of the body-wires, playing the Magician himself like an instrument. Light kindled in the icy bones of the rod-harp. A line of power crackled down its length. The Scholar wove a glissando of wild, timbreless notes into the Magician's colors. Quasar's voice, lean and husky, snapped across the weave:

> "Pick a card from Fortune's morning,
>   Turn up the Queen of Hearts;
>   Pick a card from Fortune's warning,
>   Turn down the Ace of Spades.
>
> "And fly, fly, fly
>   To that dark dealer in the sky.
>   Love is leaving, the night is coming,
>   Nova will trap you in its light . . ."

A rod shattered under sound vibrations; the Scholar kicked the fragments from underfoot as he moved, tapping and caressing sound out of the bones. A second rod snapped with a crack of light. Quasar gave another yell. The Magician vanished into negative light. The stage turned a shadowy, midnight blue. From the dark came a sweet, quiet phrase of ancient music.

Jase clapped, surprised. There wasn't a lowered head in the audience now; no one could have slept through that. He lingered, wanting to hear more. He saw Jeri Halpren suddenly, grinning at him triumphantly. But he stayed anyway.

The music wandered into warmer realms; the cubes beat a languorous pulse. Quasar sang a love ballad, slow and intimate, that made Jase remember, for the first time in years, himself sitting on a riverbank in Delta Sector, with a childhood playmate, a little girl whose eyes were green as frogs, whose hair, yellow as light, kept blowing across his mouth. The next song led them into cold, glittering space. Sounds drifted in night-darkness: the perpetual static, the murmur of icy metal from some drifting alien ship, a spattering of solar disturbance, the faint, constant throb of awareness: the heartbeat. Color passed to color down the rod-harp. The cubes flared, luminous with star-gas. Sounds gathered toward sound; Quasar's voice echoed colors shirred from the Magician's aura. A pattern struggled to emerge from the nebulosity, emerged finally as the Magician was lost in tides of changing hue: the gentle, precise music of the past.

The stage turned rose; the musicians retired to repair their paint. Jase turned back into the orderly silence of the Underworld, still surprised. I'll have to tell Sidney Halleck, he thought. I didn't expect to like it.

He returned to the Hub. One more nagging detail and he could go to bed. Everyone, he thought grumpily, is so damned innocent. Even the patroller summoned to the Underworld had no impulse to skulk in his guilt; he wanted to be entertained. If there's nothing to worry about, he thought, why am I worried? And there's nothing.

He summoned Aaron Fisher, sat waiting.

There's nothing. There's a woman in a band, there's an old cruiser that was never altered properly, there's a good and decent patroller who had his back turned to his computer at the wrong time.

There was nothing.

Or else there was something. And whatever it was revolved around Terra Viridian, the most dangerous prisoner in the Underworld.

He dismissed the two guards who brought Aaron Fisher, and studied him a moment silently. He was taller than Jase expected. His uniform was impeccable. His face, lean, rugged, was freshly shaven. He met Jase's eyes neither warily nor with challenge, but he did seem perplexed. He hadn't, Jase decided, the vaguest idea why he had been brought under guard into the presence of the Chief of the Underworld. Or else he was capable of motives and solitary actions that overrode completely every limitation of his profession.

"Sit down."

Aaron sat. Jase leaned back in his chair and said without preamble, "You're here because we put a routine tracer on a request made through the Library Bank in your district, on your computer, for top-secret information about the Underworld. Why did you request such information?''

Aaron blinked. His face was immobile a moment, probably out of habit. Then the stiffness melted, and he looked simply astonished. "I didn't."

"Who else has access to your computer?"

"No one. Sir."

"No one? Where is it? In a vault?"

"No, it's—" His voice stopped then. He looked at Jase silently a moment, and Jase thought wearily, There's something. Aaron glanced down at his hands. When he lifted his head again, the lines at the sides of his mouth had deepened.

"It's in an old nuclear shelter," he said. "On the coast."

"Is that where you live?"

"No. I mean, I have a smaller system where I live, but it's tied into this one." He stopped again. Jase eyed him.

"Are you going to make me fish for it?"

Aaron drew breath. There was a hint of color in his face. His eyes had changed; they looked inward to some bleakness. Then his muscles loosened slightly; his eyes ran over the tiny, soundless room. "No," he sighed. "I guess that would be pretty stupid."

"I guess it would too."

"It's just—I never talked about it. To anyone."

"I suggest you start."

The tone of Jase's voice brought Aaron out of his memories. He met Jase's eyes squarely. "I'm a patroller. A good one. The last thing in the world I'm interested in is classified information about the Underworld."

Jase grunted. "Then what are you interested in, Mr. Fisher?"

"I—" His hands tightened, relaxed again. He spoke quickly, his voice devoid of expression. "Seven years ago, my wife was murdered. She was a draftee serving in Desert Sector. She was killed by Terra Viridian. She was p—she was pregnant. I've been using that system in the bomb shelter for research. I don't pretend it's all been legal. I've been trying to find Terra Viridian's sister. I wanted—I wanted to know—'' His voice shook, and he swallowed, left Jase staring at his rigid face.

After a moment, Jase found his voice. "Is that why you wanted to go to that concert tonight?"

"What?" He looked bewildered, as if Jase had spoken old-world. His face was white; the backlog of emotions was crowding into his eyes. Jase straightened, a small movement, as though he were trying not to displace air.

"Revenge?"

"No."

"Then why?"

"She—nothing made sense. Why she was killed. I just wanted to understand why. To try to understand. I loved— I loved her."

Let it go, Jase told himself, with sudden, urgent foresight. Let him go back without knowing. There's no need. He's put it into words.

But there was still the matter of the docking procedures. He said carefully, "That's an unusual thing for a patroller to do, isn't it? You must have spent a good deal of time at it."

"I was assigned to it at first. The conspiracy theory, to cover up for the FWG for the trial that sent her here."

Jase nodded. "I remember the assignment."

"I told people—people I asked to help me—that I was still on assignment."

"I see."

"No one else—"

"I understand. I'm not investigating your prowling through theoretically private information, but I strongly suggest that you climb out of your bomb shelter and find some healthier activity before someone does want to investigate. You may be a first-class patroller, Mr. Fisher. Your records say so, your superiors say so. But I'd like an answer to my question. If you didn't request docking information, then who was using your computer?"

"No—" He stopped. He stared at the air between them, the color draining from his face again, even, it seemed, from his eyes. Jase laid a hand on his desk.

"Who, Mr. Fisher?"

"Only one—only one other person I know used it." His voice was husky. He swallowed, but the ache stayed in it. His face was smudged with some fresh pain, and Jase shifted, sighing noiselessly.

"Who, Mr. Fisher?"

"A woman. I brought her there. She needed information about fixing a cruiser-receiver; it wasn't working right . . ."

Jase touched his eyes. Damn it, he thought, feeling the weird stilling of time, as if they had reached the place where it ended its circle and began again. "Damn it!" he breathed, and stood up. Aaron was watching him. All the expression in his face had died. He looked, Jase thought, as if he had just become the man he had been afraid of becoming.

"The concert." His voice came easily then, without feeling. "You asked me about that. She's in the band."

Jase sat down again, weariness dragging at his bones. All on a summer's day . . .

Terra stood in front of him.

SIX

She lingered in the doorway long enough to turn Jase into stone with her eyes. She carried a laser-rifle. Aaron turned at Jase's stillness. The vision-drugged, alien eyes moved to him and he stopped moving, stopped breathing. She loosed him, melted back into the shadows, silently as she had come.

Jase, frozen for another fraction of a second, moved finally. He hit the Hub-alert, and snapped at Aaron, who was heading toward the door, "Fisher!"

Aaron, feeling the emptiness at his weapon belt, glanced down, surprised. Jase tossed him a stunner out of the desk. "Be careful!" His monitor screen was flashing different sections of the Hub: offices, computer rooms, storage, officers' quarters, all quiet, all in shadow. "Where the hell is everybody!'' The alarm was whooping in his ears. Men and women began running out of the Rec Room, out of their quarters. The screen showed him a door, welded shut with light. Then the camera eye over the door exploded.

"God—'' Jase breathed. He heard battering in the distance, shouting. Still no one came. He touched the com-light. "Get me Fiori.'' His com screen darkened suddenly, eerily, but the com stayed open. "Dr. Fiori? Can you hear me?''

"Chief Klyos! Thank God! She—''

"She's here in the Hub. Are you hurt?''

"No, but she welded the doors closed. I don't know what happened. We thought she was falling asleep, we took her out of the bubble and she just went berserk. She grabbed a rifle from one of the guards and started shooting. She shot two guards and the ceiling cameras. She shot the hell out of the Dream Machine. Then she locked us in.''

"I'll get someone to you, hang on.'' The monitor screen showed him the transport corridor and he cursed, stunned. The robot squad was scattered in pieces all down the track. "She's not human,'' he whispered, and wondered, suddenly, if Aaron were still alive. "Fisher!''

"Chief Klyos!'' Nils' voice, taut, pitched high, came over the security channel. "What's going on?''

"Nils, where are you?''

"D-Level Rec, helping the band pack up. What's—''

"Terra Viridian is wandering around the Hub with a rifle. Grab Michele and get up here.''

"Jase,'' Nils breathed. "Shoot her.''

"The thought crossed my mind. I think she's blocked off Headquarters. Get a crew to open the transport doors, get Michele in here if you have to fly her around to the Hub-dock, and get me some security!''

"Are you alone?''

"Fisher's here.''

"Fisher? That's all?''

"Quit shouting and get in here, any way you can. Oh, and get a crew to rescue Fiori.'' He glanced out; the smoky acrylic walls showed no movement in the hall. "Fisher!''

Aaron emerged from the Hub-computer room, crossed the hallway carefully. "I didn't see her," he said. He still looked startled, but his hands and voice were steady. "We alone?"

"She's got us isolated."

"How—who is she?"

Jase stared at him. Then he said, "I guess you wouldn't know. You only saw her seven years ago. That's Terra Viridian."

For a second Aaron looked at him as if Jase had told him the Earth was flat and the Underworld full of horned devils. Then the blood swept furiously into his face. He whirled so fast that Jase barely had time to get air to bellow, "Mr. Fisher!" Aaron stopped short at the doorway, as if Jase's voice had tangled around his feet. He didn't turn back, but he didn't move forward. He raised one hand, gripped the doorway, holding himself there. Jase saw him tremble with the effort.

He lowered his voice. "Mr. Fisher, if she kills you, I'll be alone here. I want you alive." Aaron said something inarticulate. "You don't know the Hub. She's not attacking us for some reason. I want to keep it that way. I saw what she did to twenty armed robots in the transport tunnel. She's got a gift for staying alive. You wouldn't fare better than the robots."

"I can't—"

"She'll kill you before you can kill her. I need you alive. She's hardly human anymore. She'll kill you, you'll die, and she won't know why you came to kill her, she won't care who you are, or what she did to you, and you won't care either because you'll be dead, and she'll still be alive in here and so will I. If you'll follow orders now, she'll be dead in five minutes and we'll both be alive."

The hand gripping the door eased a fraction. Aaron glanced back at him. The shadows had drained color from his eyes; they looked almost black. He made another sound. Jase moved toward him, said very softly, "Can you fly a cruiser?" He had to repeat the question before Aaron gave him a faint nod.

His face was chalky with the struggle to keep himself still, listening.

"The Hub-dock is above the computer room, just across the hall. There's a ladder in the ceiling. I'll drop it for you from here. Get up there and warm the engines."

"N—"

"I'm going to put the Hub on defense. That means anything that moves, that the Hub-computer can't identify by voice and code, will be destroyed. You're not on record. You'd have a better chance against Terra than against the Hub-defense. Terra will be dead in sixty seconds."

Aaron's lips parted. He took in air and managed an entire sentence. "You'll be alone."

"I need to change the docking challenges since we're on alert, and you can't be down here when the Hub goes on defense. I'll be with you in two minutes." He waited. "Mr. Fisher. You're standing in the doorway with the light behind you. Do you want her to kill you?"

Aaron's hand slid down. He turned finally. He looked, Jase thought, as if he had just been beaten for no reason. "No." His voice shook. "I should have asked her."

"What?"

"Her name. Michele Viridian. But with a rose you never ask."

"Mr. Fisher. Go."

He nodded, his face growing private again. Jase pressed a dusty button on his desk, saw the ladder descend swiftly, noiselessly, in the shadowy room across the hall. Aaron checked the hall. Nothing moved. Jase stood in the doorway, guarded him with a stunner until he had disappeared up into the dock.

The Hub was soundless. He strained to hear footsteps, heard nothing. Nothing moved. He went back to his desk, touched a com-light.

"Get me Nilson," he said softly.

"Here, sir," Nils said instantly. "Are you all right?"

"Yes. Nils, cancel bring Michele, we're flying out."

"Good. I couldn't find her anyway."

"I'm putting the Hub on defense, after I follow general

alert procedure. Then I'm out of here. Meet me at Main-dock.''

"Yes, sir."

He switched to voice command. A hundred years' worth of docking challenges had been programmed into the system: famous names, mathematical equations, quotations from old literature, videos, song lyrics, riddles and poems, phrases of obscure origin and more obscure meaning. Fifty choices appeared on-screen. He gave his name and ID code, but it was his voice pattern, inimitable as the signature of an earthquake, that was crucial. Then he gave the code that signaled all docked cruisers to log the new challenges into their systems for a forty-eight-hour alert period. He was about to read the first challenge on the list—"Oh, to be in England now that spring is here''—when he sensed movement in front of him. He raised his eyes, his throat going dry.

It was just the Magician. He had actually loosed a sigh of relief when the fact struck him. He breathed, "Mr. Restak, what the bloody blue blazes are you doing here?"

"Terra brought me," the Magician said, so calmly that for a moment those words made perfect sense. Then they made no sense whatsoever, and Jase moved his foot to push the door-shield switch on the floor. But the Magician was standing in the doorway, and bewildered as he was, Jase had no inclination to fry him.

"Come in, Mr. Restak."

He shook his head. Jase lost his temper.

"Mr. Restak, are you out of your mind? How did you get in here?"

"Terra let me in."

"When?"

"Just before she melted the transport door shut."

"Why?"

The Magician didn't answer. The expression was fading slowly from his face. His eyes widened; he looked vulnerable, absorbed, as if he were dreaming awake. The soft purple Jase had seen in Terra's visions enveloped him in a gentle haze, and Jase remembered then how he had stood in the Infirmary, gazing up at Terra, the whole time, while everyone else watched the Dream Machine.

He felt his skin prickle with shock. He heard his own voice from a distance. "Mr. Restak. If you don't move out of the doorway I will kill you. I'm going to activate the shield."

"Killing me," the Magician said, "is not in the vision."

Jase shot his stunner at an angle from beneath his desk, and like a hand, it swept the Magician out of the doorway. "God in Heaven," Jase said incredulously, and activated the door-shield.

It exploded in a dazzle of light. He flung himself backward, momentarily blinded. The soft bulk of the air-chair toppled over him, hampering his movements, like an awkward lover's embrace. Then it bore down on him, refusing to move at all. He strained against it, astonished, swearing. Then his sight cleared. He stared into a laser-rifle. Terra Viridian crouched over the chair, her eyes riveting him as much as the rifle. The Magician, weeping blood from one eye, sat on the overturned chair, pinning Jase down. His hands were poised over Jase's keyboard.

"Right," he said, no longer dreaming. "What we need now is a little Bach."

The Magician stumbled back down the transport passage a few minutes later in a dreamlike haze of amethyst and blood. The fused and shattered bodies of the robot squad lay like broken dolls along the track. The security cameras, a dozen eyes of the hundred-eyed watcher, the Hub-computer, had been blinded by Terra. The Magician had no idea where she was. She had found him; she had given him no choices. She had shown him the way through the maze of the Underworld, her mind a thread he had followed. Now she had vanished again, moving secretly before him or behind him, somewhere along his impossible path to the *Flying Wail*. He had played music for his freedom; what he needed now was an idiot's luck.

"Fool's Run," he whispered. His head throbbed; blood

kept falling into his eye. His throat burned with thirst. He saw the red sun, then, casting a bloody light across an alien world. The vision is light. God, he thought feverishly, philosophically, we drink in light like air. How would we mutate, what thirsts would we develop under a dying sun?

His footsteps rang hollowly down the passage. He had left Chief Klyos bound and gagged, but how long would he stay that way? Having freed himself, or been freed, what would he do?

Warn the docks.

The Magician increased his pace. The spoke from the Rings to the Hub seemed endless. He ran expecting to be killed at every step, expecting a fallen robot to move, turn toward him, eject light like a dying breath. But this was a wasteland, a blasted desert of fused wires, melted circuitry; nothing was aware of him. Phrases of music he had played after he had tracked down all the tones and half-tones the vast computer contained gave him a rhythm to run by.

It will work, he thought, amazed at his own genius. It will work. If only they don't kill me first. Or Terra. If only . . .

Sparks sheared the shadows behind the vacant transport cars. He slowed, uncertain. Then, with a shrug at destiny, he moved forward, the aura dissipating, until he was simply a wounded survivor of a mechanical carnage, desperately seeking his own kind.

The transport door opened with a rend of metal. The Magician continued doggedly toward it. The tech crew, faces hooded against hot metal, stared at him blindly. A small army of guards leaped past him into the transport cars. Others caught at him, not roughly but with authority. He felt a rifle behind his ear. Someone touched his face.

"It's one of the musicians."

Don't shoot the piano player, he thought madly. A finger probed around his eye and he jerked.

"What happened? What's going on back there?"

"Someone was shooting at me. I took a dive into a wall."

"Is Klyos alive?"

"I saw him alive."

"What were you doing in there?"

"He asked to see me; I never did find out why." He started to shake suddenly, realistically. "Where's a medic station? I can't stand blood."

"Let's go!" A voice yelled from the transport cars, and he stood alone suddenly, outside the tunnel, the cars already streaking away, the tech crew ignoring him, picking up their tools. He took a step. One of the hooded figures turned toward him.

"Magician!" It pointed. "Medic down that hall. Suggest you stay in your quarters."

He walked until he was out of sight. Then he ran.

Jase, buried under the air-chair, his mouth full of fabric, struggled to free his hands from the Magician's body-wire. Bach, he thought furiously. Bach. Goddamn musicians—

He saw a boot out of the corner of his eye and stopped moving. He stopped breathing. He heard a muttered word. Then the air-chair rolled off his back; hands untwisted the wire around his wrists. Turning his head painfully, he saw a grey uniform with the thin gold piping down a seam that said: Earth.

Aaron. He made a muffled protest. Aaron freed his feet, pulled the wire and fabric away from his mouth. He felt at Jase a moment.

"You hurt?"

"No," Jase said sourly. He sat up. "What the devil are you doing back down here? You might have been killed."

"I took a chance. You're not hurt?"

"No." He got to his feet, leaned over the desk, but there was nothing much left of his com-system. Aaron was still staring at him.

"She didn't kill you."

"Do I look dead?"

But Aaron's attention had left him abruptly. He was gazing down at the fine, colored wire in his hand. He opened his mouth to speak, but nothing came out. Jase touched dead lights at random; nothing responded.

"They may be still in the Hub, hiding. Let's—"

"They?" Aaron said sharply.

"That crazy musician—"

"Michele?"

"No, the Magician. Restak. We can still get to Maindock. I could put the Hub on defense, but—" He rubbed one ankle, thinking furiously. Aaron put the wire on the desk.

"The Magician."

"He reprogrammed the docking challenges. My voice command: no override."

"The Magician did."

"He's taking Terra out. But not if we have a chance to get to Maindock first. I'll have Nils put the Hub on defense when he gets in here, just in—"

"The Magician in the band?"

"Mr. Fisher, does your brain always work this fast?"

Aaron took his eyes off the wire. He looked stunned again, his eyes pained, shocked. Jase said tautly, "Now what?"

"We've been friends for years. He wouldn't—he—that makes no sense . . . Unless he's doing it for Michele. But even so—"

"Mr. Fisher," Jase said, rounding the desk, "you can stand here and speculate until doomsday if you want, or you can come with me and get some answers. If they have left the Hub, they're on their way to the *Flying Wail*, and we've got to intercept it before it gets out."

"You've got half the Underworld fleet in Maindock," Aaron said bewilderedly. "The *Flying Wail* is fast, but she can't outrun them all."

Jase felt the blood wash into his face. "The Underworld fleet couldn't outrun a flying bathtub right now. He's got them trapped. All of them. Everyone but us. Let's go!"

The Magician crossed the dock area quickly, unobtrusively, keeping his eyes off the cruisers around him, the dock crew, the men and women in the control deck above the dock who seemed, at his single, brief glance, to be unconcernedly going about their duties. The *Flying Wail* was open, fore and aft. The Queen of Hearts was carrying cube-cases up the main hatch. The Nebraskan and the Scholar were pushing the piano up the aft-hatch ramp. For a moment he felt an icy, wrenching spasm of terror. They'd arouse suspicion if they tried to leave surrounded by equipment; they'd never get it packed in two minutes; if they did get it packed, if they did leave, he'd have most of Nova with him, and how could he explain . . . They'd never forgive him for taking them; Quasar would never forgive him for leaving her behind . . .

"Don't look back," the Scholar had said. He left his fear behind him like something palpable—his body or his shadow—and picked up a cube-case as he reached the *Flying Wail*.

Michele met him coming down the ramp again. Her face looked odd without paint, smaller, younger. She stopped him, a hand on his shoulder, frowning at the cut on his face. He shook his head quickly.

"Never mind that. Get the cubes inside. We're taking off."

"Now?" Her eyes went wide suddenly, Terra's eyes, seeing into him. "Magic-Man," she whispered. "What have you done?"

He dumped the cube-case in her arms. "Fast," he said, and she turned. On the aft-hatch ramp, the piano was jammed at an awkward angle, half in, half out of the hatch. The Nebraskan heaved; the piano rolled through. The Magician followed them up, brought the ramp up and closed the hatch.

Terra, he thought. The name was a pulse in his brain. Where? Where? Anywhere. Everywhere. He had tied Klyos up and she was gone. Just gone. But she was attached to his mind like the tail of a comet; she must know where he would go. She's on the dock. She's inside the *Flying Wail*. She must be.

Don't look back.

He moved to the bridge. Quasar was there, painting her nails, and he smiled in relief. She glanced at him, brooded a moment at the state of his face and said mordantly, "It's not a color I would have chosen."

Michele came in with a cube-case. "That's it," she said. He sealed the cruiser, his hands chilly, shaking, and stepped around her cube-cases to the controls. Michele watched him, motionless, still clutching the last case. He said, "Sit down. The Nebraskan can get those."

She sat in the navigator's chair. Quasar's brush stilled abruptly. "Magic-Man, are we leaving? But our clothes, everything—"

"You want them," he said, "you go get them."

She was silent. The engines rumbled.

There was a surprised shout from the tail of the cruiser. The Magician wondered if they had found Terra. The receiver crackled instantly.

"*Flying Wail*, this is Maindock. You're not scheduled to depart until seven hundred hours GTT."

"Maindock, this is Restak," the Magician said glibly. "We misjudged our performance schedule. We're due at Rimrock earlier than we thought. We're not used to off-world time. Request permission to leave."

The control deck was silent. Right in the middle of an alert, the Magician thought. With Terra loose and the Hub sealed. Sure, Magic-Man, go right ahead. Take your leave. Take our prisoner too.

"*Flying Wail*, you'll need a dock escort," Maindock said politely. "We'll apply for permission to Chief Klyos for you. Hang on."

"Thank you," the Magician said, translating automatically: You move an inch, Magic-Man, you blow up. Salt gathered in his cut; he winced. Then he thought, Hub-com's out. He won't get through. He'll call in the troops.

"All right," he said steadily. He slid the panel away from the keyboard, as the Nebraskan, panting, swung into the bridge. "What's going on?" he asked amazedly. "Magic-Man? We haven't gotten paid yet. All our luggage—"

"Quiet," the Magician said very gently, "or we blow to Kingdom Come." There was silence aboard the *Flying*

Wail. All his thoughts slid away from the world around him, from the past, from the future, from danger and confusion, to focus on the music in his mind. He tapped out a dock code, linked the *Flying Wail* to the Hub-computer. "*Flying Wail*. Request permission to leave the Underworld."

"How?" Aaron demanded. "How could he possibly do that?" Jase settled into the Hub-craft beside him. He had seen guards finally enter the computer room, just as he'd retracted the dock ladder. But he had no time to tell them what he was doing. The Hub-craft's com-system was silent; he wasn't able to raise the control deck on it from within the Underworld. The Hub-craft was built for speed, not sophistication. It had no weaponry, no warning lights, and needed nothing but Jase's voice to permit it to leave the dock.

"Don't ask," Jase said disgustedly. Aaron was silent, staring at the red safety lights. Jase glanced at him, found time for a moment's appreciation of Aaron's bewilderment. He said, "I'm sorry I brought you up here, Mr. Fisher. This wasn't what I had in mind. But since I did, and you've already risked your life for me once or twice, I'll see that that gets on your record."

Aaron looked at him, then back at the lights. "Thanks," he said tonelessly. Then: "Lights gold."

"Klyos. Identify."

"Identified," the Hub-craft said. "Airlock opening."

"I just can't believe it," Aaron said suddenly. "Any of it. How could everyone I know go crazy in a day? How could—how could that happen with me not seeing it coming? The Magician—he even pays his docking fines on time. And the—M—" He closed his mouth, inarticulate again. Jase finished for him.

"The Queen of Hearts. How close a friend was she?"

"She." The blood mounted in his face; his eyes grew dark as the sky beyond the opening lock. "Lights go." He brought his whole fist soundlessly down on the panel and the cruiser shot into the Underworld's shadow.

Jase hit the com-light instantly. "Klyos to Maindock.

Identify. Sound dock alert. Dock alert." They were still blocked, it seemed, by the bulk of the Underworld. "No outgoing vessels. Repeat: Klyos to Maindock. Identify. No outgoing—"

"Override," Maindock said in Jase's own voice. He held his breath, then loosed it furiously and swore.

"Go."

The Hub-craft picked up speed. They were silent, hearing the Magician's voice.

"Permission to leave the Underworld."

Again, the voice of the Chief of the Underworld.

"Challenge."

Silence. Then a calm, gentle line of ancient music.

"Challenge."

Another phrase, brief, minor.

"Challenge."

A third line, sweet and totally unfamiliar. The Hub-craft rounded the curve of the Underworld in time to see the vast dome over the dock begin to open, unlock the stars beyond it.

"*Flying Wail*. Permission to leave the Underworld."

THREE

THE

VISION

O N E

The oval cracked.

The Magician, alerted by a musical comment from the *Flying Wail,* gazed in surprise at the blip on the scanner. Then a slow, soundless rain of images fell endlessly out of the oval into a purple mist, into his mind.

They were crystal-structures, delicate and varied as snowflakes. Occasionally he recognized colors: red crystal within a cocoon of yellow light, black within green, white within orange. They drifted down like confetti through still air, seemingly directionless, random. But each one was a message, and the Magician, no longer aware of what his body was doing, felt their force. Each message was precise and absolute. This was the vision. This was life. This was necessary as bone or air. If he could have responded to them, he might have changed the structure of his blood cells, or the shape of his lungs, for they were that imperative. But what were they? he wondered, fascinated. Biological or chemical messages? An alien language?

What, beneath some distant, dying star, absorbed them?

He began to see through the gentle haze. It thinned; the crystals grew indistinct, a tiny, fiery swarm, nothing. He drew breath, feeling lost, as if, bereft of vision, he had come to the end of time. Then he saw the light flashing on the scanner again, and remembered that he was Roger Restak, shooting through space pursued by a blip, with the Underworld a Furies' nest behind him.

It was, he had to admit, within his own time pattern a state almost as demanding as the alien vision.

Then he heard the absolute silence within the *Flying Wail*.

He swiveled his chair. Quasar, most of her nails green, held an unlit cigarette halfway to her mouth. Her eyes flickered as the Magician looked at her, but beyond that she gave no indication that she wasn't frozen. The Scholar was sitting against the aft-hatch, breathing quickly, too astonished to speak. The Nebraskan, surrounded by equipment, was still hugging two rod-cases upright against the *Flying Wail*'s lift-off vibrations. His face was devoid of expression; even his mustache seemed stiff.

The woman in the navigator's chair startled the Magician until he realized she was wearing an expression instead of gold paint. "Magic-Man." Even her voice was unfamiliar. "What did you do?"

"It was simple enough," he said calmly, though his wild luck was beginning to shake him. "I put all the musical tones in the Underworld computer—paging-tones, com-tones—into a scale pattern and then into code. I played Bach by number. There's a forty-eight-hour override on the docking challenges. They'll have to play Bach on their cruisers to get out of there."

Still no one moved. The Scholar breathed. "Sweet God." His dark face glistened with sudden sweat. The Nebraskan made a soft noise, as if the wind had been knocked out of him. The Magician turned back to the panel, nagged by the blip.

"Strap in. We're going to accelerate."

"Where?" For some reason no one could speak above a whisper.

"What?"

"Where," the Scholar whispered more precisely, "are we going to?"

"Oh. I don't know. Heart-Lady, what's the nearest asteroid colony?" He brooded over the blip. "It's got to be a cruiser that was just coming in, but I didn't hear—Heart-Lady, did they fix the UF?"

"Yes," she said faintly.

"Well, fix it back again, will you? I want to know what's on our tail."

"Magic-Man."

"Did you find—"

"Land's End is the nearest colony. Magic-Man!" Her hands came down flat on her control lights. The *Flying Wail* responded with a discordant complaint. The Magician took his eyes off the scanner, stared at her in amazement, and saw Terra's eyes again, Terra's face. He touched Michele reassuringly.

"She's not crazy. Neither am I. Did you compute our course?"

Her hands moved; she still looked at him, the Queen of Hearts with her mouth open, unable to find words. "Not."

"Not crazy. But we're in for a hell of a ride. All set?" He activated the cruiser's pursuit thrusters and sat listening to the musical messages. The power surge pushed him back in his seat. He heard chaos behind him and swore, remembering the instrument cases. He turned, saw the Nebraskan sprawled among them.

"You okay?"

The Nebraskan shoved cases away, struggling to sit. "My nose is bleeding."

"I told you to strap in, why were you up?"

"Because," the Nebraskan shouted through his hands, "I was going to tear your head off ! What are you doing? We're musicians! A band on a concert tour! You've got the whole Underworld after us, and all we were doing is loading equipment!" He pulled his shirt off, held it against his nose. "I quit."

"Oh, come on, Nebraska, calm down. The Underworld isn't after us. I told you, I've got them locked up for forty-eight hours."

"You locked up the Underworld," the Nebraskan said hollowly, hunched over his knees. "All we had to do was that one concert at Helios. We would have had video studios all over the world begging for Nova. We were so close to fame it was breathing on us. It was smiling on us. All we had to do was one more concert. One more. All those years of playing clubs, and all we had to do was one more. Now we'll be famous all right. We'll have our faces on the six o'clock news, and we'll have people offering us a fortune for the true story of why Nova traded an off-world tour for a mattress and a tin can in the Dark Ring and—" He lifted his head, his voice rising. "I couldn't tell it because I don't even know why!"

"The Dark Ring," Quasar breathed. "Magic-Man, what have you done?" She dissolved into old-world, came out of it, finishing, "—a renegade band, so we have to fight them, shit *alors*, we have no weapons."

"Wait a moment," the Scholar said heavily, holding up his hands. "Wait. Let's all stay calm. Maybe we're not in trouble yet. Maybe we're not fully comprehending the situation. Right, Magic-Man? We've all been with you for years. You've never exhibited signs of raving lunacy before. Now. You say you've trapped all the patrol-cruisers in the Underworld, just so we could leave a few hours early? Is that it? We're a little off-schedule for Helios? You didn't want to wait until after breakfast?"

"We have an unauthorized guest on board," the Magician said surprisedly. "I thought you saw her."

"Her," the Scholar said blankly. Then his eyes moved

from the Magician to the Queen of Hearts and back again, narrowed, incredulous. "Her." He was breathing quickly, his face glistening, as if he were in the throes of space-sickness. "What did you—" He shouted suddenly, startling the Magician, who had never heard him shout. "Did you steal that crazy woman out of the Dark Ring?"

"I'm sorry," the Magician sighed. The cut over his eye was beginning to throb. "But you were all in here. I had to leave fast."

"Magic-Man," the Scholar said furiously, "you better keep this cruiser accelerating all the way to light because as soon as I can stand you are going to be space-debris!"

"Will you let me explain?"

"You try. You just try."

"Terra," Quasar said, enlightened. "The Queen of Hearts' mad sister who has a vision."

"What do you mean," the Queen of Hearts said bewilderedly, "she's not crazy?"

"Either we're both crazy or neither of us is. Am I crazy?"

"Yes," the Nebraskan muttered.

"We rescued Terra?" Quasar said.

"Yes."

"Oh, God," the Scholar prayed.

"We freed her from the Underworld *cochons* who were performing experiments on her brain?"

"Yes."

"*Quel beau geste.*" She tossed him a green, pointed kiss from her fingernails. The Queen of Hearts closed her eyes briefly and opened them again.

"Magic-Man," she said, her voice shaking, "leaving aside the question of your sanity, which I wouldn't want to make a hasty decision on just at this moment, maybe you should tell me where she is."

The Magician opened his mouth, but nothing came out. He looked at the Scholar. "You didn't see her in the hold?"

The Scholar shook his head. "She wasn't back there. Not unless she crawled into the piano."

"Well, she was just behind me," the Magician said

puzzledly. The Queen of Hearts stared at him in horror. "Or ahead of me, I'm not sure . . ."

Quasar grinned suddenly, wickedly. "You forgot her?" Behind her, the Nebraskan made garbled noises into his shirt.

"She's got to be around somewhere. She nearly blew up the Hub to get out. She knew what she was doing."

The Scholar's voice vanished again. "She blew up—"

"The last time I saw her was when I tied up Chief Klyos with some body-wire. The blue tone. She held the rifle." He frowned at the blip again. "She must be somewhere in the hold. Heart-Lady, the pursuit thrusters will shut down in a couple of minutes. Get the UF working when you can move. I want to know who's on our—"

"That's it. That's it!" The Scholar's fury cracked across the Magician's concentration like a thunderclap, making him wince. "You tossed away our futures like last week's garbage, you plugged up the Underworld like a hornet's nest to rescue the lunatic of the century, and then, Lochinvar, you forgot the girl and came away with the goddamn buzzing hornet's nest instead! You're over the edge. You ever hear of *Mutiny on the Bounty*? Well, this is it, Captain Magic. Soon as you shut down, I'm taking over your ship."

"You can't fly," the Nebraskan said dourly.

"I don't care!"

The Magician spun his chair, arms braced against the grinding pull. "You're the one who told me," he said with sudden passion, "don't look back. You said that!"

"That's a story! A myth!"

"That's the point!"

"What's the point?"

"Remember when we talked about symbols on the way to the Underworld?"

"Symbols!"

"Listen to me," he pleaded. His voice was taut, strained so fine it held almost no timbre. "Listen. Remember the things we talked about. The wedding ring, the cross, the eye within the triangle . . . You look at them, you know what they are. They speak without words. They are a language.

Words without sound. They mean. They're symbols. Messages. Of what? Of hope, of fear, of faith, of love and hate . . . above all things, of change. Transformation. You know what a gold ring means. The meaning is old. Cultural. A circle of gold spoke of everything from daydreams to money, from ritual to politics. Now it's a historical curiosity. A fashion you wear if you think it looks good on you. But the symbolism is still there. You recognize it. It speaks to you without words, of what it once was. To us: we're human. But what would an alien see in a circle of gold? If you saw a bent oval on purple sand, what would that mean to you? Anything? Nothing. But it means, it speaks to someone, something, somewhere. And Terra sees it. I see it. And it speaks . . . What would a shower of crystals falling into light mean to you? Nothing. Nothing to me. But when they fell through my mind, they spoke. I felt the message in them, the force, the command to transform. I don't understand them, I don't know what they are. But I know what response they demand . . .

"Once the symbols we used for business logos burned like fire with meaning. Once they were something to die for. We invented them, we put our need into them, and once we needed them as much as life. Sometimes more than life. What Terra has seen all these years, what I see now, are parts of a vision. Alien vision. A vision of transformation. And within the vision, there is no choice. The strange images she sees —we see—are a language of absolute necessity. They must be responded to. Or life will not continue. I think the response is physical. I'm not sure. I don't understand the messages, I'm not the one responding, but I can see the images and I can feel the need . . ." His voice was shaking. He felt blood trickle out of the crust over his eye. "I don't know why she and I both got caught up into this need. The vision of change. But there is no way out of it. We are compelled to witness the vision, the change. There is no choice. I must witness. I want to witness. I am caught up in all the alien force of need, necessity, and I want this more than music . . .

"The transformation is beginning. It could take minutes,

by our measure of time; it could take years . . . For now, it's the only future I've got. I'm sorry I got you into this. I'll do all I can in my power to get us out of it. But within the alien vision there is no Dark or Light Ring, no hornet's nest, no human law. Only its own imperatives. The images that demand response. If you force me back to the Underworld, I'll be babbling in a bubble just like Terra, for as long as it takes to complete the vision . . .''

. . . A surface hard and clear as glass, rolled into a cylinder. A black line appeared around the cylinder at its center. A red line divided each half. A lavender line split the quarters. A green line . . . Threads of color stretched lengthwise along the cylinder, cut into it, became absorbed into it, veins of glass within glass. Gradually the colors began to diffuse through the cylinder like drops of ink in water, becoming opaque, misty . . . The light of the dying star mingled with the colors, rendering them imprecise, uncertain to human perception . . .

His arms were trembling. He loosed his grip on the chair, felt the change in gravity and sagged back wearily. He turned his chair to glance at the instrument panel. Then he closed his eyes, grateful for the silence within the *Flying Wail*, and most deeply grateful for something else. As he had spoken, or as he had dreamed, the thrusters had shut down. Michele was tinkering under the control panel; the Nebraskan and the Scholar and the rest of the instrument cases were in the hold. The *Flying Wail* still pursued its swift, arbitrary course through the dark.

No one had moved to stop him.

T W O

"K**lyos to Maindock,"**
Jase said, his eyes on
the distant blur of red
in the dark that was the
Flying Wail's exhaust.
"Klyos to Main-
dock."

Maindock, responding, sounded bewildered. "Maindock. Sir, we're receiving you on UF. Where are you?"

"I'm in the Hub-craft," Jase said between his teeth,
"in pursuit of the *Flying Wail*."

Maindock, hesitating, came up with the one comprehensible fate in the situation. "The Hub-craft is not a pursuit
vehicle—"

"I know it's not a goddamn pursuit vehicle," Jase shouted,
"but it's the only goddamn vehicle capable of getting out of
the Underworld without a harpsichord on board!"

"Sir," Maindock said, shaken, "you authorized those challenges."

"I authorized them because Terra Viridian had a laser-rifle in my ear!"

"Holy—"

"I assume she's on board the *Flying Wail*." He heard Maindock begin to snap orders, then come to an abrupt halt.

"We can't—"

"I know you can't."

"We can't get out to pursue them," Maindock said, awed.

"I—"

"We let them go. They were right under our noses, we could have melted the *Flying Wail* to slag in the dock, and instead we let them go—"

"You—"

"We just stood there and let them—they've crippled the Underworld. A bunch of musicians. I even went to their—sir, there are two incoming cruisers from Earth, both carrying prisoners. Pursuit orders?"

"Prisoner status?"

"Both Dark."

"No," Jase said reluctantly. "No. I can't have Dark Ringers flying all over hell and gone."

"Sir, are you sure they've got Terra? Phillips says he was watching the *Flying Wail* pack, he saw the Magician go in, but not—"

"Then you tell me why I'm in the Hub-craft with the *Flying Wail*'s tail in my face and you're all sitting on your back thrusters with no—"

"Yes, sir."

"Are there other incoming vessels?"

"Three incoming from the moon, one from Helios. All routine patrols, end of shift. They'll need refueling, but—" Maindock stopped.

"They can't get in to refuel." He was silent. The *Flying Wail*'s exhaust flared and his eyes widened. But Aaron had seen it; his hands played the control panel lights, finding power in the Hub-craft Jase hadn't known was there. The night seemed to intrude into the Hub-craft, exert its bulky body between Jase and the starscreen and shove. "That's illegal," Jase muttered, his ears aching. "A private citizen using pursuit thrusters."

"There's not much he doesn't know about the *Flying Wail*," Aaron said, watching the scanner.

"Order cruisers off the moon and Helios," Jase said to Maindock. "I'll track the *Flying Wail* as long as I have fuel. Did it refuel in Maindock?"

"First thing, sir. Are you armed?"

"Couple of small arms. The Hub-craft itself isn't armed. There's no way I can threaten them."

There was a slight delay, while Jase listened to static and the garbled ends of sentences. Maindock said finally, "There are eight cruisers preparing to take off from the moon and Helios."

"Good." He added to Aaron, "Start transmitting our coordinates to Maindock." Aaron nodded.

Maindock said, "You're not alone?"

"Aaron Fisher, Suncoast Sector patroller, is flying the Hub-craft. Maindock, I want the Underworld on full alert, emergency communications only, and I want those cruisers out fast, any way you can—"

"We're working on it already, sir. Trouble is the only record of the challenges we have access to is the Maindock Log-tape, and some of the notes are lost in background noise. There's no way to reproduce the challenges in the cruisers when we haven't got all the notes, and nobody up here can make heads or tails of the music. If we could find somebody who might recognize the music, maybe bring up a keyboard, we could link it to—"

"Somebody with a keyboard got us into this mess!"

"Yes, sir."

"Sidney Halleck," Aaron said. The solution was so apt that Jase took his eyes off the *Flying Wail* a moment to glance at Aaron.

"Why didn't I think of that? Does he know the Magician well?"

"Yes." Aaron's face, glowing here and there with panel lights, looked calm, but his words, to Jase's ear, had a brittle quality, as if a nutcracker were speaking. "They play poker every week."

"Poker." He turned his attention back to the *Flying Wail*. "Maindock, locate Sidney Halleck, Suncoast Sector. He's the musical genius who sent Nova up here. Get him working on this. If you can, get him to the Underworld on one of the Earth-based cruisers; if he can play the challenges on that, he can open the dock. Maybe he can talk some sense into the Magician."

"We've been trying to signal the *Flying Wail*; it's not responding. We scrambled their UF."

"Maybe they'll unscramble it. Keep trying. Klyos out." He kept the com open, listening, but heard nothing out of the *Flying Wail*. He dragged his eyes from the red glow, and said explosively to Aaron, "Why? You know the Magician. Is he a lunatic?"

Aaron's mouth tightened. "Yesterday I would have said there was no one saner. Except Sidney. Was he coerced by Terra Viridian?"

"Not that I noticed," Jase said sourly. "He came in while you were up in the Hub-dock, came in when nobody else could get into the Hub, caught me just as I started the docking challenges, started glowing purple and said Terra had let him in. I shot him—" Aaron's head turned; he made a startled noise. "With a stunner. Then the door-shield exploded—Terra demolished it—and the next thing I knew I had a mouthful of air-chair, a rifle in my ear and the Magician sitting on top of me, playing Bach on the Hub-computer."

"I saw him in a trance once," Aaron said, sounding shaken. "Playing Bach. I guess Bach."

"He wasn't in a trance, he was in a damn vision." He spoke to the com again. "Klyos to Underworld. Security."

"Security here, sir. Ramos speaking."

"Where's Nilson?"

"In the Hub, sir; the Hub-com's still not responding."

"I guess it wouldn't after that. Have there been any further incidents since the *Flying Wail* got out?"

"No, sir." He hesitated. "No more incidents. But we can't find anyone who actually saw Terra board the *Flying Wail*, or who even saw her leave the Hub. The transport spoke has been under guard since the Magician left the Hub. No one has seen the prisoner."

Aaron whistled. Jase scowled at the com. "That doesn't make sense."

"No, sir."

"She's got to be on the *Flying Wail*. But just in case, tell Nilson to clear the Hub and put it on defense. Tell him two-minute warning, and everyone out. Repeat: everyone. I don't want anyone in there when it goes off. No telling what kind of mess she might have made of records."

"Yes, sir."

"And double the guard along the transport line. If she's in there and she comes out, she'll come out shooting."

"Sir."

"Out." The drag on his body eased finally, and he drew breath, shifting in the cramped seat. He tried to raise the *Flying Wail* on different channels; no one responded. He sat back again, his mouth tight, swallowing expletives. He said abruptly to Aaron, "Why would he have any interest at all in Terra? Because of Michele? Did she talk him into it? Were they lovers?"

"No."

"Never?"

"No."

Jase eyed him. Aaron was staring ahead stiffly, not even blinking. "You asked," Jase said. After a moment, Aaron cracked a couple more words.

"I asked."

"Mr. Fisher," Jase bellowed, "we have a full-scale emergency on our hands! I need every scrap of help I can get! Will you give me answers of more than one—"

"I'm not used to—" He stopped, his back rigid, his mouth taut; Jase saw his hands tremble above the panel lights. "I'm not used to—" He had to stop again; Jase waited. "I'm not used to talking about personal things. That's all. I'll try. Just take—just take it easy on me. I won't hide anything. It's just . . . hard." He drew breath, said rapidly, tonelessly, "I loved my wife. For seven years after she died, I cou—I couldn't feel much. For anyone. I just kept searching for Terra Viridian's sister. I thought if I found her, then somehow I would understand why my wife was killed. That's all I cared about. Then—two weeks ago, I met the Magician's new cuber. She—I—we were lovers. Yes. She made me—she made me feel something. For the first time in seven years." He took in air again, through his mouth. Jase didn't move. The straightedge of Aaron's shoulders sagged a little; he added wearily, "You let one defense down and you find life's just been waiting, all that time, to haul off and hit you again, in just the same place where it hurt so much before . . . She was just using me, I guess, to get information. To get at Terra. That's all there was. I don't know why I ever had to meet her."

"You were looking for her."

Aaron was silent. He angled the Hub-craft toward a shift in the *Flying Wail*'s direction and sent new coordinates back to Maindock. "I know," he said bleakly. "But why did it have to be her?"

Jase sighed noiselessly. *The Queen of Hearts, she made some tarts* . . . For a moment a tangle of coincidences intruded itself into his thoughts, with one gold strand drifting loose, luring him to grasp it . . . But in the center of the knot was Terra's tangled brain, and he was only required to get her back into her cell; nothing in the books required him to understand her.

He muttered, marveling in spite of himself, "This is the most convoluted mess I've ever seen. I should have left you on Earth, let your station head question you about the computer business. At least you wouldn't be sitting here still pursuing Michele Viridian."

"Why didn't you?"

He said bitterly, "I had a hunch about you . . ." The *Flying Wail* changed direction again. Jase frowned. "What the hell are they doing waltzing all over the sky?"

Aaron adjusted their position, transmitted the new co-ordinates. His hands stilled suddenly; he turned his attention from the scanner to the fleeing cruiser, now heading out of the Solar System. "He's picking up the coordinates I'm transmitting for the pursuit fleet."

"On what?"

"The UF. She got it working again."

Jase hit the com-light again. "You speak," he said tersely, and Aaron's face turned to him again. It was masked under the wash of panel lights, but Jase heard his dry swallow.

"Sir—"

"Talk to him. See if you can bring him in. At least he might answer you."

Aaron drew breath. His voice came finally, loose, detached. "Hub-craft to *Flying Wail*. Hub-craft to *Flying Wail*." Silence bridged the infinite abyss between them. "Magician. This is Aaron Fisher. We're the blip on your tail. Please respond."

A husky, shaken voice traveled across the void. "Aaron? This is Michele Viridian."

He opened his mouth, closed it. He shook his head, rigid again, the love, grief and fury in him all demanding release at once, and all blocking each other, like giants jamming a doorway. Jase recognized futility, and said quickly while the *Flying Wail* was still listening, "Chief Klyos. Let me talk to the Magician."

"He's—not here."

"What do you mean he's not there?" Jase demanded. "Did you flush him into space?"

"I mean, he's here. But he's not—"

"God in Heaven."

"He's in a vision."

Even Aaron turned his attention from the darkness to the com. Jase closed his eyes. "It's a damn virus . . . *Flying*

Wail, you are under arrest. You are ordered to turn immediately and proceed in slow and orderly fashion to the Underworld where all aboard will be formally charged with conspiracy, sabotage, destruction of FWG property, and that's only the beginning. Failure to do so will render you liable to be scattered in minute fragments from here to Helios. Do you understand that?"

"Chief Klyos, this is the Magician."

"Nice of you to join us, Mr. Restak. Are you finished with your vision? Did you catch the drift of my message?"

"About blowing us up? Yes."

"Then will you turn the *Flying Wail* around, position it in front of the Hub-craft and return in a slow and orderly—"

The Magician said simply, "That's not possible."

Aaron found his voice. "Magic-Man."

There was dead silence from the *Flying Wail.* "Aaron?" He sounded stunned. "What in God's name are you doing up here?"

"It's a long story."

"Are you with Chief Klyos?"

"We're on your tail, yes. We got out in the smallcraft in the Hub-dock. Magic-Man, what the hell are you all doing? Did you blow your circuits on silver sand, or what?"

"Aaron—"

"You know there's a pursuit fleet behind you. I don't want to see you die out here. Please. Turn back."

"It's not that simple. Listen—"

"I know. You might think you'd rather die than spend a few years in the Underworld, but Magic-Man, there must be a reason why you got yourself into this mess in the first place, and if that pursuit fleet catches up with you, I'll never know why you did such a goddamn, dumb, idiotic, pointless, vapor-brained thing like stealing Terra Viridian out of the—" The Magician had said something; Jase's hand clamped down on Aaron's wrist.

"Mr. Restak. What did you say?"

"We haven't got her."

"Jesus," Aaron breathed. He sounded suddenly, amazingly close to tears. "Magic-Man, what have you done?"

"Aaron, listen—"

"That pursuit fleet is coming fast and they're armed. You can't evade them; there's no place you can reach safely without refueling, and there's no place off-Earth you can land to fuel where they won't be looking for you. The pursuit fleet will give you one choice: live or die, that's it, Magic-Man, and I don't want to watch you die—"

"Aaron," the Magician said, still patient, though for the first time Jase heard an overtone of strain in his voice. "I know. But this is all beside the point—"

"It is the point!" Aaron shouted. "You're going to die!" He touched his eyes with his fingers; his voice sank, hoarse, dogged. "Please. Just turn back. Think."

"I have been thinking," the Magician said steadily. "Aaron, I think you might have a problem. Because I don't have Terra, and the Hub, which is the last place I saw her, can't find her, and you said you flew out of the Hub, so is it possible that—"

His voice seemed to fade; Jase heard only a silence that was the abrupt cessation of all his thoughts. Then he heard the static again: the Magician, waiting for an answer. His skin felt too small for him, and cold; he wondered if even his brain had constricted. He moved his head cautiously, met Aaron's eyes.

In the tiny, shadowy hold behind them, where no movement should have been, there was movement.

THREE

Aaron turned. It was a slow turning: again he felt time elongate itself, stretch so that his perceptions sharpened to an intense, dreamlike accuracy. Death does this, he thought, knowing that the completion of his movement, the turning away from the glittering control panel, his arm lifted, swinging back so that he could see over his shoulder, might end in his final vision: a beam of light entering his eyes.

She was there. Crouched in the hold, barely more than a blur of white face in the weak backwash of cabin light. Light trickled down the rifle pointed at them.

"Mr. Restak," Jase said very softly into the com. "Mr. Restak." There was no response. "Mr. Restak."

She hadn't spoken yet; she had barely moved. Aaron

was staring at her, his own face still, his body so still she might have drawn the life out of him with her flat, dreaming eyes.

"Mr. Restak." Still no response. Jase cursed silently, watching Aaron out of the corner of his eye. He was reminded of cobras, fixed in each other's gaze, and he breathed, "Mr. Fisher, be careful . . ."

She moved then, stood up very slowly. Jase heard the Magician's voice, heavy, drained. "Chief Klyos?"

"She's here."

"Be careful. Don't hurt her."

"Mr. Restak," Jase said tautly, resisting an urge to bellow, "she's the one with the rifle."

She stepped out of the hold, soundless, bloodless as a moth, her eyes on the light that contained the Magician's voice. She was alert, no longer dreaming. Aaron's hatred, emanating like a charged field out of his stillness, spoke to her, warned her. Her eyes moved to his face; at the sudden, grey drench of her attention he swallowed. He saw Michele's eyes.

She frowned slightly, confused, and shifted the rifle, pointing at neither of them, far enough from them to swing it easily from one to the other. She saw Aaron's eyes flick to it, calculating distance: if he could move fast enough, if he could reach far enough . . . It was staring straight at him, one-eyed death, seeing his thoughts.

"The vision," she said, explaining to them why they should not stop her yet. "The vision needs to be complete."

"Terra?" the Magician said, and her eyes flicked to the light.

Aaron lunged. He felt his fingers touch metal; it jerked away from him. Then he was off balance, falling; he heard the snap of Jase's voice, the Magician's voice, rising. His hands and knees hit the floor. He waited, his mind blank but for a brief memory.

She kissed me good-bye and turned . . .

He heard his own breathing. He lifted his head slowly after a moment. Terra had retreated back into the hold.

She hadn't shot him. He was still alive. He gathered himself bone by bone, like a weary ghost out of its grave, and pulled himself back into his chair. His backbone, the back of his head still waited for fire.

"Aaron?"

"Mr. Fisher," Jase said tightly. "Don't do that again."

"She didn't shoot me," he breathed. "Why didn't she shoot? I would have killed her. She knew that."

"God," the com said. "Aaron—"

"Magician," Terra said. Her voice, thin, distant, carried clearly from the hold.

"Terra." The Magician's voice shook, steadied again. "Don't hurt them. If you shoot them, if you damage anything in the craft, you'll drift in space and die."

"It's not—" She gathered breath wearily, loosed it. "The vision. The vision is ending."

"I know. I see."

"You know," she whispered. Jase saw something almost human touch her face. "You know . . ." She added, indifferent again, "The one who wanted to kill me has Michele in his mind. Magician, the vision is all. The vision. Tell them."

Aaron closed his eyes. He heard the Magician's voice as out of a dream. "I'll try." Then, for a long moment, he heard only the static of the stars.

The cliff face black as deep space . . . It wavered, rippled, spilled like black cloth over the amethyst sand. The dim light of the rising sun touched it.

Delicate, colorless forms, like the skeletons of tiny sea animals . . . there was no horizon to judge their size against; they might be big as a hand, big as a world. They fell, absorbed by something pulsing.

Strands of luminescence, saliva or living wind, blowing in horizontal streaks . . .

The need . . . the need for integrity . . . the need to complete . . .

The vision frayed around him. He sat at the controls of

the *Flying Wail*, still feeling the need like an unquenchable thirst, a desire to redesign the structure of his eye, or the way knowledge passed into his head . . . He made a sound, a protest against his inability to respond. Michele looked up from the scanner.

Her face still looked unfamiliar to him; pale, still controlled, it revealed all its trouble and its amazement. "Magic-Man," she said gently. "Are you back?"

"Yes."

"What—what do you see? You and Terra? Magic-Man—" Her voice caught. He shook his head slightly, reading her eyes.

"It's not her. She's not doing it."

"She killed all those people. She did that. For what? What do you see that made her do that? And what could—how could—no matter what you see, how can I forgive her for that? How can anyone? It's still there, that fact, no matter what dreams you both dream."

"It's not a dream. At least not in the sense that we dream and then wake, and know we've dreamed. This is . . . a vision," he said helplessly and she smiled, familiar to him for a moment.

"A vision," she repeated softly. "You both even use the same words."

"They don't mean much, in this context. But it's the only language I've got."

Her eyes filled with tears suddenly; she stared down at the lights. He touched her shoulder lightly. "Why," she whispered, "couldn't she have had a vision sitting safe at home at the breakfast table instead of in the middle of the goddamn desert with a rifle in her hands? You haven't killed anybody yet, Magic-Man. Are you going to?" She looked up at his silence. "That's the difference between you, so far. And she's still got a rifle."

He reached out, touched the com-light, chilled. "It's that compelling," he admitted, and spoke to the com. "Chief Klyos?" He waited, gazing at the scattered, fiery points of light in the starscreen. They seemed too distant, impossibly remote, as if human heritage could only be the longing for them, and the endless darkness between suns. The silence from the Hub-craft began to alarm him. "Terra?"

"Yes," she said, and he sighed noiselessly.

"Are you all alive?"

"I am so tired . . ."

He knew which "I" she meant. The "I" seeing visions, translating messages beside the slow, dark sea, felt only its need. He knew the same weariness: the constant drain on his attention by danger, circumstance, when all he wanted was to be absorbed in imagery.

"Are they all right? Aaron and Chief Klyos?"

"They don't speak."

He felt the blood leave his face. "Are they alive?"

"Yes," she said indifferently. She added, appalling him, "There are times when I don't see them."

"Mr. Restak," Chief Klyos said cautiously.

"Are you all right?"

"What does she mean by that? That she can't see us?"

The Magician cursed silently. "I wouldn't count on it," he said at last, trying to keep his voice calm.

"The visions. Is that it? When she has one, she's not aware of her surroundings? Mr. Restak?"

"I'm not aware of my surroundings," the Magician said finally. "I can't answer for her."

"She just told you."

He felt the sweat prick at his hairline. "Are you listening at all?" he asked abruptly. "She reads my mind. She read Aaron's mind. She doesn't mean you harm. She and I are picking up an alien's thoughts. Doesn't that surprise you? Or is this routine to you?"

"Mr. Restak, I haven't had a routine moment since I set eyes on you. Right now, I feel like I've got a time bomb at my back. You want to discuss aliens, turn around and get yourself back to the Underworld. I'll listen then."

"Chief Klyos, her intent isn't to harm——"

"You saw what she did in the Underworld! She's a murderer."

The Magician closed his eyes. "She killed. Yes. But don't try to kill her while she's in the alien visions. She's still too dangerous."

'What alien? What are you talking about? You're not even on the same vessel, how do you know what she's thinking?'

"I know," the Magician said, his voice rising in spite of himself, "because I'm caught in the same bloody vision! I've been trying to tell you—"

"I don't understand a word you're saying."

The Magician took a breath and held it, searching for patience. He saw his band around him, in various positions on the furniture, absorbed into his need, unafraid because as yet he had been too engrossed in wonder to have room for fear.

His silence lengthened, misted . . .

Oh, God, no, he thought, terrified for Terra, for Aaron. Not now.

"Mr. Restak," he heard dimly. "Mr. Restak."

Terra . . .

A milk-white web, pulsing within its strands . . . It was building itself angle by angle, its sections irregular, its joints bulky, like delicate, elongated bones. Its patterns seemed random, but they were exact, the Magician sensed, complex as mathematics, and the choosing of each length of strand, each position, was as powerful and absorbing as the choice of one note after another of music under his hands. He felt himself seduced by subtleties, drawn into the pattern . . .

The lights of the control panel swarmed across his vision. His body felt stiff, older, by an uncertain measure of time. The silence around him had changed, like an angle of light; words had been spoken he had not heard.

Then he felt a hand on his shoulder, and the silence that was itself part of the vision frayed away. Michele stood beside him, drawing her other hand through her hair. The last of her heart-pins fell at the Magician's feet. Her eyes were swollen; her voice, fierce, precise, husky with pain, mesmerized the Magician.

"Aaron?"

"Yes."

"Chief Klyos? Are you listening? I want to hear your voice."

"I'm listening," he snapped.

"If you touch her, the Magician will know it, and I'll scream so loud over this com they'll hear me in the Horsehead Nebula, and Terra Viridian with a rifle in her hands is the stuff that horror videos are made of. Are you listening? Say your names. Say them."

"Klyos."

"Aaron?"

"I'm listening."

"You might think she wouldn't care about me after all these years, seven years in a cell in the Dark Ring, seeing nothing but visions. But she knows me. You saw that, Chief Klyos, in the Infirmary. She knows me. She knew I was coming to the Underworld before I got there. How do you explain that, Chief Klyos?"

"I don't."

"How would you, Aaron?"

"I don't know."

"You might ask, as long as you're up here with nothing to do but chase the *Flying Wail*. You might ask. She knew I was coming because I'm the only person she's ever loved who is still alive. She's my twin, my face, my heart, and until she picked up that rifle in the Desert Sector, there was no one in the world more loving to me. She was all my family, and I was hers. You might look for reasons why she killed, if you're even curious anymore, if anyone cares after seven years. Well, I spent seven years looking for reasons, in her past life, and you know what I found? Are you listening? Aaron?"

"Yes." His voice sounded hollow, haunted.

"Now I'm telling you the truth. Chief Klyos?"

"I'm listening."

"Nothing. That's what I found. She killed for nothing. For no reason. For no earthly reason. Seven years I hid, seven years I wore that face—the face of the Queen of Hearts, the cuber with the golden smile, who millions recognized but no one ever knew—because when I looked at my own face in the mirror, I saw Terra's face, my other face, and I was afraid that what she did, somehow I might do too . . . But now I know that that moment seven years ago in the Desert Sector is in her past, and her past belongs to her, not me, and it will never be repeated . . . Aaron—''

"We haven't touched her! She's the one with the rifle!''

"You say my name. Say it. Say it.''

"Michele,'' he whispered. "Michele Viridian.''

"All right.'' Her grip tightened on the Magician's shoulder. He felt her tremble. "You know now. What I didn't tell you. What I would have told you when—if I got back. If you wanted to listen. But you came here.''

"Yes,'' he whispered.

"Well, you'd know me now, Aaron. You'd recognize my face, now.'' Her voice loosened; she brushed back her hair wearily. "I'm not hiding anymore. You never knew Terra so you wouldn't believe me if I told you she was never a monster, just an ordinary, intelligent human being with a few gifts and a pretty face. She was extraordinary to me, of course, because we loved each other, but the most ordinary of people became extraordinary that way, by being loved. You wouldn't find it significant that she would hold me at nights while I cried for our parents, that there was always supper waiting for me when I got home from the clubs at three in the morning, or that when we came to Earth and I was so terrified of the noise, the colors, she walked through that alien planet like there was nothing left in the universe for her to fear. I loved her. But since you won't care about that, then explain to me what the Magician is doing risking his life for Terra and seeing Terra's visions . . . Aaron?''

"I can't.'' His voice shook out of control, and the Magician felt his skin tighten, as at an intimation of danger.

"You shouldn't be here,'' Michele said helplessly. "You shouldn't be here at all. I didn't want you to know all this until it was over. If you still wanted to know me. But I just want—you gave me the rose. So I want you to know, if it matters to you at all—or if it ever will matter—that I meant what I said to you when you came to say good-bye—about you, and cubing, and the Magic-Man's music—"

"Stop it! I don't want to hear this! Any of it!"

She lifted her hand from the Magician's shoulder, touched her mouth. "I'm sorry." Her eyes were stunned, bruised. "I'm sorry—"

The Magician eased her away, slumped over the com. "Aaron."

"What?" He sounded furious, shaken, stripped of an essential privacy.

"Please. Is Terra—"

"Magic-Man, that madwoman killed my wife!"

"Oh," he whispered. He couldn't find air for a moment. "God." The com went silent; he wondered if some fragile, invisible link in the night between them had irreparably snapped. He looked up suddenly, for Michele had disappeared. She was still beside him. He couldn't hear her breathe. Gazing at her, he couldn't find her. There was only her face, still, waxen, expressionless: another mask. Her grey eyes seemed drained of light.

"Mr. Restak," Klyos said.

He answered numbly, "Yes."

"Are you ready to come in now?"

He wavered, stunned by circumstances. Then he saw the human vision the Scholar had given him, out of a time and place existing nowhere but in a language passed from millennium to millennium: the Musician, stopped in his journey, turning, disastrously turning, to look back down the long path out of the Underworld to see if he had truly rescued anything of value.

"No."

F O U R

Jase wiped sweat off his face and tried to stretch, cramped and belted to his seat. "Where are we?" he muttered. They had been pursuing the *Flying Wail* for days, it seemed, months: even before he had ever seen it, it had projected its shadow from the future across his life. The dangers and tensions within the Hub-craft were, like a juggler's knives, becoming familiar.

Aaron read their position tonelessly. A precise and delicate balance of events had maneuvered the patroller into this aimless flight across the night, pursuing his friends, with his worst nightmare holding a rifle at his back. Jase, admiring the artistry of fate, would not have blamed Aaron for going berserk himself at this point and sending the Hub-craft into oblivion with Terra's rifle. But Aaron, instead of exploding, only grew more glacial.

"I'm sorry," Jase said finally, ineffectually. Aaron shook his head a little, expressionless, blinking as if his eyes were gritty.

"It's one of those things, I guess."

"God help us all," Jase murmured, "if this is what they mean by those things." He touched the com. "Klyos to Maindock."

"Maindock."

"Have you located Sidney Halleck yet?"

"Affirmative. We played him the docking challenges off the Maindock log; he's analyzing them now, sir."

"Good," Jase sighed. "I want to talk to him. And I want him to talk to the Magician. The *Flying Wail* has its UF open—"

"Yes, sir, we've heard them. They still don't respond to us, though."

"Arrange a com-link with Sidney Halleck when he checks back. I bet they respond to that."

"Yes, sir."

"Out." He sensed unspoken dissent, glanced at Aaron. "Something, Mr. Fisher?"

"Nothing. I just hate to see Sidney tangled up in this . . . He loved the Magician's music. That's why he sent Nova up here. If he ever sees the Magician alive again, he'll be in a cell with no hair and he won't be playing music." His face tightened suddenly; he looked as if he wanted to put his fist through the scanner. But his hands stayed still; he added, steadily enough, "I don't know much about music. But I know Sidney. He'll take it hard. The waste. The utter, absolute waste . . ." His eyes lifted, stared, hard, at the dark. "She's still killing people . . ."

People you love, Jase finished silently. He glanced behind them at the still figure sitting on the floor, the rifle angled toward the back of Aaron's chair. Just above the belt, Jase figured, if Aaron startled her. Her eyes moved, met his; he was not what she wanted to see. He loosed her to her mysterious waiting.

He said abruptly, "You never told the Magician about your wife."

"No," Aaron said shortly.

"Mr. Fisher, did you ever run across an old poem about six blind men trying to define an elephant by feel?"

Aaron was silent, bleakly regarding a smear of Milky Way. Then he sighed. "I'm sorry. I keep forgetting it happened seven years ago . . ."

"That's a long time for silence."

"I'm used to being silent about it . . . When I get angry, I can't talk. I bury things. Right now, I'd like to take the Hub-craft in my hands and throw it at the *Flying Wail*."

"I know."

"I remember that elephant poem. Third grade."

"That's why I'm asking questions. I've been defining this elephant as a snake with a tuft of hair at one end and a stink at the other. Michele Viridian talked the Magician into rescuing Terra out of the Dark Ring, and that's all there is to it, simple. Right?"

"That's simple," Aaron agreed.

"Probable?"

Aaron's eyes turned away from the stars to Jase. "Not if you know the *Flying Wail*. He could fly that craft by music. He says it's his soul. He'd never put it into jeopardy. Also, he's simply got too much sense. Or he did have."

Jase nodded. "That's what I can't understand. What moving mountain seems to be attached to the snake . . ."

"I keep trying to think of a word," Aaron said. His face stiffened again, but he continued doggedly, "She killed my wife. Now, seven years later, here we are, she and I, in the same smallcraft, when she should be locked away in the Dark Ring and I should be on Earth and this time she's got the rifle pointed at me."

"Irony."

"Is that it? It seems too small a word . . . I keep going over it and over it. How we all got into this position."

"What I want to know is why."

Aaron made a dry, humorless noise. "I tried for seven years to find reasons. All I came up with was this."

"Well," Jase sighed, "you certainly came up with a mare's nest."

"Chief Klyos," Maindock said. "Maindock."

"Here."

"The pursuit fleet requests latest position of the *Flying Wail*."

Aaron transmitted the coordinates, watching for the *Flying Wail* to veer as it intercepted them. Nothing happened: the cruiser was dead silent and on a straight course for a neighboring galaxy.

"Chief Klyos," another voice said. "Nilson."

"Nils! Are you in the Hub?"

"Yes, sir. We've pretty much got it in working order, though the monitor screens are still being replaced. They're also replacing your desk, your chair, all your equipment and most of the carpet."

"Did you get Fiori out?"

"Yes. He and his staff are safe. But he said the Dream Machine is beyond repair. FWGBI wants to talk to you."

"I bet they do. What did you tell them?"

"We're on alert status, but situation is stabilizing. Nothing more."

"Good."

"Also, we're getting media calls."

"How?" he demanded explosively.

"News leaks fast. We pull the fleet off the moon, people ask why."

"Christ. Maintain station silence except for mobile cruisers and emergency. Tell FWGBI I'll get back to them."

"They said—"

"Tell them to stay off channels until I have something to give them. They can fire me later."

"Okay. Sir, we haven't found Terra Viridian. Can you confirm she's with the Magician?"

"No," Jase said sourly.

"Then, she must be—"

"She's sitting in the Hub-craft hold with a rifle pointed at us." He touched the com. "Nilson. Nils."

"I'm here," he said raggedly. "What—what—"

"Other than that, we don't seem to be in immediate danger. Nils, if we don't get back, I want recommendations for citations for Valor, and for Extraordinary Performance in the Line, etc., for Aaron Fisher, Suncoast, A1A."

"Jase," Nils pleaded. "I don't want your job this badly. Code."

"No code. No orders. She's interested in the Magician, not us. Stay calm. And get me Halleck as soon as possible. Out." He added, brooding, "I can see the headlines. 'Underworld Immobilized by Dead Composer.' 'Magician Grounds Underworld Fleet; Chief in Orbit' . . ." He reached toward the com again, restively, then changed his mind. "No. He'll just tell me about visions. Has he ever gone crazy before?"

Aaron shook his head, then changed his mind. "Not crazy. Just—peculiar. I mentioned it before. The night a band in Sidney's club nearly electrocuted themselves onstage. I was on patrol at the time. There were patrollers, ambulances, broken equipment, people and robots cleaning the debris up . . . and he never even saw us. He sat on a stage playing music and never even heard us, never knew . . ."

"That's the looniest he's ever gotten?"

"In the five years I've known him."

"Then what caused this, in God's name?"

"She did."

"She who? Terra? Or Michele?"

"Not Michele. I watched them together. I needed to know. What—how they were with each other. There was only the music between them."

"Terra," Jase said incredulously, "has been sitting in the Dark Ring for seven years without even knowing the Magician existed. He saw her for about an hour."

"Something happened then?"

"He never even spoke to her! When I realized who the Queen of Hearts was—"

Aaron's head turned sharply. "How?" he pleaded. "I spent seven years trying to find Michele Viridian. How did you find her that fast?"

Jase considered the matter. "You were working with her real name. I took her stage name backward to the time when it ceased to exist. Seven years ago. I was also working on a pretty strong hunch that she was somebody whose name I wanted to know."

"So was I."

"But you weren't suspicious of the Queen of Hearts. I was."

"No," Aaron said hollowly. "I wasn't."

"Anyway, I asked her if she wanted to see Terra. I figured that was what she'd come for anyway . . ." He paused, thinking back, again struck by the odd position of the Magician among the crowd of people listening to Terra. "Michele and Terra spoke. Dr. Fiori was there, and half a dozen guards, his three assistants and the Magician. I asked him to come with Michele. We all watched the Dream Machine. It was fascinating. You could see what Terra was thinking of on a screen. Her thoughts were pretty vivid. Bizarre, some of them, others concerning Michele, their past. What I'm trying to explain, Mr. Fisher," he said, becoming aware of the chill wafting through the air between them, "is how engrossing the computer was. We all had our eyes on it. Dr. Fiori even forgot a couple of times that the machine itself wasn't Terra. All of us except the Magician. We looked at the Dream Machine to see what Terra was thinking.

"The Magician only looked at Terra."

"She's controlling his mind?" Aaron said dubiously. They both looked at Terra; the rifle shifted nervously. "Maybe," he conceded. "He's read my mind any number of times."

"He's psychic?"

"Whatever that means. But that wouldn't explain why he's obsessed. Why he's gone over the edge. He wouldn't throw away his life, his music or the *Flying Wail* just because of some—"

"Then why, Mr. Fisher? Why? What would cause a healthy, sane man to risk his life, his friends' lives—and why aren't they stopping him? Are they all in on this? Have they inhaled the same insanity virus? They're heading precisely nowhere without extraordinary amounts of fuel; if they continue on their course, the pursuit fleet will blow them into a dust-ring around the Earth. Does he have some psychological hold over them? Do they ever disagree with him?"

"It's a democracy," Aaron said. "I've seen them argue."

"Why don't they force him back? Why are they allowing this? He put their lives in jeopardy, freeing a madwoman from the Underworld, and he couldn't even manage to get her on the right smallcraft. Are they all seeing what he's seeing?"

"Somebody's navigating," Aaron said, fielding a question at random. "They can't all be having visions."

"Then what? He's coercing them?"

Aaron shook his head. "I've never seen any of them with a weapon. Not even Quasar."

"He persuaded them?"

"He must have."

"Is that likely? Does that seem credible?"

"No."

"Then what does seem credible?"

"None of this," Aaron said helplessly. Jase sat back, fuming silently.

"He's not even negotiating for freedom," he said wearily. "He's controlling Terra, I'd say, as much as she's controlling him. But he's not threatening us with her, or offering to take her off our hands. He's just—flying. Nowhere. I'd like to give them both to Dr. Fiori."

"I should have checked," Aaron said, gazing down at the controls. His eyes picked up stray colors from the lights. "I checked the whole Solar System, practically, but her. If I'd done that, this would never have happened."

"When you were searching for Michele, you mean."

"I never even did a stat-check on the Queen of Hearts.

And I did one on everyone. Everyone. If I'd done that, we wouldn't be sitting here."

"Why not her?"

He was silent for a long time. "I thought," he said finally, huskily, "that what I really wanted to know about her wouldn't be in any records."

Jase made a noise in his throat. "And what would you have done," he asked softly, curiously, "if you had found out then that the Queen of Hearts was Michele Viridian?" He had to wait again, while Aaron contemplated the barren darkness in front of him, or in the seven years behind him. The icy, colorless mask of his face seemed to melt, become vulnerable to pain, to understanding.

"It wouldn't have mattered," he whispered. "Finding Michele Viridian, not finding her. I still would have had to go on looking. I never realized before . . . All those years, it was never her I was searching for. It was my wife."

FIVE

Michele's face hung like a mask at the edge of the Magician's vision. He saw it in the unraveling dreams of alien landscapes; he saw it out of the corner of his eye as he watched the distant stars and waited. Its silence haunted him. A woman sat beside him, quietly navigating, but it wasn't Michele. Michele Viridian had vanished, leaving the empty face of a playing card to rule her mind and her bones and her expressionless eyes.

He picked up the coordinates of the pursuit fleet as they were transmitted from the Hub-craft. As Aaron had said, it was coming fast and there was nowhere the *Flying Wail* could go to elude it. Aaron's face came unbidden into the Magician's mind, taut and white, as unyielding as the Queen of

Hearts' face. Seven years, the Magician thought, struck by pity, seven years for both of them . . .

And for the dreamer under the dying sun.

And for Terra.

And how many years, he wondered, pulling his thoughts back to the problem at hand, would he himself get in the Underworld if the alien failed to coordinate its transformation with the threat on the *Flying Wail*'s tail?

Life without music. They sure as hell wouldn't let him out for a Rehab concert . . . That's if for some reason they let him live. A blind panic rose in him at the thought of his death: the transformation incomplete, failed, aborted, the death of the vision . . .

It has to end now, he thought. Now. The odds were ridiculous. He stirred restlessly, and heard, distant and harsh with static, Sidney Halleck's voice.

He leaned over the com, amazed. The Scholar was at his elbow in an instant.

"Sidney. How come they pulled him in?"

"Sh." There was a faint phrase of music, a harpsichord tinkling from the other side of the grave. The Magician's eyes widened.

"It's a fragment of the Italian Concerto," Sidney said. "The slow movement. That's the second phrase you played me. The third I haven't isolated yet. I'll run it through the music bank at the university where I teach, if you think it's that—"

"It is, Mr. Halleck. Please."

"But why don't you ask the Magician, Mr. Nilson? He knows almost as much about Bach as I do."

"Sir, that's impossible," Nils said.

"Why? He should be still with you."

"I'm sorry. I can't give you that information."

"You just want the phrases identified," Sidney said, bewildered but tolerant. "Mr. Nilson, do you realize how peculiar this seems?"

"Mr. Halleck," Nils said, "without revealing restricted information, I can tell you that's the word for it. When you've identified the third chal—the third phrase, let us know immediately. Chief Klyos will be in contact with you, then. He will ask you to come here.''

"To the Underworld? Why on Earth?"

"All I can say is that we're in need of someone with your talents. Urgently in need."

"Does this . . . does this have anything to do with—"

"Please contact us when you've identified the third phrase. We'll have a sol-car at your doorstep to take you to Mid-Suncoast Dock. Hub out."

The Magician listened, but heard nothing from the Hub-craft. He straightened, wiped sweat out of his eyes, marveling. "What's that old-world expression for—"

"Touché," the Scholar said with precision.

"What made them think of Sidney?" He answered his own question. "Aaron."

"What's Aaron doing up here anyway? Did they import him especially just to chase us?"

The Magician shook his head wordlessly. "God knows. But what could Sidney do? Bring a keyboard up, attach it to a few of the cruisers, directly to their computers. He'd know how to program the music. And how to play it . . ."

"Well," the Scholar said tightly, "there goes the tour." The Magician heard the fear in his voice, felt, all around him, tension like a blind watch-beast roused by his own uncertainty. "He'll figure out your challenges, Magic-Man. They'll bring him up; they'll explain that the band he sent on tour on his recommendation instigated a prison escape, crippled the Underworld, and is now being pursued by the Chief of the Underworld all over the cosmos. You going to tell him about aliens?"

The Magician stared at him without seeing him, terror and mystery weighing to a fine balance in his head. The moment's panic sloughed away from him, left his expression remote, wondering. He turned toward the starscreen, and the tension, unfed, dissolved.

"It'll be all right," he said, feeling it: the straight thread out of chaos to their future.

"God, Magic-Man," the Scholar said explosively. "I wish I knew what you are seeing. The rest of us can plead dumb ignorance. All we were doing was loading the *Flying Wail* when you kidnapped us, and there's no evidence of crime on the *Flying Wail*, not even a weapon, let alone a prisoner. But you. The Underworld will swallow you whole without bothering to spit out your bones. You know that. But you're not running hard enough, and you're not running scared. You're playing the card up your sleeve, the one final trick down at the bottom of your magic tricks. At least I pray so, because there sure as hell are not any wild cards behind us."

"It's the need," the Magician said. He felt it again as he struggled to explain. "Like thirst. Like breath. The overriding imperative of the changing. The Dark Ring is insignificant, a sand grain floating in the shadow of an eclipse. Nothing more. The Dark Ring is not in the vision."

The still face next to him watching the scanner turned then, almost evidencing emotion. "Terra said that . . ." Michele whispered. "So many times. You know what it means."

"I know."

"What does it mean?" Quasar asked suddenly, as if a vision without the shadow of the Underworld in it had finally snagged her attention. She looked up from the jar of glitter she was applying to her eyelids. "What are you seeing? You dream awake. Can you show us? Make us see an alien, Magic-Man."

"I need a drink," the Nebraskan said faintly. "I'm starting to believe all this."

"I want to see the alien," Quasar insisted. "Fly us there, Magic-Man."

"I don't know where 'there' is," the Magician said. "All I know is a state of mind."

"Then fly us there," Quasar said.

"That's not—"

"You go there. To this place."

"Yes, but—"

" 'Yes, but' is not an argument," she said calmly. "We're flying into nowhere as it is. I've been on this road to nowhere before. Either Aaron will capture us or the others will blow us up. Oblivion is no doubt a state of mind also. Or maybe, just maybe, there is something you see that no one else can see. Show us, Magic-Man."

"Quasar, I can't. I'm sorry."

She flicked him a black glance; her mouth curved upward, wry but not bitter. "You might kill us all, Magic-Man. And you can't give us this one little thing."

"I would," he said helplessly, intensely. "For you, I'd do it. But—" He stopped, gazing at her across the room as if she were a mathematical equation of dubious construction. "Wait . . ." he whispered. "Wait . . ."

She stared at him, surprised, trailing glitter into the air as he turned back to the com. He opened his mouth, wanting Klyos, but Sidney's voice came over the UF before he could speak.

". . . I tracked it down myself. It's a line from the Fifth English Suite: the prelude. Now can you explain—"

"Thank God," said the Underworld. "Thank you, Mr. Halleck. I'll alert Suncoast Sector. Someone will pick you up momentarily."

"Is Nova in trouble?" Sidney asked worriedly. "Mr. Nilson, is that it?"

"I can't discuss this. I'm very sorry, Mr. Halleck."

"Mr. Halleck," Chief Klyos interrupted. "This is Jase Klyos."

"Chief Klyos, what—"

"I'm sorry to inconvenience you. Mr. Nilson is acting on my orders. Due to unforeseen circumstances, we're maintaining a station-to-Earth blanket over classified information."

"Bach," Sidney pointed out bewilderedly, "is a matter of public domain."

"Unfortunately so is ignorance. All I can tell you is this: I need your help. It has to do with a nursery rhyme."

"Good Lord."

"The one we were discussing when we first spoke. You may not remember; it was weeks ago, but think—"

"The Queen of Hearts." His voice had changed.

"Yes. And would you bring something to play those phrases on?"

There was a pause. "Chief Klyos," Sidney said somberly. "I'll be waiting for that sol-car."

"Thank you, Mr. Halleck." Jase sighed.

The Magician sat down slowly, his message forgotten. He gazed at the Queen of Hearts intently, bewilderedly, seeing the mask of gold, hearing the nursery rhyme, trying to connect them both into some plausible reason for a discussion between Sidney Halleck and the Chief of the Underworld, until Michele's face wavered under his eyes, and she cried, "Magic-Man!"

"I'm sorry." He touched her, his fingers cold. "I'm just trying to . . . Did Sidney—did he know who you were? Are?"

"I never told anyone."

"That's strange . . . Was it a nursery rhyme they talked about then? Or was it you?"

"I don't know, I don't know!" He reached out, held her shoulders, but knew she wasn't seeing him, she was looking back again, dangerously far, to the nightmare of confusion she thought she had escaped from. "They are right, though," she said. "It's my fault. That's where it began: the night I painted my face and played with you. I should have known—I should have known you can't hide things. I thought I would be safe. That's all I did it for. To make myself safe. To keep myself from harm. It seems such a simple, human thing to do. One that wouldn't harm anyone else. But look at us! Here we all are in the middle of nowhere, you trapped in a vision, my own sister behind us with a laser-rifle, cruisers about to blow us up, Sidney on his way to the Underworld to play Bach, and Aaron—" She stopped; he saw the pain bloom again in her eyes. "Aaron," she whispered. And then he felt her slip away, go so far down into herself that this time not even the Queen of Hearts was left.

Something jumped in the Magician's throat. He swallowed, whispered, "Heart-Lady." He touched her hair, her wet cheek. "Michele." Neither answered. He stood up, met the Scholar's dark, shocked eyes, saw the Nebraskan's moment of hesitation before he jerked himself to his feet and hit the water dispenser. Nothing came out. He disappeared into the kitchen, swearing.

"Michele." The Magician held her cold hands, shook her slightly. "Please." She was nowhere to be found; he did not know where to go to bring her back. Then Quasar rose, her own face transformed, unfamiliar in its gentleness.

"Heart-Lady," she said, putting her arms around the Queen of Hearts. "Don't grieve. These things are always happening. The world is made of them. But it keeps on going, the old rich-ragged woman-world, who loves you one day and curses you the next. Because that's her secret: she keeps you going, because you never know—even you don't know, now—if she will hand you broken glass or gold."

The silence spun itself so tightly the Magician thought it would snap and recoil endlessly as far as there was time. Then Michele was crying against Quasar's shoulder, while Quasar murmured old-world into her hair.

"It's not your fault," she said, comprehensible again. "You did right. I know about hiding. Come away from all these lights. The Magician is navigating into his dreams. Maybe he'll pull that stupid patroller into them, maybe not. But I don't care: I want to see his alien, and I would rather blow up than be bald."

The *Flying Wail* spoke.

The Magician and the Scholar jumped. The Nebraskan, returning with coffee, spilled it on his hand. The Magician, his eyes on Michele, his mind blank, struggled with the phrase of music a moment, then gave up and checked the controls.

"What is it?" the Scholar asked tensely. "More company?"

The Magician shook his head. The yellow light that had flashed on held his attention a moment longer as if the message it gave him were more critical, more dire than a routine fuel warning. "Fuel's almost half gone. The pursuit thrusters cost us a lot." He dragged his eyes from the light. It swam in front of his vision; he blinked it away, saw Michele sipping coffee. Her hand shook badly, but she was seeing again. He held her eyes, asked her a question silently, urgently, had his answer from her before she spoke.

"No," she whispered. "Don't turn back. Please. Please, Magic-Man. You said it was ending. End it."

SIX

"Aaron?" the Magician said. "Chief Klyos? Are you all still alive?"

"Mr. Restak," Jase said wearily. "Are you aware of the course you're following? You certainly haven't got enough fuel to get to Andromeda."

"I want Terra's voice," said the com. "Terra?"

"I'm here," she said from the floor.

"Terra. Are you listening to me?"

"Yes," she said remotely.

"Terra. Listen to me. The next time you have a vision, I want you to talk. I want to hear your voice. You've done that before, at your trial, to Dr. Fiori. I want you to talk your way through your vision. Describe exactly what you're seeing. I'll be describing it too. Maybe that way they'll begin to see that what we're saying exists beyond our minds. Will you remem—"

"Magic-Man," Aaron interrupted. His voice was taut with a dangerous control; his eyes had picked up the blackness of deep space. "Don't make me listen to that. Don't."

There was a moment's silence. "Aaron." His own voice sounded unfamiliar, shaded with overtones of unexpected emotions. "You've got all the weight of justice. When this is over, you can walk away from it. I'm trying to show you something. I'm risking my life to show you. So that if they blow up the *Flying Wail*, and I'm nothing but an echo of light moving toward the end of the universe, maybe you won't be totally bewildered. Or totally bitter."

Aaron was silent. Jase glanced at him. His face was rigid, flushed to the roots of his hair. The struggle in him, between his fury, his ingrained reserves of pride and grief, and his need, seemed explosive. Jase shifted, uneasy in the currents, but when Aaron spoke finally, all feeling had been buried briefly beneath a calm professional surface.

"Don't waste time doing me any favors. Just return to the Underworld and you won't get blown up."

"Aaron—"

"How many lines do you think you can cross at once anyway? She's got that rifle at my back now. Because of you."

"I know. But, Aaron, she's just—"

The calm snapped. "You defend her, Magic-Man, I'll walk across empty space and turn you into light myself!"

Jase turned, feeling the uncoiled movement behind him before he saw it. The rifle swung across his vision. He heard the Magician shout.

"Terra! No!"

There was dead silence. Jase blinked at sudden sweat, saw the rifle wedged between Aaron's shoulders slowly fall away. Terra stepped back after a moment, sat down again. Her expression between one movement and another hadn't varied. She didn't shoot, Jase thought. Still she didn't.

He spoke into the com, feeling very tired. "How did you know, Mr. Restak?"

"I knew. What'd she do?"

"No damage yet. She made her point. She doesn't like you threatened."

"Aaron?"

Jase glanced at him. He was breathing unevenly, but noiselessly, his face colorless. From his brittle stillness, Jase surmised, he was just on the verge of trembling with rage.

"He's unhurt. Mr. Restak, this situation is intolerable."

"God, I know. Aaron?"

"Mr. Fisher is, I believe, too furious to talk. He's trying not to get shot. In the name of friendship, how in hell do you justify this, Mr. Restak? You're going to get him killed."

"He never told me," the Magician said. Jase heard him draw air. "I've known him for years. He said his wife had died. Once, he said that. He never talked about her. I couldn't have anticipated this."

I'd sooner have anticipated being eaten by crocodiles on the moon, Jase thought darkly. He kept his voice steady, groping toward some scrap of sanity, even from the Magician. He said, risking another explosion beside him, "Mr. Fisher seems to be a very private man. Did he tell you that for the last seven years, he's been secretly searching for Michele Viridian, to see if he could understand from her why Terra killed his wife? Using all our highly sophisticated and thorough records systems, he still failed to find her, she hid that well."

"He found her," the Magician whispered.

"That's why I brought him up here. Because she used his computer to request restricted Underworld information . . . She found him, Mr. Restak. If she hadn't done that, he wouldn't be sitting here with Terra at his back."

"She—"

"Michele Viridian is liable to some very serious charges. But you never knew her name?"

"She never told me. She never told anyone. She was

terrified of it." He added, after a pause, "In the Underworld, she told me that seven years ago, Michele Viridian painted her face after Terra was sentenced, so that she could cube one last time without being recognized. Then she was—she would have killed herself. That night. From despair. She's not the hardened criminal you describe, Chief Klyos. She was alone on Earth, with no other family except Terra then. And Terra was on her way to the Dark Ring."

"That night," Jase said curiously. "She didn't kill herself. What happened to make her change her mind?"

"She found—she found one last band to cube with. Mine."

Aaron's head lifted involuntarily; he swallowed, stared down again, his eyes hidden, unblinking.

Jase shifted in his seat. The tiny Hub-craft cabin felt even closer, crowded with overlapping events, too many details that prismed into complexity.

"The Queen of Hearts," he said without inflection.

"The nursery rhyme," the Magician said, startling him. He felt, furiously, that his mind had been read.

"How did you—"

"I was listening, when you talked to Sidney."

"Mr. Halleck . . . did he know the Queen of Hearts long?"

"He met her seven years ago, not long after she first played with me."

Jase was silent. "Mr. Restak," he said wearily. "Every time I try to make sense of this, I just get tangled tighter and tighter. That pursuit fleet is just about on your tail. A while ago, after you tied me up and played hell and Bach with my cruisers, I couldn't have cared how many pieces you were scattered into. But now, before they blow you up, I'd certainly like to know what's going on. If you've got anything to explain, I'll listen. If you want Terra to talk, I'll listen; I'll try to keep Mr. Fisher from killing himself. Just tell me how in God's name a nursery rhyme got us into all this trouble."

"It didn't start with a nursery rhyme. It started—"

"When?"

"That day," the Magician said carefully. "In the Desert Sector. I know why Terra massacred those people."

"You know—"

"It has to do with the visions in her head. The transformation. I can see it."

"Mr. Restak, every time you start talking like that you make me uneasy. I want to go give my brain a shower."

"Please. Listen." He paused again. Jase felt him picking at words. He heard then the deep underlying weariness: the Magician juggling with tables and scarves and coffee cups, and one knife too many. "When I went with you and Michele to see Terra: you remember?"

"Yes."

"There was the computer, showing images in her mind. We walked in there; we looked at Terra, because that's the first thing you see, the bald madwoman in the bubble. Then you looked at the screen. And she looked at me. And I saw in my own mind all the images she's been seeing. And it's—it was overwhelming. It was—Chief Klyos, what's the one thing you want most out of life?"

"A transfer."

The Magician paused. "All right," he said, with inhuman patience. "What's the one thing in life that touches you most deeply?"

Jase was silent, struck by the unexpectedness of the question. "What is it you're trying to say, Mr. Restak?"

"That what she—what we're both seeing is that important. That vital. Not to us. Not on a human level. On a—"

"Oh, Christ, you're not going to start talking about aliens."

"You saw those images."

He saw them again suddenly, the strangeness of them, always on the wrong side of the broad boundaries of his experience. Forms pelting down like rain, hurrying away down an amethyst shore. The bent oval, serene as a moon dropped on the sand. The red sun . . . The colors are all wrong, he thought. But she had insisted on those colors.

"She killed because of those images. Because whatever

makes them, I think, felt an overwhelming urge for light. The urge was probably biological, instinctive. Like animals or reptiles born on land who are driven to water or they die. They're driven. What happened in this case, I don't know. Maybe it had something to do with the dying sun. Terra was in the desert in broad daylight. But the image in her mind was dark. She saw dark. She felt dark. She made light."

The outrage in Aaron's voice jolted Jase like an electric shock. "Magic-Man, this is unbelievable! You hand me fairy-tale crap like that and expect me to forgive and forget—"

"Mr. Fisher!" Jase snapped, seeing light glance across the rifle out of the corner of his eye. The Magician's voice, worn with strain, snapped back at them, stilling them all.

"Then, goddamn it, you explain it! You tell me what you're doing up here, still tracking the woman you tracked for seven years, furious with her, furious with me, wanting to kill a woman tried and sentenced years ago—seven years, Aaron! You've got questions, I'm pulling out my back teeth trying to give you answers, and you can't even listen because after a seven-year diet of bitterness and hatred, that's all you remember how to feel!"

"You—" The word came out of Aaron on a rush of breath, as if he had been kicked. "Magic-Man—"

"Mr. Fisher, will you calm down?"

"She's the one who killed! Why am I on trial?"

"Because all this is your fault as much as anyone's!"

"Mine!" he said incredulously. The rigid control was gone, but so was the fury; he looked, Jase thought, genuinely hurt by something not in his head. Terra had set the rifle down. Jase saw it, then repeated it to himself with amazement. She put the rifle down. Then, with even greater astonishment: She's listening to this.

"While you've been tracking Michele Viridian all these years, you've been giving her something to hide from, to run from as hard and as fast as we're running now. You're what she hid from in the first place: all that secret fury. It's dangerous to hide things like that in this world. If you don't put them into language, they transform into other things; they surface when you think you've got them buried, you find them where you least expect them: the madwoman with the rifle at your back, the mask across the face of the woman you cared for—you found exactly what you were looking for, Aaron: the things you hate.''

Aaron's lips moved soundlessly. He stared at the com-light as if it would suddenly produce the Magician like a hologram. There was little expression on his face; it had faded away with his color.

"I'm trying—Aaron, I'm trying to show you a different way of looking at the thing you've been staring at for seven years. I don't want to hurt you. I'm just trying to show you that you could never have explained Terra's killings, Michele couldn't have explained them—you were never looking for the right thing.''

"I know," he said, his voice so faint the Magician almost didn't catch it. His eyes caught light oddly, filmed with tears or memories. His hands were loose; his whole body was loose, as though he were accepting the empty air. Jase's throat stung suddenly. Seven years, he thought. It took him seven years to let go. God help us, how do we manage to survive, with our sorrows and brief loves?

"Magician," he said, shrugging the problem at hand back on his shoulders like an old familiar boulder. "You've got our attention. Now can you be more explicit—''

"Pursuit-cruiser *Hero* to Hub-craft," the com inter-rupted abrasively. "Fleet approaching last transmitted coordi-nates of *Flying Wail*. Please transmit new coordinates—''

"They're practically under your nose," Jase said irrit-ably. "Now—''

"Orders upon approach? Do you want us to fire on them?"

"I want you to get off—negative. Match speed and escort.''

"Sir," *Hero* said incredulously. "Code 5?''

"Negative Code 5. They're unarmed.''

"Sir, are you certain?"

"Just—I'm negotiating a return. Maintain silence; clear channels. Escort and wait—"

"Code 8?"

"Negative," Jase shouted. "Negative Code 8. No force. Re—" He broke off as the Magician said something incoherent in the background. "Mr. Restak," he said, suddenly, deeply uneasy. "Magician." He heard Terra's breathing behind him, hard, unsteady. "Mr. Restak! Will you respond? Damn it, *Hero*, will you get off—"

"The need," Terra said tightly, freezing Jase's vocal cords, "is for light."

SEVEN

Dark. Not the dark behind closed eyes, with its random shadows of color, not the dark of night with its distant fires, but the soundless, motionless midnight of emptiness . . . She stood in it. Was enclosed in it. Buried in it. She held darkness between her teeth, breathed it into her lungs. Her bones were carved of night. Her eyes held no light. She might have been beyond the edge of the universe, in a place where light had not yet been conceived.

"This dark," she whispered, to the Magician lost in his own blindness, to the vague, shadowy men, hardly more substantial than memory, whose gazes were riveted on her. "This dark . . ." A line of old poetry drifted through her head. " 'And dark on dark is dark . . .' It is cold, this dark. And too small. The dark is . . . a skin that needs to be shed . . .''

An eye opened in the dark. A pinprick of light.

"The yellow star . . . Too far. Too cold. It means nothing. It is no message. It is . . . not real. There is no fire, but the memory of fire. The need . . . and the memory of need.'' She felt the Magician's mind, struggling, like a small insect in the corner of a gigantic web, to break free of her voice, her vision. The struggling ceased gradually; the fear she sensed all around her, within her—fear and the memory of fear—was no longer in him. He was truly swallowed in the dark, in no-time, under the cold gaze of the yellow star. She—a time-bound part of her—still remembered fear. Someone's heart beat raggedly in terror at a memory; someone's hands, clinging to a rifle, were slick with sweat.

The need grew, the star grew, a sweet and dangerous flower in the dark.

"The need is for light . . .''

The cold star ate away at the dark. Existing nowhere, in no-time, it caused no shadow and gave no warmth. "It is a star of memory,'' she said despairingly. "It gives nothing.'' Her hands shifted on the metal she held. Someone said something: a word existed in another world, another time. A memory of light was filling her own mind, light from the past. "No warmth,'' she whispered. "Not in memory.'' But she carried light.

A movement in front of her, stilled. She tasted fear like a pellet of metal. "Again,'' she whispered. "Again.'' But there was no desert sun above her head, nor did she stand on pale, heat-drenched sand. This was a tiny bubble of air enclosed against a vast dark. Two men breathed noiselessly in front of her, their faces turned away from the panel lights, shadowed as they watched her. They were so still they might have been trying to hide the sound of their heartbeats from her, or the meaningless murmurings within their minds.

"Terra,'' the dark said gently, pleadingly, and for a second she was outside of the vision, and the only light she saw was the tiny com-light on the panel between the two men. Her lips moved soundlessly: Michele.

"Terra."

"The need is for light . . ."

"No light you make can reach into a dream . . . No light you make can reach across such a darkness . . . You will only die. This time, you will die. And so will I because you will destroy my face, my heart."

"Michele," she whispered. And then she felt it: the quickening, the terrible hunger for warmth, for light, for life.

Her hands tightened on the rifle. She flung a light across the dark . . .

There was not enough warmth in the desert sand. The light soaking into it, burning the skin, was not enough. The sun-filled sky, so lucent it hurt the eyes, was not enough. He hungered for it, ached for it, wanted to wrap himself in fire, net the sun like a fish and haul it toward Earth until the sand melted underfoot and yellow fire stretched overhead from horizon to horizon.

He lifted the laser-rifle.

He heard the screaming, like the cries of seabirds in the distance. It meant nothing. The need was for light. Stones exploded around him, walls and equipment lost their shapes. Fire billowed up between the Earth and the sun, gave the desert a reddish cast. The red sun was not enough, the need was greater. He made a world of fire, he painted all he could see with light. Until there was nothing left of it but fire . . .

He stood in a red night. It was soundless but for the fire still licking at the bones of the barracks. His hands were welded to the rifle. He freed them finally, dropped the rifle. It made a small sound in the emptiness around him. He wondered a moment what dream he was in, whose dream. Then he began to see the shapes scattered across the ground, washed in the red light. The light of the red sun. Charred, fused, broken nightmare figures. An attack, he thought. I'm the only one left alive.

And then his sweating, shaking body, his aching hands said what he had done.

He made a sound. He was kneeling, blinking away sweat. Grey. Grey floor angling up to form the control panel. A swarm of lights. Under the lights, a keyboard.

He expelled a breath that was not dark, was not fire. The *Flying Wail* was as soundless as his vision had been. He saw boots, black, scuffed brown, a glittering orange reptile skin that hurt the eyes. The sweat chilled suddenly on his face.

"Oh, God," he whispered. Then he heard her voice over the com.

"Magician."

"Terra," he whispered, afraid to move. Grey boots entered his vision; a dark hand reached down to him. He looked up, saw a living face.

"Magic-Man?" the Scholar said tentatively. "You in there?"

He nodded, let the Scholar pull him to his feet. He stumbled to the com.

"Aaron?"

"I'm here." His voice was barely more than a whisper.

"Chief Klyos? You're not—she didn't—"

"She didn't shoot," Jase said. He seemed, to the Magician's ear, to be handling words cautiously, as if he were astonished he still had a voice. "She didn't shoot."

"You know—"

"She talked. You told her to talk so she talked. You didn't."

"I was—I was— The need was for light."

"I know."

"She made light."

"Not in the Hub-craft. Thank God."

"No," the Magician said. He felt himself still trembling and sat down. "In my head. The only safe place for her to do it without harming Michele. She saved us," he said, still incredulous, to both the Hub-craft and the *Flying Wail*. "She kept us all alive."

Jase's voice came again. "Is that where you were?"

"In Desert Sector. Making light."

"Mr. Restak—" He sounded shaken.

"There wasn't enough light. I felt it. Not enough light in the entire Desert Sector, not in the entire world . . . not for something under a dying sun, needing light to be born."

"Now?"

Images formed at the edge of the Magician's awareness, seducing his attention . . . A cliff face black as deep space. A dim, reddish sky beyond it. An oval bent back on itself, all colors or no color, lying on amethyst sand. A concave vision of a red star. The cliff. The oval. The red sun. Terra's voice.

"The vision."

She spoke to the tiny star of light that was the Hub-craft's com. She still held the rifle, but she was no longer aware of it. The men had turned their faces away from her, toward the fire and dark beyond the starscreen as if her words and her thoughts were coloring their minds, creating visions among the stars.

"The purple sand ripples. Something moves beneath its surface . . . The black cliff. The need is to reach the black cliff. The need is . . ."

The Magician's voice across the dark, struggling with the language of the dream: "Heat. The need is . . . to change. To transform. But the need is not in the sun. The black cliff . . ."

"The cliff is a door, a gateway . . ."

"A passage to fire."

"The vision is fire."

The rippling continued, a methodical undulation of amethyst particles, a vibration against the cliff. The cliff itself began to vibrate.

"It's not easy to estimate," the Magician said tranquilly, "the perspective within the vision. Is the cliff a mile high? Or as high as my hand? Is the vibration enough to move a fist-sized stone? Or enough to disturb a thousand miles of surface?"

"The gateway must be broken open."

Shock waves undulated across the sand. The gentle sea began to stir, water heaving onto the shore as from a boiling pot.

"The gateway is immense," the Magician said. His voice was hushed. "Any seed on Earth might have such an intense, explosive reaction when it finally splits itself open, driven toward light, but would it be able to perceive the source of light? The sun in this vision is as we might see it, on our horizon, though it is huge and dim . . . On the horizon beneath the dying sun, the cliff itself is huge. So is the thing beneath the sand, driving toward heat, disturbing the sea . . ."

"Fire and water."

"It's a hazardous beginning to life . . . a balance of fire and water, heat and cold. The black cliff contains the forge. The crucible."

"The need . . ." Terra whispered. "The need . . ."

The center yawned open: a cave of colored teeth or a mouthful of jewels. It swallowed its own debris; it swallowed the last, frantic surge beneath the sand. The reflections of fire within the cave beat the jeweled walls like wings.

"Fire . . ."

A million messages, all at the touch of the planet's inner fire. Joints sealed, surfaces smoothed, energy crisscrossing along elegant patterns of framework. White heat exploded out of the cliff in a rain of stars. Then the tidal wave struck.

"Water."

"The healing," Terra said. The word came from her in a soft sigh.

Jase looked at her. She sat on the floor, one hand resting on the rifle beside her, though she seemed oblivious of it, of the Hub-craft, of everything and everyone within it. Her eyes were distant, defenseless, luminous with visions.

He turned back to the starscreen, feeling light-headed, dislocated, his head full of the subjective and approximate imagery of dreams. The two voices supported and overlapped each other, the language never quite precise, always dancing on the surface of the vision itself, light on water, illumining but never encompassing. A transformation by fire and water . . . of what?

"What are we seeing, I wonder?" the Magician mused. "Or how? Out of alien eyes, an alien mind watching? Or is this thing watching itself as it forms? Are we seeing its own biological blueprint, watching its heritage of genetic messages, its inner vision of commands that it must respond to? The cliff, the sun, the sea, inherited memories, a code of transformation, so that the sun we see is in its cells, its being? The true sun may have changed even more since this message was inherited . . ."

Steam poured out of the cliff. It obscured the sea, the sun, hung like a dense tropical mist over everything. Long waves curled like scrolls above the sand, unrolled to the lip of the cave, withdrew slowly, heavily, dragging the sand with it. Layer after layer of amethyst, coloring the water a twilight purple . . .

"A wave," the Magician said. "Another wave . . . Another : . ."

Jase glanced at the chronometer, but the time didn't register in his mind. It meant nothing. That's it, he thought. That's what I've been feeling. Time is different. All my time-habits are suspended. He was aware of Aaron's silence beside him. Concentrating, he could hear Aaron's breathing, slow and almost noiseless, timed to the Magician's counting of the waves. He wondered if he should become alarmed, fight his way out of the general hypnosis. Then he thought: To hell with it, I asked for an explanation.

At last, after many waves, the Magician said, "There are contours beneath the sand."

"Sir," *Hero* interrupted. "This is *Hero*. Fleet has matched speed and is escorting *Flying Wail*. Request orders."

"Just stay with them," Jase said calmly. "Maintain silence."

"Patterns in the sand," Terra said.

"Spiderweb filigree . . . A lacework all down the shore . . . It's huge, whatever it is."

Metamorphosis, Jase thought, remembering one of Terra's inexplicable references. Only this was a thinking larva and its cocoon was made of amethyst and it plunged itself into fire and water as it changed. It is aware of its own construction, and it sent out a blueprint of its transformation across God knows how many light-years.

"Sir. *Hero* again," the fleet commander said edgily. "We're picking up some weird chatter from the *Flying Wail*."

Jase sighed noiselessly. "Log it," he suggested. "Might be some kind of code. Keep listening."

"Sir," Aaron breathed, roused out of his trance. "What the hell's going on? I can't stop seeing—imagining things. I don't even have an imagination. The Magician—he makes me see the things he's saying. So does she. What—how are they doing it?"

"I don't know. Wait."

"Bones," Terra whispered. "Bones of crystal."

The fragile, glittering skeleton lay limply across the sand, catching fire now and then from the weak sun as the steam thinned. The sun glowed like a hot coal in shadowy red smoke. Another wave fell, withdrew. Another.

"The heat," the Magician said, "must have glazed its framework. It was still so hot when it crawled back out of the furnace, it melted the sand, minerals, whatever else was down there. It formed a membrane between each—each bone. I don't know what it's made of. It looks like wings of lead crystal and stained glass. But that can't be, if it's meant to fly."

"Dark," Terra said, but this time there was no anguish in her voice. "The need is to see. To see the sun."

"The main body is still buried. The brain."

Jase caught himself trying to imagine an alien brain and stopped. Beside him, Aaron stirred slightly, as if troubled by the same image. He turned briefly to look at Terra, amazement struggling with the hostility in his eyes.

"Is it true?"

"God, I don't know," Jase said. "Aaron, what is more imperative at this moment? Law? Retribution? Our fuel supply? I don't know what's true. But I do know what's got my attention."

"The need is to see . . ."

"The timing is astonishing," the Magician said. "The needs are precise, crucial . . . a moment of fire, a moment of water, the sun . . . the well of magma, the sea to cool it, and enough wave action to unbury it, and all in daylight, never at night . . . Seven Earth-years to ready it for a few perilous moments."

But what is it? Jase thought, fascinated. What?

"The body contours are beginning to show. It looks—" His voice broke off in a murmur of surprise. He tried to speak again, failed. "I can't—" He was panting suddenly, raggedly. "Too much . . . too fast . . . I can't—I can't—"

"Magician." Terra raised her voice slightly. "It's not for you. The knowledge. Don't listen to it. Let it go. The knowledge is not for you. Only the vision."

There was a long silence; Jase gazed absently at the com-light, as if he might hear, beneath the static and faint chatter, the masses of information rushing through the Magician's head.

"My God," the Magician said shakily. "That thing's programmed like a—like a—"

Like a what? Jase shouted silently.

Waves were washing the cylinder free. The cloudy surface was divided with a spectrum of color. Waves flowed over it, withdrew down the long, glassy lines of it, wearing away slowly, carefully, every particle of sand.

The sun, seen under a blur of water . . .

"The sun," Terra said softly. "The red sun."

"The sun is a direction finder," the Magician said surprisedly. "A point of reference. That would explain all the star-charts it swallowed. The need—"

"The need is forever," Terra said simply.

"It's the home-sun. The parent sun. The need goes deeper than intelligence. Even dim and dying, it's—" Language seemed to fail him for once. "It's a symbol. Long ago it must have been more than a symbol. The young star must have been the heat source, the process itself. But the star aged; the transformation imperative evolved a different pattern. Even so, the evolutionary memory is long. The instinct is for that sun."

Jase drew breath, loosed it soundlessly. The yellow sun, he sensed, next time he saw it, would be, for a fraction of a moment, unfamiliar.

"It's moving," Terra said. "The wings are moving."

They lifted to the steam, things of air and light, almost invisible. Very slowly they furled, tucked close to the body, then unfurled, the long, glittering length descending over most of the shore. They furled again, opened gently, almost sensuously in the warm, damp air.

"It's beautiful," the Magician breathed. "Enormous, beautiful, intelligent and—"

"What?" Jase said, though he knew the Magician wouldn't hear.

"Feeling. That's part of its information patterns. It's amazed at its life, it's content in the steam, it's lonely, it's aware of itself, it's awed by the sun and in need of it, like a child; it's capable of loving and being deluded . . ." His voice broke suddenly, hoarse with strain and with his own emotions. "About the only thing it isn't is hungry." He gave a faint laugh, half in awe, half at himself. "It fed itself down in that fire . . . It's fueled and ready to fly."

Jase's blood ran cold with wonder. A ship? he thought numbly. A living ship? Star-charts in its brain, wings like solar sails . . . "God," he whispered almost reverently. Beside him, Aaron was motionless again; he gazed out the starscreen at the red glow that was the *Flying Wail*, and all the burning worlds beyond.

"The need is to fly," Terra said. She saw nothing around her; her eyes were full of the great, delicately winged creature conceived under crystal sand, born of fire and water, who was gathering into its wings the light of an alien sun. A tear slid down her cheek.

She's waited long enough for this, Jase thought. Will it end here? Or will she fly with it, inside its brain, as it roams the universe? And who is inside whose brain? Is she telling the story to the Magician? If she is, it'll go on and on, because there's nothing here for her to come back for. She invented this thing and she's making us feel it, and she'll stay with it until she dies. It's the only escape from the Dark Ring.

"Sir," *Hero* pleaded. "What's going on?"

"Just wait," Jase said quietly. "Follow your orders."

The wings, spanning their full length, stiffened. The enormous single eye tested its capabilities: infrared, X-ray, ultraviolet, visible light. Intense heat made the sand run liquid, scarred the cracked face of the cliff. The water roiled with steam. The wings, at the last moment, curled again, tucked close. There was a blur of light.

Silence . . .

Far away in the dark between worlds, it opened its wings again, soared on the solar winds, delicate, immensely powerful, and, for the moment, absolutely free.

Jase became aware, slowly, of internal noises: cross chatter from the Underworld and the pursuit fleet, a creak from Aaron's chair, a soft warning tone that the Hub-craft's fuel was nearly half expended. He reached toward the com, then paused, gazing at his hand, wondering for a second where it had come from and what it was for. What an amazing creation, he thought. It feeds you, it's useful in making love, it fixes a leaky pipe, it plays music . . . The Magician. He blinked, awakened, and met Aaron's eyes. His face was bone-white; his eyes, in some strange mingling of surroundings and emotion, were the same color as Terra's.

Terra.

They both turned. She could see again; she was watching them, taking slow, weary breaths through her mouth. As they looked at her, her head tilted back, came to rest against the cabin wall, as if it were too heavy for her to carry any longer. She closed her eyes, stopped breathing a moment. When she opened them again, she looked completely unfamiliar.

Jase swallowed dryly, motionless in his chair. One woman

had entered the Hub-craft; a total stranger had taken over her body. Her eyes, he thought. That's what changed. The thoughts in her head changed the expression in her eyes. She glanced around the Hub-craft, then at Aaron. Her eyes were filmy with exhaustion, but they were no longer focused with such terrible intensity on private, invisible events. She looked relieved of some great stress, aware of her surroundings, watchful but not frightened. She looked—

Normal, Jase thought, feeling the skin tighten on his face. My God, she just went sane.

"It's over." The voice was the same, fragile and tired. Then she looked at Aaron.

She nearly dropped the rifle, picking it up; Jase saw her arms trembling. She stepped across the cabin, slowly as if she moved underwater, or against some dark rushing wind. Her head swayed; her face, in the cabin lights, was so pale it seemed blue-white. Aaron seemed spellbound under her gaze; he made no move to stop her, even when she came close enough to touch him. She let the rifle slide into his arms.

"Forgive me."

She seemed to Jase to fall for a long time before he caught her. He reached for the com. Aaron, moving finally, hit the light first. "Michele," he said. His voice grew ragged, insistent, sending the name like a heartbeat across the void. "Michele. Michele. Michele . . ."

E I G H T

The return to the Underworld was, Jase thought, the quietest journey through space he'd ever had in his life. The Magician had turned back without a word; the *Flying Wail*, surrounded by the pursuit fleet, followed the Hub-craft slowly and in a funereal silence. Aaron gave up trying to speak to Michele. He spoke to Maindock in monosyllables; he spoke to Jase only once.

"What are you going to—"

"Later," Jase said succinctly, and Aaron let it go.

They pulled aside near the Maindock to watch the *Flying Wail* enter the Underworld again. The challenges the Magician played sounded over the UF with a delicate, eerie beauty. Maindock opened, swallowed the *Flying Wail*. The pursuit fleet headed back to the moon, and Aaron dropped the Hub-craft neatly into the Hub-dock.

There were guards, doctors, morgue attendants waiting for them. Jase got out stiffly, without a backward glance at the body lying on the cabin floor. Dr. Fiori caught his arm.

"What happened? Did you shoot her?" He reddened at Jase's expression. "I'm sorry. I should have said: Were you forced to shoot her?"

"I wasn't armed," Jase said icily. "Neither was Mr. Fisher. She just died."

"Of what?"

"You're the doctor." He took a step toward the ladder, then relented. "Take a look at her. When you're finished, come to my office. Aaron—"

"I'd like to speak to you," Aaron said.

"Not now. Go talk to Michele."

Aaron lingered, looking bleak. He swallowed. "I don't know if—"

"You just spent seven years looking for her! You could at least explain to her what happened to her sister."

Aaron stared at him, a little color coming at last into his face. He was wordless a moment; Jase waited. "You tell me," Aaron said finally, explosively. "What did happen?"

Jase was silent, hearing the unspoken challenge. Fifty-six, he thought wearily. For nine years, Chief of the Underworld. A somber but respectable career, by the book, without ambiguities. And now I get this.

"Go," he said softly, inarguably. Aaron went.

Nils handed Jase a cold beer when he finally reached his office. He downed most of it before he spoke. He leaned back in the air-chair as far as it would go and sighed.

"Pleasant trip?" Nils asked genially.

Jase stared at the carpet. "It's blue."

"Supplies was out of grey. So what killed Terra Viridian?"

"She stopped breathing." He was silent a moment, picking at the label on the beer bottle. Nils sat down on the edge of his desk.

"That's it? Visiting musicians help prisoner escape, Chief recovers prisoners and felons without a shot fired, prisoner drops dead, everyone else goes to jail. End?"

Jase rubbed his eyes. "Sounds easy, doesn't it?"

"Simple." He paused, watching Jase. "So what's the problem?"

Jase dropped his hand. Dr. Fiori stood in the doorway. "Chief Klyos?"

"Come in." He straightened.

"Chief Klyos, I'm sorry I jumped at you with a question like that, I just—"

"Never mind. Dr. Fiori, I'd like to run through the tapes you have in the Dream Machine of Terra's—Terra's vision."

The doctor made a soft, bitter noise. "She destroyed them."

"Who did? Terra?"

"When she fought her way out. There's nothing salvageable of the tapes or the computer." Jase muttered something. "Pardon me?"

"I said it figures."

Dr. Fiori took a step closer, studying him. "Why? Did she do—did she say something, or do something while she was with you, that you thought significant? Important?"

"You might say." He leaned back in the chair again, wearily. "I think she—became sane, just before she died. She came to the end of her vision, and became—normal." He added to Nils, who was looking vaguely pained at the nebulous language, "It's on the Hub-craft log-tape."

"What did she do?" Dr. Fiori breathed.

"She handed Mr. Fisher her rifle and asked him to forgive her. She'd killed his wife in Desert Sector, seven years ago. That was the last thing she said. She simply stopped living."

Nils whistled. "We brought Fisher up here to go through that?"

"Nils, don't even start thinking about it."

"But why?" Dr. Fiori demanded. "Why did she do it? She acknowledged her crime, she accepted guilt, responsibility for another person's grief—the woman I studied here could never have done that. Why did she change? Chief Klyos, what happened out there? Something happened."

Jase eyed him. "What would you say might have happened to cause her to do that?"

"She realized her sister Michele was imperiled by her escape, she saw through her own imagery of guilt, accepted responsibility for her actions. She stopped running, turned to face what she had done, and—I don't know—maybe decided she didn't want to live with it."

Jase grunted. "That sounds plausible."

"Is that what happened?"

"Close." Nils glanced at him sharply, then rose and wandered to his own desk, his back to Jase. Dr. Fiori gazed at Jase puzzledly, chewing his lower lip.

"She came to the end of her vision," he repeated. "You said that, Chief Klyos. You used her language."

"So I did," Jase said, surprised.

"What did happen?"

"Dr. Fiori, when I figure it out, you'll know. I promise you that. Now, if you'll excuse me, I have a few decisions to make."

Dr. Fiori turned to go. He paused at the door. "Chief Klyos, if that's all it was—if it was all this simple—then what possessed the musician?"

"That's a good question," Jase said, and didn't answer. He asked Nils' back, when Dr. Fiori had gone, "Is Sidney Halleck still on his way?"

"No. I had the Earth-cruiser head back home again when you said the Magician was returning. It didn't seem necessary to bring him too." He turned to face Jase finally, asked curiously, "What did happen to Terra? What happened to you?"

The Magician, under heavy guard, was taping three fragments of Bach for Maindock on the *Flying Wail*'s keyboard when Aaron wandered aboard. Guards stood outside the open hatch; their eyes followed Aaron up the ramp, but they didn't stop him. Two more guards, carrying rifles, were inside.

"I'll watch him," Aaron said. They eyed one another; he added, "I brought him back, didn't I? In one piece so you can get your cruisers out? Give me ten minutes."

"Five minutes, Mr. Fisher," one of them said finally. "But let him finish the tape first."

Aaron leaned against a wall, not feeling much like sitting. He closed his eyes; for a moment he rearranged past and future. He was back on the dock in Suncoast Sector; the Magician, morning sunlight on his back, was playing music; for a moment there was still a future. He opened his eyes, hearing the com crackle.

"I think we've got it. Stay there until we're sure. Replaying it."

The Magician sat still, listening. The challenges were repeated, note-perfect, from the Maindock tape. He nodded.

"That's it."

"Thank you, Mr. Restak. We hope you enjoy the rest of your long stay in this idyllic spot full of recycled air, artificial light and coffin-sized accommodations. Say goodbye to your keyboard."

The Magician gazed down at it. His shoulders jerked slightly as at a cold touch. Aaron realized suddenly that the Magician had not even heard him come in.

His throat closed, aching, but he forced himself to speak. "Magic-Man."

The Magician stood up. One hand hovered over the keys, pressed them gently, making no sound. Then he replaced the panel over it neatly, cast a glance around the cruiser, and finally looked at Aaron.

"Fly it home for me, will you?"

Aaron, slumping against the wall, was mute again. "I'm sorry," he whispered. "I'm sorry."

The Magician regarded him, or the situation, dispassionately. "Don't sell it yet." His eyes were wide, as if he were still seeing visions; his face was very pale.

"There's no way Klyos can put you away. I'm a witness. There's the Hub-craft log—even the pursuit fleet heard the end—" The Magician shook his head slightly and Aaron stopped.

"I can't think yet," he pleaded. "When she—when Terra died—"

"You felt it?" Aaron breathed.

"I've never died before."

"Most people—most people don't. Die before they—" He gave up with a gesture. "Klyos—"

"There is no way that Klyos can stand up in court and talk about an alien on another planet and still remain Chief of the Underworld."

"I'll make him. I'll badger him. We're talking about truth, justice, law—"

"We're talking about an alien," the Magician said patiently, "and no matter how we say it, we'll still sound exactly like Terra. This was in the vision. This was not in the vision. The vision is ended."

"Is this something you're guessing at?" Aaron asked recklessly. "Or is it something you see will happen?"

The Magician looked at him silently. "I'm making an educated guess," he said wearily. "I'm too tired for more visions. The rest of the band is probably safe. That's all I care about at the moment. It's me they want." He glanced toward the hatch at the sound of footsteps. Aaron did not move, refusing, for a moment longer, to yield all the Magician's past to the Underworld.

"No."

Something broke through the unfamiliar darkness in the Magician's eyes. He touched Aaron lightly, looking almost human again. "Have you talked to Michele?"

"No." He frowned down at the floor, sensing the Magician's surprise. "I'm scared to," he admitted baldly. The guards stepped back into the cruiser. They motioned silently, peremptorily. "Where are you taking him?" Aaron asked, watching the Magician descend the ramp. He blinked a little, midway, as if he had walked suddenly into light.

"LR Security, level B."

"Is that where the rest of the band is?"

"They're back in VIP quarters," the guard said over his shoulder. "Under guard."

Aaron lingered at the hatch until the Magician, flanked by six guards, crossed the dock and disappeared. He did not look back. A strange emptiness yawned behind Aaron: the *Flying Wail*, stripped of all its magic and music, just another old, rather tired cruiser. He moved, impelled by overwhelming need.

He felt the light, cold sweat on his face as he stood outside the VIP quarters. The guards, recognizing him by his Sector uniform, unlocked the door. He caught Quasar midpace, swallowing smoke, the Scholar slumped glumly in a chair, the Nebraskan breaking off a gentle, melancholy wailing from a small rectangular instrument at his mouth. Michele, curled in a corner of the couch, raised her head, sliding the long hair back from her eyes.

All the words vanished from Aaron's head. He met her eyes, helpless, inarticulate, incapable of moving. He could not see the expression on her face; it had blurred a little under his gaze.

"I looked—I looked for you for seven years," he heard himself say finally. "I don't know why walking the last six feet to you is so terrifying. I guess there's something I need to say. The last thing Terra—Terra said to me." He heard her voice faintly, in the distance, a question. "Forgive me."

Then he could walk blindly toward her, hoping that she would be there to meet him where his past ended and his future began.

Jase sat in his office, scowling at words on his console screen.

Conspiracy . . .
Assault . . .
Destruction . . .
Failure . . .
Death . . .

All applicable. None false. Yet somehow, none precise.

Nils, handling reports, trying to maneuver available cruisers where they were needed while Maindock was still inaccessible, worked quietly at his own desk. He seemed oblivious to Jase, and yet when Jase cleared his screen to start again for the fourth time in an hour, Nils commented, "It usually doesn't take you this long to make a report. You usually do it once, speaking."

"I'm tired," Jase snapped. Nils' head came up, his expression carefully neutral.

"Just say it," he suggested. "Just say what happened. You've got evidence enough to lock the Magician away for most of his life."

"I know."

"It's true."

"I know."

"Aaron Fisher—"

"Aaron," Jase repeated softly. Nils took a breath or two, quelling confusion, or, Jase thought, anger at something that wasn't performing flawlessly, that had betrayed a bewildering weakness. He knows, Jase thought. He hates knowing, but he knows. That the language I need for this report is nowhere in the books.

"Aaron Fisher was at your side the whole time. He'll make his report; he'll back you. Everything is clear, right down the line."

Jase leaned back, feeling his own temper rise. "God damn it, Nils, the one thing that's clear in this whole business is that if I tell the truth I'll lose my job."

Nils stared at him. His face flushed deep red. "No," he said. "You can't tell me that. You can't even suggest that. That this—this vision business—that Terra was—wasn't—"

"I may not say it," Jase said, holding his eyes, "but my guess is Aaron will."

Nils half rose, subsided again into his chair. Jase watched the fury in him calm slowly. Nils lifted his hands to the keyboard, touched it, then dropped them again. He leaned forward, pushed his face into his hands; when Jase could see him again, he looked groggy.

"Shit."

"It's messy," Jase agreed.

"I don't want to know."

"You're the one who told me just say it."

"It can't be true."

"Okay." He shrugged. "I'll put the Magician behind light and that will be that. Or, I'll tell what really happened, and you can have my—"

"You say that," Nils warned him, "you'll lose teeth." Then he sighed, his face patchy, all the strain of the recent hours showing. He glanced at his screen, typed a couple of orders. His shoulders slumped again; he stared at Jase.

"There are five dead bodies in the morgue. Terra put them there before she left."

"I know," Jase said.

"She demolished the robot-guard. Not to mention a few dozen monitors and this office."

"I know."

"The Magician effectively shut down two-thirds of the operative cruisers in the Command Station for this area. We could have had a disaster on our hands."

"Yes."

"You and Mr. Fisher tracked him, alone and unarmed. You brought him back."

"Yes," Jase said patiently.

"Well," Nils said, his voice rising again, "they won't give you a medal for talking about visions! Just stick to the facts. That's all you have to do. That's all anybody wants out of you."

Jase was silent, staring at his dark reflection on the empty screen. There's the Hub-craft log, he thought, and memories of the rich, vivid, alien imagery drifted into his mind. Fire and water . . . the giant red sun glowing through steam above a disturbed sea . . . the great, living ship, wings slowly lifting . . . Would some patroller years from now, on a routine cruise in the space around the astonishing planet he came from, spot it and become inarticulate in terror and wonder? We are born surrounded by mysteries, he thought. We make our compromises with terror, with wonder, so that we can go about the business of simply surviving from one day to another . . . We achieve a balance on the high wire, take one slow step after another, while the wire shakes and the wind blows, and nobody wants the unknown, the unexpected, with wings like some alien insect out of a gaudy, gargantuan jungle to sail by and sweep us off balance . . .

"Jase," Nils said, and he blinked, startled. "Message on-screen from FWGBI. They want to talk to you."

"Stall them."

"How long?" Nils asked tightly. "How long?"

"Long enough," Jase said, making one decision at least, "for me to talk to Mr. Restak. Get him up here. Please. And—"

"I'm not leaving you alone in here with him. I just got this place cleaned up from the last time he was here."

"I want you to stay," Jase said mildly. "I'm just trying to do what you suggested. I'm trying to do my job."

The prisoner came escorted by half a dozen guards. There was a filament around his wrists. He looked pale, unshaven and exhausted. He stood quietly, expressionless, while Jase said to the guards, "Take that off him. Wait outside." He was silent until they had gone; the Magician glanced at Nils once, then waited, resigned, for Jase to lean back in his air-chair and contemplate the problem.

"Mr. Restak," he said finally, "do you realize, when you're put on trial, what you're going to sound like?"

The Magician looked surprised. A little color came back into his face. "I've thought about that," he said.

"Once in a lifetime, somebody babbling about that, is a bizarre curiosity. Twice in seven years—" He shook his head. "It might be disturbing. Might be. I don't know." The Magician regarded him silently, as if trying to hear what Jase wasn't saying.

"The vision ended," he said at last, softly. "Terra died.

I turned around. There was no communication between the Hub-craft and the *Flying Wail* after that."

"No."

"So I have no idea what"—he paused, searching—"how much you understood."

Jase leaned over his desk. Out of the corner of his eye, he saw Nils hunch farther over his work, trying not to listen, not wanting to listen. Jase sighed. "Mr. Restak. I don't get paid for understanding. I get paid for dealing with things that happen or don't happen. I know what happened on the Hub-craft. I'm just trying to figure out how much it's worth to me."

The Magician started to speak, stopped. His eyes had changed. "You believe—"

"No. I saw, Mr. Restak." He paused, repeated gently, almost to himself, "I saw." In memory he saw it again, the image Terra and the Magician had put into his head, unfurling its glittering sails across the black, black sea between suns. The Magician, the terrible weariness fading in his eyes, seemed to read Jase's mind, watch it too. For a moment the office filled with an infinite, tranquil silence. "The point is, Mr. Restak," Jase continued, "that I'm sitting here in my office and you're standing there with six guards waiting to escort you back to Security. The Hub-craft log is ambiguous, and Mr. Fisher is, after all, your friend and therefore biased. The point is, Mr. Restak, what in God's name am I going to do with you?"

The Magician shifted slightly, as if Jase's question had thrown him off balance. Nils was no longer even pretending not to listen. "Well," the Magician said finally, his face impassive, masking hope, as he played one last wild card, "you said you wanted a transfer."

N I N E

Jase and Sidney Halleck sat at the mahogany bar in the Constellation Club, sipping beer. It was three-fifteen in the morning. The club was empty but for the Magician, playing something gentle and complicated on the stage nearest them. A year had passed since Jase had last heard him play. He had thought that exposure to Earth, with all its riotous color and noise, would dim his off-world memories. But he still found himself trying to drink beer through gritted teeth.

"I just put a new piano on that stage," Sidney said, watching it and the Magician fondly. "An old German make, very fine. He seems to like it."

"It's big enough," Jase said politely.

"Nova performed here tonight for old times' sake. If

you'd gotten here earlier, you could have heard them. The Magician forgot to stop playing . . . They'll leave tomorrow for Archipelago Sector."

"I just came from there."

"Beautiful, isn't it."

Jase nodded. "I guess I left just in time."

Sidney's eyes wandered from the stage to Jase's face. "I can ask him to stop," he said. Jase shook his head, feeling himself relax under Sidney's tranquil gaze.

"No," he sighed. "It's just that . . . I never really feel safe around Mr. Restak. To look at him up there, he seems harmless enough. But things happen around him . . . I haven't seen him for nearly a year. I retire from my job, I wander around the world awhile, one day I get on a shuttle for a five-thousand-mile flight to Suncoast Sector, I have a six-hour stopover in the middle of the night, and so I come here to pay you a visit. I walk in the door and I find it's the one night the Magician and Nova have come to play. I've never been paranoid, or even very imaginative. But that man makes me uneasy."

Sidney leaned over the bar, pulled a fresh glass off a rack and set it under one of the antique draft handles. Dark beer trickled slowly into the glass. "That's quite understandable, though. His freedom cost you your job."

"No," Jase said fairly. "I wouldn't put it like that."

"You refused to press charges."

"That's not what cost me. The Magician's stat-sheet was so clean it squeaked; there was a speeding fine on it, maybe a docking fine. That's it. The patrollers were furious with him for being smart enough to lock them up for a few hours. But they were the same men and women who had gone to hear his band play. He didn't hurt anybody. I was the one who took Terra out of the Underworld. The Magician had transgressed, but he wasn't a criminal, there was no deep feeling against him. And I had Aaron backing me, when I refused to press charges. As well as my own reputation. That carried some weight. No. There was just one detail that cost. And that cost blood."

"The alien," Sidney said gently.

Jase nodded. "The moment I suggested that Terra Viridian might not have been crazy, that's the moment they decided I was crazy."

"Was there one?"

"One what?"

"An alien?"

Jase gazed across the floor at the Magician, absorbed in his music. "I let him go, didn't I?"

Sidney made a soft sound. He set the full beer glass on the bar; Jase took a swallow. Chilled, the color of molasses, with a head on it like whipped cream . . . it gave even the Magician's music charm, for a moment. Jase wiped his mouth. "That's all I wanted."

"What?" Sidney said, smiling.

"Nine years, Chief of the Underworld, and all I really wanted was a cold draft beer."

"Maybe," Sidney murmured. The smile faded from his face; his eyes, grave, contemplative, sought out the piano player again. "But for you, he would still be there. In the Underworld, note by note, forgetting all that music . . . As his friend, I'm very grateful that you were there. Anyone else would have—"

"Ah—" Jase interrupted him, shrugged. "I was trapped up there. I wanted out. My deputy-in-chief was a good man to leave the Underworld to, so I did. I told FWGBI he'd make a terrible administrator, and they went for him, hook, line and sinker. He's not fond of aliens, but other than that, he'll do a fine job."

"What will you do? I can't believe you'll be content being a tourist for the rest of your life."

"When I find a quiet spot with some sun, water and good fishing, I'll do a little private business, detecting, consultant work. I enjoy working with people . . ." He took another swallow of beer. A phrase of music drifted into his head, so sweet and precisely measured it seemed he heard it with the Magician's ear. He recognized it; like a key it unlocked memories. He looked up, half expecting to hear his own voice challenging the phrase.

It was the Constellation Club he stood in, not the Underworld. His hands were linked tightly around the glass. He felt Sidney watching him. He said softly, "That night . . . that long flight into an alien vision . . . with a madwoman holding a rifle at my back, with the Underworld paralyzed, while I chased a man who'd invented laws to break, there was a moment when I was compelled to look with wonder at the structure of my own right hand . . . That's the moment when I had no choice, I knew what happened."

"I looked at Aaron," Sidney said simply. "I knew something extraordinary had to have happened."

"Aaron . . . He would have been on my back for the rest of my life if I hadn't let the Magician go. And what he goes after comes to him."

"He's not here anymore," Sidney sighed. "They transferred him south."

"I know. I keep an eye on him."

"They made him a station commander. So I don't see him or the Queen of Hearts very often. He said it was your fault he got transferred, you got him so many commendations."

Jase shook his head. "I couldn't give him enough, not enough to make them forget that when I refused to make formal charges against the Magician, he backed me all the way. That'll shadow his record. The FWGBI knows something more than routine went on up there during that flight, and it doesn't want to hear what. An Underworld Chief going softheaded is one thing, but an Earthside patroller with an impeccable record agreeing with everything he says can't be so easily explained. No matter how many commendations I got him, what they'll see is that I recommended them."

"You had an impeccable record too," Sidney argued.

"Until I said a five-letter word. Funny how that word makes people jumpy . . ." He washed the bitterness out of his throat with beer, found himself listening again to the Magician's music. "Doesn't he ever quit?"

"I'm surprised he's not aware that you're here."

"Everywhere I go," Jase said grumpily, "I hear their music. I find the tiniest, darkest hole-in-the-wall bar that looks like it hasn't been swept since the FWG took over, and wouldn't recognize sunlight if it fell all over the floor. Someone turns on a video and there they are. Nova."

Sidney smiled. "You had your chance to stop them. You made them famous, letting them continue the tour."

"I know. And I could have been a hero, too . . . pursuing dangerous criminals in the Hub-craft, getting everybody back to the Underworld—the FWGBI would have sent me flowers and a plaque."

"It would have been easier for you," Sidney said gently.

"After they quit giving me medals and laughing at me about the Bach, they would have left me sitting up there for the next ten or twenty years. Chief of the Underworld, with no way out. I like the way Earth smells . . ."

"Aaron and the Queen of Hearts and the Magician have all given me bits and pieces of what went on that night," Sidney said, getting two more glasses. "That's all it feels like to me: bits and pieces. Maybe, without the Magician's vision, it will never seem more than that. But I still don't understand why you brought Aaron of all people up there at that time on such a vague business. Or why you connected the Queen of Hearts with Michele Viridian. Or where Dr. Fiori sprang from, just in time to move Terra out of her cell. You were a busy man. Why such attention to such small details as a broken cruiser-receiver?"

"Do you ever have hunches?"

"I have a hunch you're going to tell me a long story."

"Do you have time?"

"And the beer."

"It all started," Jase said, "with a nursery rhyme."

By the time he finished, the walls of the club had changed color twice, and there was a pyramid of glasses on the bar. The Constellation Club, to Jase's eye, was Earth at its most harmonious and civilized; even the Magician's music, he conceded, might sound good to some people.

"Good heavens," Sidney said blankly. "You mean, I might have been up there playing Bach to a fleet of patrol-cruisers so that they could capture the *Flying Wail*?"

"That's what we wanted you for. Luckily, the Magician's vision ended and he turned back before you reached the Underworld."

"And that's what you saw, that was your premonition of disaster: Terra Viridian escaped from the Underworld." He blinked a little, lifted an empty glass, then found the right one. "I remember now. The Magician had a premonition too."

"The hell he did. When?"

"The night before you and I first talked. He was in here playing the piano. For hours. I'd never seen him like that. He never stopped, he never spoke . . . He said later he'd been watching the Underworld orbit as he played . . . It was very odd."

Jase grunted. He felt the soothing fumes of beer in his brain slowly abandon him, leaving him adrift in the small hours, sleepless and unshaven, in the same stale clothes he'd worn for five thousand miles. Reluctantly, his eyes moved beyond the mellow gold and wood around him, out across the floor to the stage where the Magician still played.

"He doesn't usually do that, then? Play for hours like that."

"No."

"Like he's doing now."

Sidney shifted on his stool. "It's after five," he said surprisedly.

"He was watching the Underworld orbit?"

"That's what he said."

They both watched the Magician, moving tirelessly, frowning slightly in concentration, or like someone deep in an engrossing dream. Jase said without hope, "Maybe he just likes the piano."

Sidney gathered empty glasses between his fingers, poised them over the floor and dropped them. Jase jumped at the crash. But the Magician's eyes did not even flicker.

"Mr. Restak!" Jase bellowed, praying for the Magician's head to snap up, his fingers to tangle on the keys. The Magician, deaf as a hologram, paid no attention.

"It could be anything," Sidney murmured. "It could be . . ."

"It could be anything," Jase said grimly. "Except for one thing. I'm here."

Sidney looked at him. They rose simultaneously.

Onstage, standing on both sides of the Magician as he played, they were still beyond the periphery of his vision. Sidney touched him, spoke his name. Finally, gently, Jase reached out, caught his left hand in the middle of an arpeggio and lifted it from the keys.

"Mr. Restak."

The Magician's right hand halted. He looked up at Jase, pale, his breathing audible, but showing no more surprise than one awakened, but not yet fully awakened, from a dream. He said, "It's watching us orbit."